*"Got caught
digging for idols
when I should
be reaching for the sky."*

- Road Craft Song, *Reach*

BOOKS BY RANDOLPH LALONDE

Brightwill

Dark Arts

Spinward Fringe Broadcast 0: Origins
Spinward Fringe Broadcast 1 and 2: Resurrection and Awakening
Spinward Fringe Broadcast 3: Triton
Spinward Fringe Broadcast 4: Frontline
Spinward Fringe Broadcast 5: Fracture
Spinward Fringe Broadcast 6: Fragments
The Expendable Few: A Spinward Fringe Novel
Spinward Fringe Broadcast 7: Framework
Spinward Fringe Broadcast 8: Renegades
Spinward Fringe Broadcast 9: Warpath
Spinward Fringe Broadcast 10: Freeground

For more information please visit:
www.RandolphLalonde.com

DARK ARTS

Randolph Lalonde

Cover Image Licensed from iStockPhoto, art by Kirill Semenov - http://skirill.deviantart.com/

Print ISBN: 978-1-988175-00-3

EBook ISBN: 978-1-988175-01-0

Prologue

July, 1976

Montreal

"You have come for the Libro de Puertas," said the monk ponderously. The drooping sleeve of his threadbare robes hid all but the corner of the small leather bound book.

Maxwell stood in the doorway of St. Peter's Chapel. It was less than a tenth the size of the last St Peter's church Maxwell saw months ago. He pulled a nearly empty package of Marlboros from his jacket pocket and popped one out into his hand.

"No smoking in this house, son," the monk warned, standing slowly.

"No bother on me. American fags are shite anyhow," Maxwell griped.

"Not bothering to tame that Cockney, either. Your father would be embarrassed."

"Da died trying to be something he wasn't. Didn't even get the book he spent most of his life looking for. That one there, the one you murdered for." Maxwell pressed the smokes into his leather jacket pocket. "Like you, on the verge of excommunication while Clergy and law alike go looking into a few torture victims in Seattle."

"I was in the vicinity, not the perpetrator," the monk replied.

"Heard the girl's father caught up to you. Is that what you're hiding under that hood? A few new scars?" He hoped to rattle the middle aged former monk, to get some kind of feel for who he'd become since he started wandering across the continent. The word was that he'd gone severe; following the ways of the inquisitors.

Drawing demons to him as much as seeking them out so he could pry secrets from the lips of their possessed victims. Didn't believe any of it was possible, Panos was just a sick asshole the Catholics tossed aside who liked to torture people. "I hear he tried to take your nose. Can't believe he didn't just kill you."

Panos the Monk didn't show any sign of irritation, he didn't flinch. "Are you any better? Riding around America with your band, collecting religious baubles to keep them on the road?"

Maxwell looked around the chapel, taking note of the fairly average stained glass windows, worn pews and humble Christ carving at the front. The savior seemed to stare at the altar, his expression locked between pity and a cringe. Whoever carved it did the church a disservice, the work was good, but the expression was all wrong. "It's enough to keep me and my boys on the road," he said. He needed to buy enough time to figure out the situation. Why had Panos spent so much time in Montreal with the authorities after him, and was it coincidence that Maxwell spotted him going into the church nearest to the bar they would be playing in?

"Who is paying for this relic, Maxwell?"

"Angelo's the broker," Maxwell said quietly. "Told me that you stole that, and it wouldn't be good for you if you were found with it. Don't know how, but he knew you'd be here. Said it was most likely I'd find your corpse."

"Nearly," the monk answered. He tugged one side of his hood, making certain it hid his face. Max could see the merest hint of bandages crisscrossing Panos' face.

"Best hand it over. You may be standing in His house, but I'll guess He's on my side." Doubt weighed on Maxwell with regards to the wishes of the Almighty. He believed in his Zippo and tin of lighter fluid much more.

"I can't give it to you," Panos said. "Not unless you have something to offer, something worth trading. Something that will empower me even more."

"Like what?"

"You've seen the Eternity Ankh, where is it?"

"When I was barely past my da's knee," Maxwell scoffed. "He sold it for weight, it was pure gold. You think you need something like that to keep you breathing?" He couldn't stand most of the people he met while he did his job. Superstition and zealous ideals infected most of the collectors. "Buying in to the folk tales in that book is not healthy."

"This book you're after is keeping me alive, boy."

"World doesn't work that way," Max said.

"You think you know that much about the world? At the ripe old age of what, twenty?"

"Life lived, world seen, and I've never seen what you're telling me," Maxwell said. "If you're really walking' around at room temperature, maybe you could prove it. I'm sure hanging boy over there won't mind if you borrow one of his nails, show me your blood doesn't run."

"Crass," Panos said. "I've no mind to prove miracles to thugs."

"I've got five hundred dollars here, it's yours if you come back to reality, and give me that book," Maxwell said. He watched the other man, who only spared him a glimpse at the mention of so much cash. "That much green could keep you liquored for a while. Miracle enough for a drunk, monk or no."

"I haven't had a drink since I found the Libro de Puertas. It's about the covenant. Angelo shouldn't have it. His customers don't deserve it, and it shouldn't go anywhere near Sudbury."

"Angelo isn't the most trustworthy type, but he's a good collector. He knows what he's buying," Maxwell pulled the wad of twenties from his back pocket and held it up so it couldn't be missed. "Pays honest, too."

"He should have come himself," Panos said.

"Can't get him out of his store these days." Maxwell couldn't help it any longer, he had to ask. "What's under the hood, Panos? Give us a peek, mate."

"The covenant is delicate. Someone like Angelo's customers can't be allowed to know the details as they are translated here, you understand?"

"Five hundred dollars," Maxwell enunciated loudly, wiggling the thick green wad between them. "Enough for you to drink yourself to sleep for days. It's a good time for you to find a hiding place, this'll get that done."

"You don't understand," Panos said earnestly. "I have been saved. This book comes with a purpose; it needs to be protected until a new covenant is needed. It must be carried by someone who knows."

Maxwell pressed the cash into his inside jacket pocket. It would make a hell of a bonus if he could get the book without paying for it. His hand went to his right outer pocket then, and wrapped around the tin of lighter fluid.

"You're not getting the book," Panos said, starting for the side door.

In three long strides Maxwell closed the distance between them and gripped Panos' brown robes beneath the back of his hood. In a glimpse he could see someone had torn out tufts of his hair, leaving scabby patches of scalp. In Maxwell's other hand he held the lighter fluid tin high. It was pocket sized, but there was enough to set the man's clothes on fire.

"Let me go!" Panos shouted. He wheeled around clawing.

Maxwell withdrew just quick enough to get away with the slightest scratch on his cheek, spraying the monk in the eyes with lighter fluid. He continued to spray even as the man retreated, almost emptying the can.

Panos screamed, recoiled, and fell backwards over a pew. The book fell out of his sleeve.

"Should have taken the cash," Maxwell said as he picked the book up and secured it inside his jacket. "Mad geezer."

His boots echoed as he crossed the chapel to the front door. Maxwell hoped Panos would stay down, but listened to the rustling behind him as the man struggled to his feet. Cringing and whining sounds echoed behind him, the most noticeable thing in the church until he heard the faintest click.

Maxwell had heard that sound before, and in an instant he hurled himself between old pews. The small church became an echo chamber for Panos' furious .45 as two shots rang out. "Give the book back!" Panos cried. "I'll keep shooting! You can't hide!"

Without a second thought, Maxwell tossed the book over the nearest pew in Panos' direction.

"And the money!" cried the monk.

"Wanker," Maxwell muttered. His ears were ringing. He produced the wad of cash and held it up so Panos could see it. "Do you want me to throw it?" he asked.

Panos didn't answer. Instead he crossed the distance to the book. Maxwell watched the man's shaky hand pick it up from where he lay on the floor. The monk quickly shuffled over to Maxwell's row and pointed the gun at him.

"No worries," Maxwell reassured, holding the money up as high as he could. "Just take this and we'll go our separate ways. Just like before, I'll leave you no worse than I found you." He had an opportunity to look the monk in the face, and saw that the bandages over Panos' nose were soaked equally with lighter fluid and blood. That's why the Monk was in so much pain; whatever terrible wound had been bound up probably felt like it was on fire.

Panos snatched the cash and started to run.

"Ey, mad Monk!" Maxwell called as he pulled his Zippo from

his jeans pocket, lit it, got to his knees and tossed the little torch.

The monk began to turn back towards him, aiming the gun.

The Zippo couldn't have landed in a better place if Maxwell had an eternity to try. In a split second Panos' expression turned from rage to panic as the flaming lighter landed in a fold of his fuel soaked hood.

Maxwell ducked as the gun went off. Panos went up in a blue and yellow plume. One, two, three shots sounded. Even though his ears rang like tinny bells, he could hear the monk's shrieks as he fell forward rolling, trying to put the flames out.

Maxwell picked up the book and kicked the smoldering man over. One more shot rang out as Panos rolled onto his back. He wondered at his luck, an instant later when he realized the shot missed. Maxwell kicked the gun out of the monk's hand and was tempted to keep kicking, but bent down and snatched the wad of cash instead. Panos was more interested in wailing, his hands over his face, than stopping him.

"I've been using that lighter fluid gag for a couple years now, you're the first I've actually set on fire," Maxwell said. "I have to admit, you didn't go up as bad as I thought you would, and you put it out quick. Might be time to find a better way to scare the wits out of your sort."

He was just over twenty miles away, riding his Harley Davidson Sportster in the cool night air when he realized his neck was soaking wet. He reached up and felt a bloody trail leading to his ear. Maxwell winced in pain, nearly losing control of his bike entirely as he touched an open wound where his earlobe had been. "Shoulda dragged his arse out of that church and made sure he burned," he said through gritted teeth as he accelerated down the street, the roar or his Harley Davidson filling his ears.

The pain had lessened to a throb by the time he downshifted and turned down the side street behind the Wild Side, an old pub repurposed as a rock bar. Bernie was behind the wheel of their converted school bus, smoking and listening to Mississippi Queen. The early 60's bus had been repainted black on the outside, and the interior cab lights were upgraded with brighter, bare bulbs. Bernie's cousin, Scott was hanging out inside, leaning against the dash. They both got out of the van, Bernie flicking his cigarette down the alley, and met Max as his motorcycle came to a stop. "We're ready for our set, getting ripped off by the owner though. They're only paying us a hundred because the other band just dropped an album," Scott said, running his hand over his recently shaved head. "I remember when that was us."

"Anyone I know?" Maxwell asked as he leaned his Harley Davidson Sportster onto its kickstand and pulled the antique book he'd just taken from his jacket.

"No," Bernie said, lighting a fresh cigarette. "Some band called the Racer Kings. Good rhythm section, God awful singer and a guitarist who thinks he's Clapton."

"Everyone wants to be Clapton," Max sighed.

"Guess you'll have to show him," Bernie replied. The tall, lanky man was by far Max's favorite Canadian, the only one he told all the details of his hunting excursions to, and the only one he trusted to back him up. His cousin Scott was a close second, but he was easier to unnerve. Max snatched the freshly lit cigarette from Bernie and popped the filter into his mouth. "I'll be having that," he said.

Bernie started lighting another. "Did you get it?"

"I did," Maxwell said. "Had to fight for it, but we stay on the road." He carefully opened the book and almost failed to catch a small object that fell out. "Nearly lost my head for it, but Angelo's five hundred is all ours."

"Five hundred?" Bernie said. "I thought you were kidding before, five hundred doll-" he stopped, noticing the mess on the side of Max's head, even in the dim light of the alley. "Is that blood?"

"I said I nearly lost my head for it," Max replied.

"What happened? Is it bad?" Scott asked.

Bernie reached out to touch Maxwell's ear. "Holy shit, what did this?"

"Oi!" Maxwell said, recoiling, the sliver that fell out of the antique book clenched in his free hand. "I'm good to play, just need to get some whiskey on it so it doesn't infect. Get some in me first though." The wound burned and stung at the same time. He tried to ignore it, holding up the hard sliver that had fallen out of the middle of the book so he could inspect it in the scant illumination of the streetlight. "Petrified wood?" he muttered to himself.

"Let's hurry up and get this taken care of, Zack'll start puking if he sees this," Bernie said.

"I might start," Scott said. "Is it the whole ear? Did you get stabbed? What happened?"

"Bugger started shooting," Maxwell said, chuckling at Scott's boggling. "Monk with a gun, figures he ends up over-piercing my ear."

"Are you sure the bullet didn't go in? I heard a story about this guy, didn't even know he got shot until the X-Rays."

"If he didn't know he got shot, why was he getting X-Rays?" Maxwell asked. "Didn't go in, don't worry your little head," he said, patting him eight times on the top of his scalp so the slaps rang out in quick succession.

"C'mon, I've got the first aid kit in the back of the bus," Bernie said. "What is that?"

"Bonus," Maxwell said, pushing the sliver into the inside pocket of his leather bomber jacket, "maybe part of the book, don't know."

I

The bus and the band were well behind in North Bay, the boys decided to sleep in after a raucous night at the Nipissing Inn. They played until one in the morning, then invited a few old timers – Gib Frost, Vernor Newman, and Maria Townsend – on stage for a jam that pushed the noise until three, an hour too late for the local police.

The party started after the police left and the doors locked. It was an old hotel, recently upstaged by a newer establishment so the rooms were empty. Max did as he often did, kept his guitar in hand so he reached for the constantly refilling pint glass less, and passed on ladies who wouldn't mind taking the place of his instrument on his lap. He had a big payday coming, the kind even his father would envy if he were still alive.

The music of the night before still rang in his ears as the wind blew through his long hair and the sunlight painted the road in hues of gold. The two lane concrete connection between North Bay and Sudbury was anything but pristine. He had to pay close attention for large cracks, potholes and animals ahead. He knew he was getting close to Sudbury when he started seeing dead trees instead of the thick green wood.

The country in Canada was staggeringly beautiful to Maxwell, except for certain parts, like Sudbury. As the road rolled under the wheels of his Harley Davidson motorcycle, vistas of green woodland gave way to bare black and grey stone. This was the part of the trip he tended to forget. A century of mining and smelting made Sudbury and the area around it look like the crater it was.

He throttled up; passing a car with reckless weaves in and out of the opposing lane and didn't slow down after. He tried to focus on the road as the trees along side changed color from lush green to rust red, then grey. The vista opened up to each side, revealing a dead marsh with fallen trees, still water and decades-old, thick tree stumps that would have been removed from the landscape by the organisms that flocked to rotting wood, but that process never took place, the organisms were as dead as the fallen grey trees that surrounded the still waters. A pair of smoking stacks rose up on the horizon, and Max couldn't help but feel like he was returning home.

He was raised in England, bouncing between cities there with his father until they moved to Sudbury when he was eight. He met Bernie and Scott then, and his years of playing with his guitar instead of other children paid off. They were inseparable from that point on, ignoring the strange pursuits of their artifact-seeking fathers as much as they could while they played music in the barn. Other kids joined in when they could, especially when they got a little older. Every girl in the neighborhood seemed to want to take their turn singing like Brenda Lee, or some other radio siren, but they got bored before long, except for Miranda, who wanted to sing songs from the Beatles and Rolling Stones. She was the little girl with the big voice, and the fourth member of their barn band. That was until her mother died, and she left with her Aunt when Max was thirteen.

Bernie was a rhythm section magician by the time he was fourteen, pounding on the drums like a cross between Bonham and Pert before those gents were famous. He wasn't as talented on the bass, but he loved the instrument much more than the drums, and Max learned to accept that Bernie would rather play bass than drums. Scott, who was never far behind his older cousin, learned to play drums from Bernie, and said so little about playing with the band that it was years before Max knew for certain that Scott enjoyed it. He loved it, in fact, and found playing any other instrument intimidating, singing included.

So they wrote music together and eventually formed their band – Road Craft. The name had a ring to it, but Maxwell didn't like where it came from. Bernie's entire family was life long nature worshippers, and, like Max's father, believed in superstition, magic, and the power of spirits. While Max had an appreciation for nature, he had no use or belief in those other things. He enjoyed dark music like Black Sabbath, loved playing in the devil's scale on the guitar, and horror movies, but that was as close as he got to believe in the occult. For him, the closest he got to believing in the occult was artifact and book hunting. Scraping after rare artifacts and forbidden books was a way to earn money, and he'd learned from one of the best seekers on two continents – his father.

Max slowed down to turn into a curved section of road that had been cut through high black stone. Flat, unforgiving faces of rock rose up along either side of the curve, they were driver killers, regardless of whether someone was in a car or on a motorcycle. Fly off that corner, and the unyielding stone would turn man and machine into a terrible wreck, he'd seen it more times than he could count. You could test yourself, find out how fast you could make it down the road, but you couldn't test stone.

He made it through the dark corner and accelerated until he hit ninety miles an hour, nearly twice the posted limit. He shifted his shoulders so the guitar case strapped to his back was centered and watched the road carefully. The dead stone and fallen trees along side the road were ignored, slowing down for rock cuts; bad sections of road and turns were his focus.

Before long he arrived in Sudbury, the highway becoming the Kingsway. The road was newer, straighter, cut in a better line through the dark stone the mining city was built on. Instead of dead trees, there were car dealerships, their lots brimming with glittering vehicles.

The single yellow arch of the Deluxe Hamburger place made his stomach rumble, but he pressed on, headed for the down town center of the city. He slowed down as he came around the last corner, and sat up straight in his seat. After seeing Montreal,

Ottawa, Toronto, and so many smaller cities between that summer, Sudbury seemed small and dirty.

Even so, the brown brick buildings of the modest downtown center, a few rising as high as four and five storeys were a welcome sight. The place was alive with shoppers on Elm Street, so much so that he slowed to a cruising speed, catching the eye of more than one pedestrian through his dark sunglasses. Leather clad motorcyclists weren't common, were sometimes completely unwelcome, and the low rumble of his Harley drew attention.

As Maxwell passed the Woolworth's and turned onto Durham Street, he noticed a dark figure in the crowd; Miranda, looking right at him with her brown eyes, her long sable hair stirring in the air. He flashed her a grin the instant before his front wheel caught a pothole, nearly ripping the handlebars from his grip. He recovered and rolled on, finishing his turn. "I'm a bloody git," he said under his breath.

Seeing her on the street corner, years after her sudden departure when they were children, in a black leather jacket with long fringes, wild long hair, and the full figure of a woman was a shock. Those eyes were instantly recognizable, but the wear on her leather, how she wore it, and her steady gaze on him, however brief, spoke of a worldliness that he already found seductive.

He decided to look for her later. They both stood out, it wouldn't be hard to find her. For the time being, he had business to attend to at Harmony Music. The place stood out from the other shops, marked by a two story G-clef. Max drove into a side lane, stopped, and dismounted, trying to put the vision of Miranda out of his head. He loosed the homemade straps holding his guitar case to his back and carried it by the handle down the street.

The sound of the bell on the door of Harmony Music sent several heads turning in his direction. All Along The Watchtower was playing softly inside Sudbury's largest music store. Brass and wind instruments were along one wall, the drum section was in front of that, with orchestral strings to the right. On the opposite side of the store were guitars, basses, with stools in front of the racks. Bins with music notation books filled a space between the door and the guitar section, with a glass case between the counter and the door. A stairway by the door led downstairs, where there were pianos and more sheet music. "Max, you've got to see this!" said one of the younger patrons standing in front of the case.

Max wiped his boots on the mat at the door, a habit that didn't much matter to the store, since the brown carpet was in fairly bad condition. Paths were worn from the door to the counter and to the three walls of guitars to his right. There was much less wear and tear towards the drums and orchestral instruments. "Hey, Toby, what'd they find for the case this time?"

The high schooler with shaggy blonde hair waited for him at the case with two of his mates. Inside was a pristine white Fender Stratocaster guitar. "New Strat," Max said, looking into the case. "If that's your love." He looked around the store and didn't see Angelo, so he moved to the side where he could see the only guitar in the shop he wanted. "There's a beauty," he said, not surprised that it was still there. It was grossly overpriced.

"You and Les Pauls," Toby said. "Clapton plays nothing but Fender."

"Everyone wants to be Clapton," Max said under his breath as he eyed the ebony Les Paul Custom in the case, his focus drawn towards the golden hardware almost as much as it was to the price tag, $999.99.

"Man, Max is right," one of the teens said. He had no idea who the shaggy kid was. "Besides, I was in here the other day with my dad and he said that Fender was like a girl who's too pretty – if you're afraid to play dirty with her, there's no point."

"I wouldn't repeat that around town," Max said with a chuckle. Freddy Mann, one of the owners of the shop came towards him with the keys for the case in his hand and a grin on his face. "Oh, no need to open it up," he told the shop keep. "I'm here to see Angelo. He's expecting me."

"You sure you don't want to try her again, Max?" Freddy asked, twirling the ring of keys around his finger. The bell on the door rang, Miranda and a friend with long blonde hair in a summer dress entered. They both flashed him a smile and walked downstairs. "I'll let it go for nine hundred, c'mon, have a seat with that Gibson and fall in love all over again."

"Came to get paid, not to fall in love," Max said. "Angelo?"

"Upstairs," Freddy said, thumbing towards the narrow staircase behind the counter.

Max met Angelo half way up the stairs and looked him in the eye. The man's forehead was wrinkled with worry, an exaggerated expression thanks to the pocked, loose skin on his head. "Just coming down to get you," he said quietly.

"I got the number one item on your list," Max said as he followed the man upstairs to a small office. He was in his late fifties, and seemed too thin. The ledger and checkbook were out on the desk. The small sofa in the room was covered with paperwork. There was an old French horn hanging over a window overlooking Durham Street. Angelo closed it. "Lost part of an ear for it, almost lost my head."

"Close the door, Max," Angelo said.

He shut the ill-fitted old door behind him then put his guitar case down on the sofa. Max opened it, lifted his old Airliner guitar and retrieved the book he'd taken from Panos. "Here it is."

"Oh, my God, you really got it?" Angelo said. "I mean, I don't even want to know how, but you got it?"

"Sounds like you sent me on a fool's errand, Angelo." Max held the book out between them, but didn't cross the two feet to the desk. "Why don't you want to know how?"

"Listen, I got a request from someone in town to get that, someone none of us like, not you, your friends at the farm, or anyone you know, and it was so much money that I couldn't believe it. I put that on my list just because the client was willing to pay so much."

"I know about the money," Max said. "You made sure you told me about the money before we went on tour."

"I know, and I know your dad could find anything, that's how he made a living, and you've done really well since," Angelo stopped himself and swallowed nervously. "You've done really well, and you got paid, I got to keep providing certain groups of people with some interesting stuff, and there are people around town who know how good you are at this. They even feel they owe you something, but this is not the same. I never thought anyone would be able to bring that back when I put it on the list, and when I heard that your band was making its way back and I didn't get a call, I was assuming you didn't get it. I already told the interested party that they weren't going to have it."

"But this is it," Max said, holding the book up. The leather cover wasn't stamped, but branded with symbols from seven cultures from what Max could determine. "I managed to read it from cover to cover – the English translation, anyway. This is the kind of shit that would get a Catholic schoolboy tossed out of school, home and church. It's yours, for that ten thousand you put up for it."

"I don't want to know what's inside," Angelo said, putting his hands up as though he was pushing the idea of the contents away.

"It's all translated, old text on one line, the Queen's English on every other. Just like you described, just like your man wanted. So, cash, money, paid – that's what I want to be."

"Listen, Max," Angelo said, turning red. "A lot of people have been by the last couple months since you've been gone south with your band. I don't know how, but they knew you were looking for that, that most of the people who can find that sort of thing were looking, and they told me it couldn't be here, it couldn't be in

Sudbury. They say bad things would happen, bad things like –"

"You keep your superstition, your fucking twisted midnight shite, and give me my money!" Max shouted, slamming the book onto the table. "I've seen oracles, old friends of my Dad's who I've never wanted to see again, even a shaman, and then I had to set a bloody gun-toting monk on fire to get this fucking thing! Paid! That's what I'll be as soon as you write some numbers down on that fancy cheque book of yours!" He riffled the pages of the large business class cheque binder and shoved it towards Angelo. "Then we're done, it's been a good ride, but there are other dealers down south who don't get the jitters when they see old writing about resurrection and life eternal. There was a reward of five thousand dollars beside this book's name on the list, and here it is."

Angelo pulled a ring of keys out of his pocket and fussed with it. "I can't use the company cheques, I keep the music and the magic separate." He opened a drawer and retrieved a battered lockbox. It was unlocked and flipped open in seconds, revealing a modest pile of bills. "I can't give you the five thousand, but I can give you something for the running around."

"I went to Detroit tracking this, you wanker, and we only managed one gig while we drove a week out of our way."

"I know, you had to do a lot of research to get that," Angelo counted out a stack of fives, tens and twenties.

"Research? If I believed what the oracles told me about that book, I wouldn't have even come back to Sudbury. The last one said I should give up on finding this and go to California, take Bernie with me. California! Didn't sound too bad, if I'm honest, but I'm here instead."

"What else did she tell you?" Angelo asked, deadly serious.

"Cash!"

The sounds of hurried footsteps on the staircase were too short a warning before Freddie opened the door. "What's going on up here? The customers can hear you," he said, brows furrowed.

"Your partner here is refusing to pay for delivery," Max said.

"Here, it's three hundred fifty seven," Angelo said. "Keep the book, I don't want it."

Max let Angelo put the money and the book in his hand, speechless at the shortfall. He glanced at Angelo, who was staring at him, sweating, then looked to Freddie. "Your uncle owes me five thousand and he pays me three hundred bloody fifty seven."

"Keep the book," Angelo said.

Max regarded Angelo and asked; "Who wanted it? I should just sell direct, yeah?"

"I can't tell you," Angelo said. "I'll lose my business, both my businesses. Too many people want that out of Sudbury."

"You believe this?" Max asked Freddie, who was turning red like his uncle. "Can't get paid properly, can't find whoever wanted this in the first place." A thought occurred to him then. "Freddie, go get the case for the Les Paul, the one I was just staring at. Get it out from behind glass, put it in the case and in my hand."

"The Les Paul? No, I mean, that belongs to the store," Freddie stammered.

Max picked the ledger up off the desk and shook it in the air. "Then fucking pay me!" he thundered. "Or find a way to grow the bottom part of my bloody ear back."

Angelo was startled, whether it was just the sound of shouting, or the ledger being rustled to pieces, Max didn't know. He was happy to have found a raw nerve. "Go ahead and get that ready for Maxwell, Freddy," he said.

"But it's the Les Paul," Freddy said.

"It's all right, go and do that for me," Angelo reassured.

Max put the ledger down and folded the stack of bills before putting them in the inside pocket of his jacket. His finger brushed the shard that he'd found in the book. "Oh, and I've found something else inside this book. Maybe you'd like to take a look." He held the thing up. It was the first time he'd seen it in raw daylight, and he was immediately sure it was petrified wood.

Angelo's eyes went wide. "No, I don't know what that is," he said. "Can't be important."

"Are you sure?" Max said, aware that the appearance of the thing made Angelo nervous. "Looks like you swallowed a bug."

"Your father was right, you're a thug," Angelo said. "No more business from me, there are other people who can do your work."

"You sure?" Max said, happy to be out of the man's address book, but eager to taunt him one more time. "Bernie's not going to go running for you, his father would never have it, and no one from the Circle will talk to you."

"I'll make do without hiring thugs," Angelo said, slamming his lockbox shut. "Take that with you." He pointed at the book on the edge of the desk.

Max took it and slipped it inside his jacket. "I'll go get my guitar now, you can have the Airliner in trade, overprice that too."

The teens were gone when he arrived downstairs, and the black Les Paul Custom was in its velvet lined case on the counter. Miranda was standing beside it, a little smile on her lips.

"Here you go, Max," Freddie said, gesturing dismissively and retreating upstairs.

"Never heard anyone give someone shit like that, and I've lived in Italy," Miranda said as she watched Freddie disappear upstairs. "Owed you a lot of money, huh?"

Max closed the guitar case and slapped all the latches shut, trying to cool down at the same time. "Sorry, luv, I'd have a sweeter first meeting after not seeing you for so long."

"Hi, yourself," Miranda said. "Always loved your accent, it's better now though."

"So are you," Max said, pushing through the nervousness that was replacing his anger. "You need anything?"

She stared at him for a moment before comprehension dawned on her. "Oh, here? No, I left my gear at the farm. I'm staying with the Webbs for the Gathering."

Max's heart sunk a little at the thought of Miranda believing in the occult. Some of his nervousness at seeing her subsided. "We'd best be off, don't know if they'll change their mind on this," he said, hefting the guitar case a little for emphasis. He grabbed a handful of picks, stuffed them into his pocket, leaned over the counter, grabbed a pair of harmonicas, then helped himself to a few sets of strings and finished filling his pockets. It lacked class, but made him feel better.

Miranda's smirk didn't subside as she watched him take a few things. He could feel her eyes on him, and the only thing that bothered him was that he couldn't tell what she was thinking, but he was pretty sure she was amused at least. "Well, it's not five grand, but I'll be good on supplies for a bit."

"Right," she led the way out of the shop.

"My bike's just here," Max said. "I have to get to the farm, meeting the band there later." He walked past her, immediately regretting it, feeling rude. He turned back towards her after walking into the alley, and she bumped into him. "I'm a prat," he told her.

Miranda didn't step back much, but settled against him and looked him in the eye, that expression of mild amusement still on her face. "Just bad timing," she said.

"We could start over, yeah?" Max asked, trying desperately to be calm and cool as her nose was two inches from his.

"No," she whispered. "I heard everything, won't pretend I

didn't. I think this is the side I was meant to see of you first. You notice I'm not shying away?" Her smile stretched into something a little more interesting, as though she'd just given him a dare, or taken and fulfilled one herself. She glanced over his shoulder after holding his eye for a long moment. "That yours?"

"My favorite thing in this world," Max replied as smoothly as he could, but his quiet response was gravelly, not gentle.

"Give me a lift to the farm?" she asked.

There was nothing he wanted more in that moment than to ride back to the farm with Miranda on his bike behind him, but there was one detail he couldn't forget. He raised the guitar case a little. "Don't know if I have room."

"Me, or that guitar?" she asked, arching an eyebrow.

"Wait, I have straps, if you'll wear 'em," he said.

"Straps?"

Max stepped back and pulled the homemade straps and loops he used to ride with a guitar on his back off the seat and wrapped them around the guitar case.

"Yeah, I'll wear that," Miranda said, walking down the alley to his bike and zipping her black leather jacket closed. She turned around and let him put the arm loops around her, then tied them tighter. "Not bad," she said. "Now kick that thing so we can get down the road."

"As my Lady wishes," he said, straddling his bike and giving it a hard kick-start. It turned over and roared right away, not something that happened every time.

Miranda climbed on behind him, wrapped her arms around his waist. "My life's in your hands, Max" she whispered against his good ear.

He revved down the alley and onto the street, breaking out between two cars and roaring towards Elm Street.

II

Even though Maxwell's motorcycle rushed through the air down the highway, he could still smell her: sweet vanilla and rose. He'd taken women for rides before, but she fit. Her feet landed where they were supposed to, her hands were around his waist, but holding, not gripping or locked tight.

When they took a turn, they leaned together, and when they were on a long straight stretch, she wasn't afraid to rest against his back. He paid close attention to the road, taking no risks, giving her no reason to doubt her trust in him as a passenger. The highway to Azilda was far from perfect, and he made sure that they didn't hit anything that would interrupt their smooth ride.

The girl he knew was fading away, and the reality of the woman Miranda had become was replacing it. He didn't know this lady he'd met, but she still felt so familiar that it was mind-boggling. He felt as though they had found a completely different place to exist separate from the rest of the world, a space that was easy and comfortable. Maxwell had never experienced anything like it, but he still reminded himself of one simple fact – they had just met.

The barren stone landscape started to become green again; they had passed through town and made it to Azilda. Forty minutes of their ride had passed, and it felt like fleeting moments. The last stretch of highway passed even faster, then they turned onto a dirt road. In minutes they were rolling on a two lane, kicking up dust behind them, surrounded by tall, green trees. The rising heat and humidity of the early afternoon made the air smell rich, alive.

Maxwell liked thinking he was a creature made for the city, but when he returned to the Webb Farm it really was home. The woods made him feel like he was surrounded by life. The smell of the damp soil, the underbrush, and thick trees were a warm embrace he'd learned to miss.

They took the last turn onto a well-tarred dirt road and he slowed down. There were a few twists that could make trouble for them. She moved with him as they made the turns and then they came to the top of a hill. Miranda gave his waist a squeeze and he throttled up in response, sending them down the hill at an alarming speed. She laughed against his good ear as they went down, the slightly smaller hill ahead rising up, blocking the sun.

They made it up the other side, mostly on the speed they'd accumulated on the way down, and then they could see the farm. Cars lined the road leading to the large grassy green opening and there were at least two dozen tents on the empty field around the main farmhouse. The main house was a large, expanded building with nine bedrooms and at least five other rooms people could sleep in. If that was so full that people needed tents, then there was more to the Gathering than he expected, much more.

A few people picking things from the trunks of their cars turned to see him and Miranda ride by, and they greeted them with smiles. An old Wrought iron gate, large enough for two lanes, marked the boundary of fenced in land. He rode towards the barn, where there were at least a dozen people he didn't recognize moving in and out of the building.

That barn hadn't been used for livestock for decades, but they did keep feed and a workshop there. When Bernie and he were teens their dads spent a weekend building them a modest stage with enough space for a band of five or six at the back. It was years before Max saw the wisdom in that. They knew there would be partying as the two boys approached twenty, and giving them a good place to do it close to home kept them within reach, and it worked. The other barn was further down the road that was for livestock and farm business. Past that, down a well-travelled gravel road there were cabins and the lake, a major source of income for the Webb farm. The cabins were normally booked for most of the year, even through winter. Scott couldn't help but prattle on about how the band had been given the big cabin for the week, a four bedroom rental that dwarfed the rest of the quaint one and two room log structures.

"Stop here," Miranda said into his ear.

He could see what she may have objected to, a pair of women who were all smiles, breaking from the group headed into the barn with trays and pitchers. One was short, a plump older woman, and the other was taller and thin. They both had the same dark hair as Miranda except for an invasion of a little grey. The shorter one with the bigger smile caught them with her Polaroid camera, practically tittering at the act. She pulled the instant photo off the front of the camera and waved it in the air.

Miranda gave him a final squeeze. "See you later," she whispered before dismounting and pulling the straps off her shoulders so he could get his guitar.

He accepted the guitar and said; "Take it easy," immediately wishing he'd chosen any other words. The private space that separated them from the rest of the world was gone. As he watched her walk towards the two older women who were only a few feet away, admiring her shape through tight fitting jeans, he realized he wanted it back more than anything.

"You don't have to gloat every time you're right," Miranda said as she walked past the pair of women. The taller one rolled her eyes and followed her, speaking in Italian.

Maxwell knew he had been caught admiring Miranda's retreat towards the main house, as evidenced by the shorter woman grinning at him through momentarily narrowed eyes. He smiled back at her a little and tended to his bike, doing some fine adjustments before he let it down on it's kickstand so it wouldn't topple over onto the gravel. She approached, admiring the image forming in her photograph. "I knew you two would match," she said. "Look at that."

He glanced at the photo and returned his attention to setting his kickstand down on more stable gravel. "Think she just hit me up for a ride, if I'm honest," he said.

"Look," she said, putting the photo in front of him.

The pair of them matched, both in dark leather and denim, and it didn't look like Miranda was simply wrapped around him, it looked like they were riding his shining motorcycle together, sharing one space. Their expressions were passive, relaxed as they stared back at him through the photo.

"Yours," she said, putting it into his pocket. She had an Italian accent that was unmistakable, and a manner that made it impossible to refuse her insistence. "You don't recognize me, but then, we only met once when you were thirteen or fourteen."

Maxwell took another look and recalled immediately. She'd visited the house within weeks of his father's death. "You were here to talk to Allen." He said, remembering the late night, when Bernie and he came in from the barn to find her and his father at the kitchen table, talking soberly. They thought little of it at the time, but he didn't see Miranda after that.

"I took Miranda in after her mother passed," she said. "We returned to the old country, that's Italy, we're Sicilian. After a few years there we moved to Spain to meet her father, then New York. Two years there was enough, too fast, too busy, and Miranda had enough time to know our people there, so it was time to come here, at her mother's house in Chelmsford. Back just in time for the Gathering."

Maxwell looked to the barn, where people from the tents were beginning to congregate for lunch. Many of them were dressed in the loose dresses and bellbottoms of the sixties, and they were all ages. He faintly recognized a few from the year his father and he made the journey to Canada from England. As he returned his attention to Miranda's Aunt, he thought he saw his father out of the corner of his eye, standing in one of those half button-up collared T-Shirts he wore all the time and his dark framed glasses, puffing his pipe by the main barn door. He looked back immediately and saw nothing but bare barn door. He shook his head. "I'm sorry, I can't remember your name."

"Gladys," she told him. "And my sister there is called Susan. I understand, it was a long time ago, and you weren't interested in some woman visiting. You'll have to get used to me now though," she said with a wink.

It had been a long time since Maxwell felt he was in a situation where he felt he had little to no idea as to what's going on. When he caught sight of Bernie's father, who was only a slightly thicker, greyer version of his tall son, he was relieved. Allen waved him towards the large gazebo off to one side of the barn, and Max got off his bike. "Looks like someone wants an update on his son," he said.

"And a few other things," Gladys said, falling in step beside him. "Miranda missed you, you know. She never forgot you, sent letters to Bernie a few times. I was always surprised that she never sent one to you."

"Bernie never said he got letters from her," Max said, allowing the stout woman to loop her arm through his.

"She was a shy girl until a few years ago. I suppose I can't call our Miranda a girl anymore," she chuckled to herself. "New York will show anyone their shouting voice, except for our Miranda. She found her singing voice there, but I think she wants to see what is here for her, for now. New York can be tiring for people who are bred for the country."

"I've never seen traffic like I've seen in New York," Max said. "Wish I'd known she was there, I'd have dropped in."

"You would have been able to see one of her shows," Gladys said.

"Think she'd sing after things are set in the barn? I hear there's some band playing, locals I think."

"Your band," Gladys said, poking him. "You're funny, I didn't expect funny. If you don't play that disco music, then she would, I'm sure. She should, I'll tell her later."

"Good bands don't play disco," Max said.

They arrived at the Gazebo and Max's stomach rumbled at a tray of sandwiches in the middle of the table. He shook Allen's hand; it felt calloused from fingertip to wrist. "Your son's coming in a couple hours. He had to mind Zack and Darren into the wee hours last night."

"And you didn't?" Allen asked, amused.

"I've got a remarkable constitution," Max replied. "Mind if I?" he asked, pointing at the neat stacks of sandwiches on the table. For the first time he noticed a wrinkled old man sitting at the back of the gazebo in shadow. He smiled and coughed once when he looked up at Max. The ancient's blue eyes looked as young as a child's.

"Go ahead. How was the last leg of the tour?"

"Sold the rest of our records," Max said before chomping into what turned out to be a cucumber and mozzarella sandwich. He hazarded picking another quarter sandwich from the other end of the tray up and finished chewing. "Zack's an-" he consciously changed his mind about how he was about to finish his sentence. "He's been difficult. Wants to be the next big disco star or something, Darren's leaving, the Grand will be the last gig he plays rhythm guitar for us. His girlfriend is expecting, waited five months to tell him, so she's popping in a couple of weeks." Max decided to stop there; he could feel the frustration that his long ride to Sudbury and the subsequent ride with Miranda had relieved coming back.

The ancient fellow in the corner found that particularly funny, laughing so hard that his cane rolled off his knee and clattered to the floor. Max didn't hesitate for an instant, but retrieved it and offered his hand. "I'm called Maxwell, Max to friends."

"Samuel Hamilton, you met me a long time ago, when you and your father came for your first Gathering here. You call me Sam, and it's not his child," he said, his voice thin and wheezy. "Don't tell him that though, or she'll end up alone, and she's a good girl, except for the one time. Darren's chosen a woman who does not do well alone, he should stay close, and they'll be happy, especially if you don't tell him her secret."

Max was frozen in place for a moment, then straightened and took a bite of his sandwich. He chewed slowly. This was one of those meetings. He'd overheard dozens of them, been shooed out of the room and told to go play, as many times when he was younger. This was the kind of talk that dealt with portents and old magic, the kind of thing his father wasted his life on. This time he was the subject of the meeting, they were waiting for him, and he would not get away without ruffling more feathers than he could afford to.

From the groups of people outside and how many he recognized, he came to one conclusion. This was a gathering of people who believed in witchy ways. There was a High Summer Festival every August on the Webb farm, and there were people who stood in circles, praising whatever pagan deities they chose to around midnight at every one. None of them had the attendance he was seeing, and few of them had a name – The Gathering. The last one he remembered attending that seemed half as large happened the year his father brought him to Canada.

There was some special significance to the year, or the month, or the day, that he missed because he didn't believe, and he tried to ignore all things occult. The true consequences of that special time was this – a rare call to the Webb farm for the week, he would be neck-deep in spiritualism, and this gazebo meeting in the growing humidity of the late morning was where it would start for him. He inwardly admonished himself for not paying more attention; he could have avoided it all together. But then, he might not have run into Miranda.

Something so good happened to his father during their visit during the last large festival that he decided to move in to the farmhouse and become a Canadian citizen, dragging Max through the whole process. He objected as a child of seven would back then, but since then he'd learned to love his father's decision. He'd never had friends like he did in Canada, or felt as free as he did in its wilderness.

So, the act of walking out of that gazebo, of quietly avoiding all things mystic could come with serious repercussions. He would be alone, everyone else there was most likely a believer, and Miranda was among them. He would at least have to listen to what they had to say. They were staring at him, the quarter sandwich he'd taken – this one was salami and some yellow cheese – had been chewed to unrecognizable pulp as he put off what was about to happen next. He swallowed. "I'll be sure to keep Darla's details under my hat when I see Rick," Max said quietly.

"Her name's Pamela," the old man croaked.

"Bloody hell," Max said. "You got that from Allen."

"You slept with her sister, Franca when you were in Barrie, kept it from everyone. She's doing well, by the way, got into University of Toronto," Samuel said, shrugging. "She's not pregnant, even though the thing broke."

"The condom," Allen said, catching a wide-eyed look from Miranda's aunt.

Her gaze switched to him as Maxwell sat down in an old wooden chair. "So I'm believing for a second while I figure out how you know that, my good ear is wide open to whatever you're sellin'," Max said.

"What happened there?" Allen asked.

"That piece sacrificed itself so the rest of me could go on," Max said, fixing Allen with a withering look. "On with the show, what's the spooky thing you've brought me here to talk about?"

"You're on the verge of making a mistake, Max," Samuel said. "In a few days-" he was interrupted by a rattling cough.

"It's all right, Sam, I'll tell him," Allen said. "Max, what would you give to be as famous as Jimi Hendrix, or Jim Morrison? To be recognized for your style of music and your talent?"

"I've given plenty already," Max said. "You should know, your son and your nephew have been along for the ride." He was already irritated that his music was being brought into the conversation. "If this is about me playing in the devil's interval, then I promise to write something more cheerful for the next record. If there is a next record."

"No, it's not about that, everyone here has heard what you and my son do, and I think we all like it," Allen paused for a moment, looking to Sam, who was nodding.

"Vivaldi could not have written the Four Seasons without the Tritone," Sam said, taking a moment to wheeze before going on. "There are no objections here."

"I haven't heard the record," Gladys said. "But my niece has loved it, Bernie sent her a copy when she could not find it in New York."

"And I know," Allen said, "You guys have been paying the price for the dream you share on the road for three years. I've watched you start with a school bus rotting from the inside that you fixed up, do a turn across the northern states, then get a record deal. Everyone was excited, I think I was as excited as both of you, then you were back on the road, pushing that vinyl, and you started on a low when you found out most stores didn't get the record. It's been harder ever since, I've seen it, not the whole story, not how low things have really gotten, but I get it from the tone of my son's letters, from his calls. You've been doing your father's work to keep the wheels on the road, everyone here knows it, and it was all right, he taught you everything whether you liked it or not. Members of the Circle have actually benefited from your skills, placing orders through Angelo, or through Grant. It's been good, watching you work connections, bring things to the region, but now things are different, now you've found something and you're headed for a dangerous path."

"This book," Max said, reaching into his jacket.

Samuel lurched into a coughing fit, Gladys took a step back, clutching a small bag hanging from a string around her neck, and Allen put his hand on Max's. "You can leave that where it is."

Maxwell withdrew his hand without taking the book out and poured a glass of iced tea for Samuel. He accepted it gratefully. "I've come by that, and a piece of stone, looks like wood, but I've never seen the like."

"That explains more than you know," Allen said. "That book is powerful, have you read it?"

"From cover to cover, it's fully translated," Max replied. "Completely mad too, a lot of laws, rituals, and a list of names, a few I remember from lessons. Not all bad, not all good, like it's written by someone who just didn't care how the book was used," he replied, consciously making an effort to accommodate their apparent belief in the book. "Not recommended for summer reading."

"That's what we were afraid of," Allen said. "Is there a section on the Covenant?"

"At the end," Maxwell said. "It's what my father was looking for on and off most of his life, lives up to the lessons he gave me. The section refers back to a lot of the previous parts of the book, how those passages break the rules. Doesn't' always go into details about consequences though. I guess to a believer it's either a horror show, or a kind of 'how to break the world' manual. That Covenant deal is simple, but strict, not easy to play with."

"It exists?" Gladys asked quietly. "The pact between the High Lords and the Gods? The laws are there?" She pointed at his jacket, where the book was neatly tucked into his inside pocket.

"Laid out in fine print. A man proves his power by resurrecting himself, then surrenders to the will of the Heavens – that's the translation, none of this 'Gods' business – and the heavens take him, restoring him to a natural death. For their part of the deal, the Masters of All keep the primordial darkness, the power of all things and the cycle of life in balance, so mankind can't monkey around with the order of things on their own." Max cleared his throat then and recited one of the final lines. "'Upon the hill, Witnesses chosen during a new dawn beheld their Master ascend as a being of light. All gathered felt the whole love in his being, the truth of his heart, bathe them and hold them. Then the Witnesses did travel, sharing the light that followed them.'" Max took a moment as his head spun and his fingers tingled. He shook it off and nodded slowly. "The end is brighter than the beginning," Max said quietly. "Horror show of darkness and things that hunt human like a lion hunts elk."

"No more quotes for now," Samuel said quietly. "Especially from the beginning. The first translator died before he reached the end, transferring the text from Ancient Greek to Latin. I know you may not believe it, but that book contains knowledge that can unlock a fount of power in someone with the right upbringing."

"I've heard that before," Maxwell said, his back straightening. "My father wouldn't let me forget how incredible I could be if I minded my lessons with him, if I took a moment to be open to it. I know his books and lectures better than I knew him, thanks to all this."

"He was his lectures," Allen said. "Whether we like it or not, that was his life, and he was hard to deal with sometimes because of it, but he was a good man on the whole."

"Helped a lot of people," Samuel said. "Helped me too."

"I knew him differently," Maxwell said. "Too tired to get in a row about it, so we'll leave it at that. Now, I need a buyer for this, and Angelo isn't touching it, he isn't telling me who made the order either. So if any of you could help me, I'd appreciate it. This cash is a new life for Bernie and Scott," Max said forcefully. "I can sell this, give them each four thousand for whatever schooling they want, because this band is going nowhere, and I'll take the other two thousand to figure out what I want to do. It's the least I can do after dragging them on the road with me for a couple years."

"Max, I had no idea," Allen said.

"This last tour was hard," Max said. "Zack is on his way out, and I'm pushing him on, good riddance, and we're not finding a new howler, so that's it. I'll quit so they don't feel like they're leaving me, some dreams just gotta end before they start taking what you love away."

"So, you were going to give most of the money away," Gladys said, a strange expression on her face that seemed joyful and sad at the same time. Max hadn't seen it before. "So they could have a future."

"The plan," Max said, nodding. He started pulling his cigarettes out of his pocket, then remembered he was sitting beside Samuel and put them back.

"We'll pay you to keep it then, get a collection," Samuel said, his breath rattling.

"No, you'll just make the connection between me and the customer, then he'll pay me. Doesn't make sense to pay me to keep this thing," Max said.

"That book and the stone both have power of their own, aside from the knowledge the book contains," Allen said. "It's important that they stay with you because you were trained to handle exactly what those things can do. As much as you hated every minute of it, now that training is important in the presence of something so spiritually influential. The book and especially the stone have most likely already imprinted themselves on you. Things that powerful do that, and it's not good to have them passed around, the fewer people they're attached to, the better. You have to be the bearer, I'm sorry."

"This stone couldn't be more dead. If it's petrified wood, then it's been a tree, got cut off, died, then got old, and turned to stone. It couldn't be more dead, it can't know anything, it can't do anything," Max said, so irritated by how ridiculous it was that these people, one of whom he'd respected for over a decade and saw as an adopted father, were so concerned with superstition.

"All right," Allen said. "I've always respected your point of view, Max. Now I'd like you to give us just a minute to listen, then you can ride off, or go drop yourself in the lake, whatever you like."

"All right," Max said, leaning back in the old wooden chair until it creaked.

"Spirits follow the Dawn Shard around, it is used to attract them for rituals. No one knows for sure where it came from, we don't know exactly how it got to North America, or why it was brought here or by who, but we do know that it has been in the wild for too long. We have seen it in pictures with politicians, musicians and artists over the last few years, and then we heard it had been brought together with the dangerous book you're holding, which is actually perfectly safe as long as it is in your hands."

"Why is it safe with me, but it nearly gave Samuel here a coronary?" Max asked.

"You read what it said," Gladys said. "You don't believe, and even if you start believing, you'll never use it. Your father trained you too well, and you are too strong to be tempted."

"I've come to call that a stubborn streak," Allen said. "But it's true nonetheless. That book will tempt anyone in this room many times more than it would you. We've all lost people we'd be tempted to break the natural order for, and some of us would want to extend our lives. We'd like to think that we could resist, but you never know until the opportunity presents itself."

"If you followed most of the non-sacrifice passages in this book, nothing would happen, because it's a fiction. All it did was cost me gas money, force me to talk to some unsavory characters that each had a unique and terrible smell, and get me shot at while I was looking for it. If that's power, then it is massive, but other than that, it's a book, just a bloody old book."

"Max, just try to believe for a minute," Gladys pleaded.

Max put up his hands. "Fine, because I know you're good people with some strange business, but the good sort nonetheless."

"All right, to the point. That shard has a demon attached to it," Allen said. "We don't know it's name, but it is an inhuman who has never been alive on this earth. It collects the souls of the talented and desperate. We've managed to find evidence of it and the shard together going back to 1938, but that's just for musicians. Gladys found evidence that one of the earliest people to have dealings with that demon was Pope John the Twelfth. All of them rose to high power or fame, and they were all twenty seven when they died."

"I'm not twenty seven," Max said. "Safe for a few years."

"This is when we think you'll be approached, right now."

"I knew it was going to happen before the Dawn Shard was a part of this, thank you," Sam said.

"Yes, we know," Gladys said. "Not everyone has good sight in both worlds."

"I'll trade my third eye for a good lung," Samuel said. He turned towards Max, gravely serious. "It's on you, son. That demon is going to approach you with temptations you cannot imagine, and it will be just as you're starting to believe. You've tried for a while to be famous on your own, to get recognized for all your hard work, and you see that road coming to an end. I know what that's like, more than you know."

"All right," Max said quietly. "That's as much as I can take. I'm sorry you've got fewer days ahead than behind," he told Sam. "But I'm going to take a few of these." He pointed at the platter on the table. "Then I'm going to get some gas from the shed, top up my bike, and disappear for a few hours." No one said anything more as he pushed one-quarter sandwich in his mouth and took two more in each hand then left.

III

Maxwell didn't intend to ride to his father's gravesite, but he was rolling down the pebbly drive into the old graveyard before he realized it. The once whitewashed church standing by the graveyard was being reclaimed by the forest, abandoned before Max arrived in Canada. One wall had fallen in, and the eastern side had fallen outwards. Rotting pews were barely visible beneath the wreckage of the simple old wood shingle roof. The entrance, really an archway thee feet deep set into the low front wall, still stood, its door absent now, though Max could remember the finely carved cedar of the heavy door, with its iron handles. He drove onto the flat stones that marked the end of the graveyard path in front of the church, grabbed a blanket from his saddlebags and walked to the quiet plot where his father was laid to rest.

A few dead branches had fallen across his father's grave and those surrounding it. The grass was a little long, but lush and green. Max took some time to clear the branches away from several plots, throwing them into the bush surrounding the quiet site.

When he was finished he looked at the simple grey stone. There was a pentagram with oak leaves around it above his father's epitaph, which read:

> Charles Foster
> Father
> Community Leader
> He will be missed.
> 1910 - 1969

There was a ritual his father insisted on when Max was given the first ring that didn't have much meaning beyond the aesthetic. Anything that didn't have religious meaning had to be left by the door. Max maintained a version of that ritual, pulling a silver ram's head, a pentagram, the circular Seal of Julius, and a treble clef ring off his fingers. The Seal of Julius and pentagram were religious symbols, but they meant little to him other than looking flashy and feeling good on his fingers. He put them all on top of his father's rounded gravestone, hung his leather jacket on one side, and lay down beneath it, using his folded blanket as a pillow.

The smell of the earth and humid air surrounded him, he listened to the sounds of birds and rustling leaves for a while before beginning the next part of his visit. The long shade allowed the grass to grow thick and richly green. With the tall trees surrounding the small graveyard, it was difficult to tell what time it was, but Max knew it was early afternoon. To him it had already been a long day.

"Miss having you around, old man," he said, looking through the clearing in the trees to the scantly clouded blue sky. "Don't know what they want from me this time, but I'm pretty sure it's my fault for picking up the trail you were following most of your life. Got what you were looking for, what you didn't even tell Allen about. I think they actually believe it can resurrect the dead, change the world." He never knew his father as a young man, he was forty-five when Max was born, still vital, but turning grey. Most of his memories of his father were of him leaving and returning.

There were the lessons, which were unavoidable. Max learned about different religions, their origins, the laws of the magical universe, and the 'old ways' as Max's father and his friends referred to them. He enjoyed most of the history, but the so-called practical side seemed pointless, as good as well wishing and hand wringing while looking up at the stars for a response.

In all the rituals and so-called magical circles Max was forced to attend, the most magical sensation he had was a case of the goose bumps. The most common feeling he endured was having to go to the bathroom after the first forty minutes. None of the high magic, incantations, prayers, invocations, charms, or anything else seemed to do anything in the world. He could recognize the comfort faith brought to some people, and that there brand of paganism seemed to keep a large community together, but that's where the benefits ended for Maxwell.

When he fell asleep exactly, Maxwell didn't know, but he started awake when his head rolled onto his recently healed ear. He opened his eyes in time to see the headstone begin to move, and rolled out from under it. The granite fell forward with enough weight to crush his head and shoulders. He got to his feet and stared at the blank side of the stone, wide-eyed, a rotten, churning feeling in his gut.

A chill wind pulled at his shirt and hair. Looking up, he could see the church standing as upright as it was when the congregation was in service, and the wrought iron fencing standing around the small graveyard. At the end of the lane was an arching tree with people hanging from nooses on three main branches. The men and women slowly twisted in the wind, and Maxwell recognized the scene from an old picture, but couldn't quite remember why they were killed.

A slender hand landed on his back, and he turned. It was a young boy. The family he hung with was around him, looking to Maxwell mournfully. "Free us. Take us to water. Give us peace."

A movement caught Max's eye, and he looked to the doorway of the church. The boards weren't white the way a whitewashed shingle building should be, they had the glisten and yellow color of bone. The figure in the doorway was square-shouldered, tall, his narrow face stern, and the clothing he wore shifted as though it was made of shadow. It felt as though the man's steel grey gaze weighed Maxwell down. He took a step back and tripped over his father's downed gravestone.

The clear day had returned, the cool air replaced with the thick, humid heat of the afternoon and the tree at the crossroads by the end of the church's drive was gone along with the people who hung there.

Maxwell picked up his rings and tried to pull the corner of his jacket free from the stone. "Fucking geezer!" he shouted as he fought to retrieve his leathers. "I'm either stoned or you were right, but it doesn't matter now, because I'll never be back to clear your grave!" he freed his jacket and put it on.

The thought of those sandwiches being drugged seemed ridiculous, but less so than having waking visions of dead families, so in a demonstration of distaste for everything his father believed in, he bent over and shoved two fingers down his throat. He gagged and vomited up less than half of what he ate, mostly forcing bile up. By the third try, he was down with one knee on the tombstone and one on the grass. He didn't notice a car pull in on the side of the road behind him.

The light touch of a hand on his shoulder startled him out of the desperate act of trying to regurgitate the quarter sandwiches he'd had possibly hours before. He spun around, falling backwards.

It was Miranda, beautiful with the blue of the sky behind her, wearing a summer dress so light he could see the bathing suit she wore underneath. It was in a new style, flashy, the sort of thing Farrah Fawcett would wear. She looked almost as worried as Bernie, who was standing behind her. He dropped to one knee to attend to Max. "What'd you take? What's the reaction? Was it the LSD?"

"Fucking sandwiches," Maxwell replied, still stunned enough to reply honestly, but not so out of his mind that he couldn't recognize how ludicrous the answer was. "They must've drugged me with the sandwiches," he explained. It still sounded ridiculous aloud, and he surprised himself with an involuntary snicker.

Miranda was frozen to the spot, confusion slowly replacing her expression of alarm. Bernie checked Max's pupils then fixed him with an irritated look. "You're fine and clean. Wait, did you say sandwiches?"

The whole situation sunk in for Maxwell. The likely possibility that everything he fought to disbelieve was true, that he was nearly killed by his father's downed headstone, and that he just spent ten minutes trying to upchuck sandwiches that he suspected may have been poisoned under the supervision of Bernie's father, a man he saw as more of a father than his actual dad. It sunk in, and all he could do was laugh. It was a high-pitched, raspy, unrestrained kind of heel-kicking laughter that put him flat on his back when Bernie let him go.

"You asshole, I thought you'd taken something and it was going wrong," Bernie said. "It's going around today."

"Does he do that?" Miranda asked, unable to stop herself from smiling a little in reaction to Max's unrestrained laughter.

"He does magic mushrooms sometimes, some weed, but chemicals," Bernie said, shaking his head. "No, not for a year, probably longer. The last time he did acid we couldn't get him out from under the bus until sunrise. You all right, mate?" the last he asked with his own terrible impersonation of a British accent.

"Is he okay?" Miranda asked, still looking amused.

"No, I think he's lost it this time. I don't even think he's been into the weed, his pupils are fine," Bernie said.

"Okay," Max said, taking a deep breath and recalling the sobering scene he'd just witnessed in his vision, or hallucination, he wasn't sure. "Okay, I'm all right." He turned away from Miranda while he wiped his nose and mouth, then tried to clean his hands in the grass. He put the pentagram on his left middle finger, and the heavier Seal of Julius on his right middle finger then pocketed his other rings. "It's been a hell of a day," he said, standing up and turning around. "Everything's gone strange today, but not all bad," he looked to Miranda then. "Glad to meet you again after all the bad news this morning, then dark sprits and murder attempts from beyond the grave. My head was under that a second before this geezer turned his stone down," he said, kicking his father's headstone.

"Bad omen," Miranda said. "Lucky you got out."

"Bernie, you know I do everything I can to step lightly around what you and your dad believe," Maxwell said. "I want to believe that these are just patches of dirt, with people's old bodies under 'em like old clothes. All used up, nothing hovering around or moving on."

"You're good at stepping around that, it's cool," Bernie said.

"If that's how you feel, I'll tell my Aunts," Miranda said. "They'll back off."

"Right, well listen. I don't want to say I'm a believer, because I'm half way to checking myself in to the special wing of the hospital, where they keep people in padded rooms, and half way to cracking one of your dad's books to find out what I just saw here. Who I just saw here."

"Why? What did you see?" Bernie asked.

Maxwell ran his hands through his long hair and sighed. "All right, all right, let's pretend for a minute that I believe everything your Circle are into. Ceremonies are important to the seasons, there are as many spirits as there are stars in the sky, and the moon's a big cheese wheel."

Miranda sighed and rolled her eyes.

"Okay, not the last bit, of course," Max said. "So, I fall asleep there, and when I wake up I'm about to be pancaked by my father's gravestone. I narrowly avoid that, and when I look around it feels a bit like fall, chilly, and the sky is grey. I see a family, six, maybe seven men women and children hanging from a great old tree there," he pointed to the crossroads at the end of the graveyard drive. "Just where the old fence post is. That church is in fine condition, some old priest is standing in front, glaring daggers at me, and one of the hanging kids turns me around to tell me I have to free him over water."

"Then you started throwing up?" Bernie asked.

"Well, that's all gone, the suns down over the treetops, so I must have been asleep for a couple hours, at least, and I'm thinking the only thing that could do that – logically – are drugs, so I try to empty the tank."

"Well, it makes sense, but you're fine now," Miranda said. "If you were high enough to hallucinate that, well, you'd still be tripping hard."

"She's right," Maxwell sighed. "And I wasn't dreaming, I woke up first. So, let's say all of it was real, face value."

"Then you saw spirits trapped in a terrible event," Bernie said. "They're trapped here, maybe by the priest you saw. It's also doubtful that this is consecrated ground now, if that's what's happening here. Something was done to desecrate the area a long time ago, but that's just a guess."

Miranda closed her eyes for a moment, visibly relaxing, then tensed as her eyes opened again. "We have to leave," Miranda said, looking across the aged tombstones as though realizing where they were for the first time. "There is something wrong here."

"We can look it up later," Bernie said. "Our family library will have something about it, there are records about the whole area."

"Now, I'm just temporarily believing, playing along, you understand," Maxwell said.

Miranda fixed him with a patronizing smile and kissed him on the cheek, her lips' touch was feather light. "Uh-huh, you cling to that as long as you can, sugar."

"So, what you got from Panos is the real thing?" Bernie asked, looking slightly worried. "That could be a part of this."

The trio began walking towards Max's motorcycle. The memory of the dark pastor in the church's doorway made him wary of the fallen structure. "Your father and her Aunt tells me that what I've got on me will draw spirits from their shadows and graves, then I pay my dad's grave a visit and have a full-on vision? Either that's proof positive that the book and stone I got from Panos is real, or nothing is. Don't tell anyone I said so. I'm still clinging to sanity here."

"Would you rather be crazy or wrong?" Bernie asked, hesitant. Max knew that his friend had always wanted him in the fold, amongst the believers.

"Well, if I'm stoned, someone drugged me, because, I haven't taken or smoked anything today. I haven't even been smoking, not since this morning. I want a cigarette so bad I could smoke my sleeve."

"So, not drugs," Miranda said.

"And I know you're maybe a little off center, but you're not crazy," Bernie said. "I'd testify to it."

"So I've got visions, a book that could break the world, and a piece of petrified wood that could have come from who knows what, maybe even the first Sun Prince," Max finished.

"Is that what it is?" Bernie asked, alarmed. "You brought that here?"

"First Sun Prince?" Miranda asked.

"Great story, ancient history stuff. There was a young man who claimed to be the son of a god sometime around five thousand B.C. and he was murdered by a pharaoh because he was afraid the boy would threaten his power. The boy rose from the dead to prove to his followers that he was really god-like, or a god himself, then retreated into the desert never to be seen again. They say he was born again two thousand years later, named Amun, and he struck down a corrupt slave master before he was killed, did the same resurrection act as before, but then ascended into the heavens, joining or merging with Ra, he Sun God, known as Amun-Ra for a few centuries until the cult of Ra was eventually disbanded, but temporarily, so Ra rose again later." Maxwell said. "So, the first Sun Prince had a staff, and there's suggestions that this petrified wood is a piece of it. I have a doubt, and I don't care, to be honest. If it really does what the Circle says it does, then I'd rather drop it in a deep, dark hole and be done than carry it around like an unlucky rabbit's foot."

"Wow," Miranda said, wide-eyed.

"My Dad never stopped teaching, the whole Sun Prince thing is the kind of bedtime story he'd put me to sleep with. I had some strange dreams growing up," Max said.

"I wonder how much of his lessons you actually kept up there?" Bernie asked.

"Old geezer tested me on whatever I had to read, whatever he told me. It was like coming home from school to another school, you were there, mate," Max said.

"I was, but your dad was never as hard on me," Bernie replied.

"I had traditional teachings, practical things, and some history. Most of it was about Europe since the fall of Rome, and how our people survived as pagans," Miranda said. "I've never heard of a Sun Prince. I'll take the car this time," Miranda said as Max got onto his motorcycle. "If my aunt sees anyone else driving it, I'll get the evil eye from her for the rest of the weekend."

"Everyone's gone lakeside," Bernie said.

"Good enough, just run interference between me and everyone who wants me to be a believer." He strapped his guitar onto his back. "I need to look some things up, see if I was dreaming."

"Keep me in on it, none of this is safe if you're doing it alone. You know the rules: There is always a conjurer, a weaver and a watcher."

"Yeah, I never thought I would have to pay any attention to them myself," Max replied. He looked to the roadside then, where Miranda was getting into her Aunt's Skylark. It was a beast of a green car with a great, frowning grill. "Could have warned me that she was coming."

"You two were separated when her mother died for a reason, Max," Bernie said. "Your father had a vision before he died, and my dad carried his wishes out."

"Fucking geezer," Max said. "That goes for both of 'em."

"You guys were always hanging out when you were kids, and she was my other best friend. I wanted to tell you she was still writing every few months, but my Dad made sure I didn't say a thing. I don't have all the details, but my Dad used to tell me that you two would be too much of a distraction to each other growing up."

Max turned the situation over in his head. His father was always manipulating people, and it didn't stop there. He grew up overhearing conversations about portents and visions, listening to his elders talk about how to prevent this, or to ensure that. It all added up to self-serving nonsense to him. If a vision predicted that something was going to happen, why would it take so much work to make sure it did? That was only one of the many questions that no one ever answered, and it fortified his disbelief. "I missed her." Max looked at his old friend, who looked worried. "I still remember strummin' to her singin', and I never forgot her laugh. Now she's something else, we missed all that time between."

"It was hard, man, keeping everything I knew about her away from you, especially at first, but I guess I just started having faith in the plan after a while. By the way, what's in the case?"

"Half your first year college tuition," Max replied. "What's the plan?"

"I don't know, they just had to keep you two apart, that's why I fell back on faith. She wasn't happy to move either, she tried to get her Aunt to take her back for years, if that helps. New York was close though, she almost stayed, but things are going disco there too, not much of a future for a singer like her."

"So, she's going to stick around?" Max asked. "Don't think I can stay away now, don't think her aunts want that for us either. They were grinning like they had clothes hangers in their mouths when we rolled in on my bike. Not the reaction I'm used to when someone's daughter is on the back of my bike."

"Be careful, Max. I know she's grown up foxy, but she's your match, man," Bernie said. "Like your equal, just as cool, seen more of the world, and done just as much as us in it. She was on her own in New York for a year."

"Miranda," Max said her name as though slowly rolling it over in his mind and his mouth and watched as she started the car twenty feet away. "All this spiritual shit's getting me sideways, but that ride has been in my head since this morning. Be careful," Max shook his head once and sucked air in between his teeth. "Too fucking late, mate." He jumped down on his kick-starter, and the engine failed to turn over.

"Careful, she's cooling off. On the way to the graveyard she was saying you didn't seem to enjoy that ride you can't forget," Bernie said. "Let her know, man, let her know."

"Stop talking about me and get in the car!" Miranda said, leaning out of the window and honking the horn.

"Think she heard us?" Bernie asked.

"Not bloody likely," Max replied, trying to kick start his bike again and failing.

"Oh, yeah," Bernie said, starting to walk away. "You've got a mess to clean up, Zack's tripping hard on some LSD he picked up. The guys have him cornered on the bus, but who knows how long that'll last."

"I'm kicking him out of the band," Maxwell said. "I know we're retiring anyway, but firing him is the best way to make sure he doesn't disco all over our songs."

"Saw it coming," Bernie replied, jogging to the car at the sound of Miranda blasting the horn again.

"C'mon, old girl," Max said under his breath as he kicked his starter again. The engine turned over and he increased throttle. "There it is." He reached into his pocket for his pack of cigarettes and tried to pop one out only to find that the last one had been crushed to paper and crumbs. "Days like these," he said as he crumpled it up and tossed it into the wreckage of the church in front of him.

He spun his tire, spraying the yard with dirt and gravel until his bike was turned around one hundred eighty degrees. He couldn't leave the graveyard fast enough.

IV

"I hate when one of my aunts are right, now that both are right, there will be no living with them," Miranda said. She drove a car like Maxwell did, her foot down, and her front right tire right along the outer edge of the road. On the highway it was quick and a little alarming, but on dirt roads it was terrifying. It made him wonder if she was a better rider than a driver like Maxwell too.

Bernie gripped the dash with his left hand and the edge where the door met the window with the other as they made a tight corner. Max passed them as soon as they were past it, roaring by. He tried to ignore the shared insanity between Miranda and Max. "What do you mean?"

"They've been telling me for the last year that Max was my destiny, trying to get me all worked up about visions of him and me getting together now that we're both ready." She huffed, flicking her hair over her shoulder. "They actually cursed me with a memory spell for two weeks. I kept having dreams that were just memories of Max and me. You know, him playing that old acoustic and me singing along beside the barn. A few where we're just running around like the kids we were, having fun. There was one, it must have been when Max was eight, I was seven, we were all snuggled up in the yard in one of those night time family circle ceremonies and my mother wraps a blanket around us. When I woke up I could remember how sweet and comfortable and safe that moment was. Riding his bike with him was just as good. No, better, because there was more, like our auras were merging, it was just amazing and right. Then it's over and he says 'take it easy,' like I was just another saddlebag, and my aunts are standing there grinning, because they know I won't be able to stop thinking about him, and I can't, even though I should be just as happy to see both of you, we grew up together, until I got kidnapped off to

Italy, and Spain, and New York. Maybe I should just stay away from him to make a point," she actually made a growling sound as her lips pressed together with such tension that they were drawn across her face in a straight line. Meanwhile, her foot was getting heavier on the accelerator.

Bernie was rattled in his seat as the car went over a section of road that was recently flooded, small potholes and loose stones. "Easy, these roads aren't nice to speeders."

She slowed down to a slightly more reasonable speed and turned the radio on, Wish You Were Here was playing, one of only a few songs that Bernie sang on stage every once in a while, usually to buy Zack time to get on stage or decide that he was finished pitching a fit over the latest slight.

"You heard me, right?" Miranda said.

"Oh, yeah, destiny, you didn't want to like him," Bernie said, realizing that Miranda was paying more attention to him than she was the winding road. "Road, road," he said, pointing over the dash.

"I'm a great driver, never had an accident. Then again, I didn't drive in New York, and I don't have my license here, but this isn't much different from Italy or Spain, lots of dirt roads there. Anyway, you had to know why they separated Max and me back then."

"No, I just heard your mother died and you were going to live with your aunt," Bernie replied. "I was sad about it for a few months, well, maybe a few weeks, but Max was pissed. First, at loud, slamming doors and skipping school to play guitar, then he didn't talk about it, he was just low, you know? I knew why, but no one at school did, so we started high school and he was just this quiet, dark, kind of unpleasant English guy to them."

"Wait, when I left he was what, fourteen, fifteen?"

"He was about to turn fifteen," Bernie said.

"So, how long did his pouting last?"

"It wasn't pouting," Bernie said, emphatically shaking his head. "At first, when he was loud about it, yeah, but then he got quiet and didn't come back up unless you counted the noise he made with his guitar. He wrote some amazing stuff back then, we played constantly after his father died. Music was how he connected to people, and I think he jammed with everyone who could play three chords or more. He just never really got happy again, like when we were kids."

"So why would my Aunts and his dad agree that I had to go half way across the world and pretend he didn't exist? I mean, I guess I wasn't distracted either, they taught me everything they knew, and other than not having too many friends I had a great time growing up, well, until New York, things were okay."

"Let me guess," Bernie was momentarily interrupted as they struck a pothole dead on and he was bounced in his seat, his head brushing the ceiling. "You started rebelling, getting into trouble."

"I took off with a band for a while, Aunt Susan nearly cracked me over the head and chained me to the radiator when she caught up with me four months later, but I was out of high school, I didn't see the problem," Miranda said.

"How old were you?"

"Seventeen, I just graduated," Miranda replied.

Bernie could see that she honestly didn't see the issue with a seventeen-year-old girl running around the New York area with a band without telling her guardians where she was. The parallels – Max spending his college fund on their old school bus, road money and a demo around the same time, acts which infuriated Bernie's dad, but there was little he could do. The only real differences were that Max was eighteen when he ran off, and that Bernie went with him.

"What?" Miranda asked after a stretch of silence.

"You're perfect for each other," Bernie said.

"I didn't want a boyfriend, I'm here to figure out the next act," Miranda said. "Can't think about that though, not since that ride. The Gathering was all I came for, I love nature, and connecting with the universe the way we do, so I couldn't skip this. I was looking forward to reuniting with you and Scott too, and it's good to see you both after so long. Max has stolen the scene though."

"Stolen the scene?" Bernie asked.

"I was in a few plays in New York, mostly background stuff, it means…"

"I get it," Bernie said.

"But if he's going to be all broody and quiet the whole time, I don't know," Miranda said. "I'll hang out until he cracks, if he cracks."

"He will," Bernie said. "I think if anyone can connect with him, you know, aside from me and Scott, you can."

"Cool, but what's with his British accent? It's even thicker than before."

"He spent four months in England with his Great Uncle before he died," Bernie replied. "Must have been three years ago now. He brought back a small library and that accent."

"Oh," Miranda said. "At least I can understand him, most of the time."

"So, instead of proving your aunts wrong, you made sure you were one of the first things he saw when he came into town?" Bernie said.

"No," Miranda said, shaking her head. "They both had a vision, and they told me, where he'd be and when," Miranda confirmed.

"Then you go there,"

"To prove them wrong," Miranda said. "I wanted to get right up to him and take a good look, so I could go back to my Aunts and say; 'nope, I checked him out and didn't even get a buzz.'"

"Then-" Bernie started to reply.

"Then I'm asking him for a ride out of no where, I didn't plan it, I didn't even think about how it would look to my Aunts, who are gloating,"

"I heard that the first time," Bernie said, patiently. He was glad there would be dozens of people to talk to once they got back to the farm. People other than the love-stunned Max and Miranda.

"Yeah, so I just forget everything and ride with him, like we're tucked into that blanket together all over again, and time passes so fast, and we're at the farm and I remember – shit! I was supposed to turn my nose up at this British-Canadian hick, not throw myself at him! Then he says; 'take it easy!'"

"Do you want advice? Or are you just talking to blow off steam?"

"Oh, suck an egg!" Miranda shot at him.

"That's what I thought," Bernie said. They were finally getting close to the farm, and he wondered what trouble awaited him there. He was the peace keeper between Maxwell and Zackary, the lead guitarist and lead singer, but sometimes, especially when Zack had gotten into a terrible substance and was on a bad trip, Max was the only one who could calm him down. He had a way with the inebriated and insane.

"Sorry," Miranda said, slowing the car down to a reasonable speed, probably for appearances sake.

"Don't worry, I like eggs."

"Max," Miranda said. "Did he forget me? Is he all right with women? I mean, I saw a lot in New York, people treating girls like they were nothing, guys who just did their business when they got an opening, wiped it off on the sheets and left the door open on their way out."

"Damn, who did you hang out with?" Bernie asked, taken aback by the mental image.

"That's another conversation, focus," Miranda said as she parked the car at the back of a long line of vehicles along the farm roadsides. "Should I just suck it up and enjoy the Gathering then go back to my Mom's house, or is he worth my time? I know you're his friend but, you're mine too."

There she was, the young girl Bernie remembered from when they were thirteen, right before she had to leave. Those brown eyes may have been decorated by a little mascara since then, but he could still see innocence, and a person who didn't want to be hurt. That's why he told her the truth. "Max has done well with his strong, silent, exotic British routine on the road," Bernie said. "But he's not a pickup artist, he picked and chose from what came to him, maybe nine times since we started touring three years ago."

"Nine times?" she asked, her expression unreadable.

"Well, he could have had ten times that, I mean, sometimes they really threw themselves at him, I'm not even exaggerating. Look at Zack, his night isn't finished if he hasn't dragged some girl into a bathroom stall."

"Nine is low," Miranda said. "I had two boyfriends in Spain, then there were three guys in New York."

"I don't need to know," Bernie said, getting out of the car.

Miranda laughed, "I don't get that. Guys can talk about who they get it on with, where, how and how many but the moment a woman says she's had a bit of fun, she's a slut, and no one wants to hear it."

"I didn't say that," Bernie replied. "I just don't think of you like that, I always pictured a little girl when I read your letters, all eleven of them."

"Well, me and my last Spanish boy went through condoms like tissues in a flu epidemic," Miranda said, taunting Bernie. "He worshipped me like a Goddess, and followed me around like a puppy, and he had just as much energy. It was amazing."

The sound of a car door slamming behind them made them both jump. Bernie watched as a couple old enough to be their parents walked past, the woman staring daggers at Miranda. "Hello, Miss Parillo," he said, forcing a smile.

"Good day," she said as she shuffled past with a small cooler in one hand and her purse tightly clutched under her arm.

"You know her?" Miranda asked.

"Lives down the street from you," Bernie replied. "She's probably just visiting for the barbeque tonight, seeing how her daughters are settling in. You'll be seeing her around."

"Wonderful," Miranda said. "They probably think Max is an angel on two wheels too, while I'll be known as the harlot of Chelmsford. Just pin a scarlet letter on me."

"Oh no, Max is not what you'd call a community favorite. That bike of his and stubborn streak have gotten him into a few fights, one with a councilman's son. He didn't start that one though. Actually, Max has never swung first."

"Does he know what's going on with him? That he's going to wake up to the brighter world whether he likes it or not?"

"Yes, I think he's starting to realize that he's opening up to the spirit world, mostly thanks to those things he picked up. Why?"

"I can't be with someone who doesn't believe," Miranda said quietly. "I've known him for less than a day, and I want him to be one of us, I want to know him," she stopped voicing her thought and for a few minutes they just walked down the drive between the parked cars. Most of the cars would be gone that evening. They belonged to the parents who had come from across North America, all people who knew of the Circle, all people that Bernie had heard of through the letters to his father preceding their coming. This was the festival that celebrated the deepest kind of connection to nature and the spirit world. An earlier Gathering brought Maxwell and his father to their shores. Practitioners everywhere agreed that the world needed more healing, and the few festivals that celebrated nature were becoming larger and larger.

"I think he wants the same thing, Miranda," Bernie said.

"Good," she replied. She stepped in front of him then, barely giving him enough time to stop, and looked at him, deadly serious. "I've been having visions too, just a couple."

"About you and Max?"

"No, I can't see Max, I can't see myself," she replied. "About you. I want you to promise me something."

"Sure, what?"

"Seriously," she said. "You promise me that you be careful if you see something that's too good to be true. Remember the rule: if it seems too good, it's rarely true."

"You're unforgettable, babe," Bernie said with a wink.

"Seriously!" She pounded his chest.

"Fine, I'll be careful."

"Okay." She hugged him and kissed him on the cheek. "So, what is Max like now? What's the one thing I have to know?"

"Well," Bernie said as they started walking again. The school bus was just in sight, painted black, parked on the lawn just inside the farm fencing. "He has no idea, but sensitive people can feel him coming. It's like there's a low rumble only a few people can hear. He's really all heart underneath all that leather and British, more of a gentleman than he wants anyone to know. Doesn't like swimming much, sorry," Bernie said, glancing at her swimsuit.

"Okay," Miranda said. "I'm sure I can lure him into the water if I want to."

"Maybe, but the cardinal sin with Max is trying to talk about his father. He'll talk about him on his own when he wants to, but he saw all those lessons in mysticism and history and the occult as a kind of torture. Maybe that'll change, but he's still going to resent his dad for it for a long time. I was there, I was interested most of the time, and the way his father shoved it into our heads, it wasn't good. Then he'd leave for weeks, or months and come back with something that just didn't matter to Max. Even the money his dad made, a lot sometimes, didn't impress him. He wanted a dad, and I think that's why he's a brother to me, because my father took care of most of that, even before Charles died."

"Okay, groovy," Miranda said. "I mean, I'm curious, I've read everything Max's dad published, but I won't bring it up."

"Other than that, I don't know, just watch him. My father told me to stay close because he knows Max is about to hit a wall, he's refused to believe in spiritualism all his life, now there's no way he'll get around it. He's going to need us." He looked at Miranda, realizing that he'd just said 'us' instead of 'me.' "You are going to help me watch him, right?"

"You think he'd take help from someone he barely knows? It's been years."

"From you? Sure," Bernie said. "I mean, does it feel like you've been gone for years? I mean, other than a few obvious changes-" he was interrupted by the sight of his Scott running out from the bus, slamming the rear door shut, then pushing the motorcycle ramp up over it and trying to secure the hooks that were meant to keep it there.

"I see the agenda of our system! Corrupt! Corruption!" they could hear someone shout from the inside. "Idolatry! The man with the brightest eyes rules the day, and we are dazzled!"

"That's Zack, he's gone off the deep end," Bernie said, breaking into a run towards the bus. He was surprised to see Miranda pass him.

"Man, oh man," Scott said. "I'm glad to see you!"

Bernie helped him finish closing the latch to the motorcycle ramp that Max used to store his bike in the back of the bus. It also kept the back door closed tight. People were starting to gather, to witness whatever bad trip was taking place inside the black bus.

"Max chased him onto the bus," the drummer said. "They're in there now."

"How much LSD is he on?" Miranda asked.

"Well, the fuzz stopped us this morning," Bernie started.

"More like noon," Scott added. "They searched us, thank god we finished smoking my weed last night, so they didn't find anything on me, but Zack bought a whole vial of LSD from some bikers outside of Ottawa, and it was almost full. He told the cops it was eye drops, and then he puts a drop into each eye, I think one took two drops, but I wasn't close enough."

"Yup, one eye took two," Bernie confirmed.

"Black leather heathen!" Zack shouted from inside the bus. "You have me cornered, but you come with envy in your heart, and so your lies may as well be told to fish! No ears! They go pwah, pwah, pwah!"

"Yes, you're the greatest lead singer the world has ever seen," Maxwell could be heard saying through the open windows on the side of the bus.

"Flatterer! Pimp! Ennnglishmaaannnnn!" Zack screamed as the sounds of bottles and other random articles were heard being jostled and tipped.

Bernie came around the side of the bus in time to see Max stride all the way to the front, then through the folding doors. He pulled them closed behind him and put a broom handle through the loop on the front so they stayed that way. "Git!" he shouted over his shoulder. "Does anyone have a cigarette? I'm not calm enough for this," he said, pulling his leather jacket off. Bernie took it and hung it over a nearby lawn chair.

"Nothing to see here!" Maxwell shouted to the two dozen people beginning to gather. "Man's diabetic, just needs his shot, and someone's coming with it now."

"Diabolical!" Zack shouted, poking his head and one shoulder through an open window. His eyes were wild, his long hair was disheveled to the point of looking like three sparrows' nests. "He'll castrate all of you!"

"Very bad reaction," Max countered.

Miranda's Aunt Susanna added; "Please, go for a swim, it's too hot to stand around in the grass. Shoo," and to Bernie's surprise, they listened. She carried an open tin with cheese, crackers and sandwiches inside. The bottom had a separate compartment for ice. "Is it peyote?" she asked, her Italian accent in full evidence.

Their drummer lit a cigarette and handed it to Max, who took a long draw and let it out slowly. "Worse," he said as he finished. "About half an ounce of LSD. May I?"

Susanna brought the large tin container forward and raised it as it swung a little on its handle. "You must be hungry."

"Famished," Max said. "Not just for me though." He took a slice of cheese and a half sandwich and stuffed half of both in his mouth.

"Can you really calm him down from this?" Miranda asked.

"I am the model of calm!" Zachary barked. "Clouds and naked babies singing harps!"

"He can," Scott replied. "But he can't if he's high strung. Man, you gotta loosen up, what's got you tense?"

Bernie barely caught Max's glance towards Miranda, and silently wondered what could be so wrong about her that his best friend would see her as a source of stress. She didn't say anything but walked away, towards the main house.

"Ooh, who's the new girl?" Zack asked from the window. "Sad to see her leave, love to watch her walk away!"

Maxwell stabbed two pointing fingers towards Zackary with a murderous look. "Git!"

"Retreat!" howled Zachary as he fell back into the bus.

Maxwell put the second half of the sandwich back and hurried the rest of his chewing as he walked after Miranda in a hurry. She turned towards him when he'd crossed half the distance. "I'm glad you're here," he said. Not the greatest thing he could have said in that circumstance, as far as Bernie was concerned. "Best thing about coming home is meeting you again."

"I enjoyed our ride," Bernie barely heard her say. It wasn't in her nature to look nervous, it didn't seem like something that happened to her often, but she definitely seemed like it then, even though she had turned around and was closing the distance between them.

"When did Max get a new girlfriend? She's right and tight," Scott said.

"Thank you," Susanne said. "Isn't my niece lovely?"

"Um, sorry, ma'am," he replied sheepishly.

Maxwell and Miranda came back down to the bus's side door. Both of them looked more contented than he'd seen either of them all day. "Feeling better," Max said, taking another pull on his cigarette. "I'm afraid mental boy inside is going to get the rest of those sandwiches," he told Susanne. "It'll give him something to do once he calms down. Mind if I take that peeler too?"

"If I can have it back when you're finished?" Susanne said uncertainly. "What are you going to do with it?"

"Don't worry, I'm the sane one, you'll get it back," he reassured her. "Might be tomorrow though, but we have a few in the main house." He finished the second half of his sandwich, then his cigarette and took the orange peeler out of the bottom of the tin. He looked to Bernie and nodded. "Get that ciggy and follow me."

Bernie snatched Scott's freshly lit cigarette out of his mouth and followed Maxwell onto the bus with Miranda in tow. Scott closed the folding doors behind.

There were two slim bunks in the middle of the bus with a narrow bed behind. Zack was sitting cross-legged on the bottom left bunk in his underwear. "The heat frees me," he said, wiping sweat off his chest with a tattered sheet. "I shed my sins and inhibitions simultaneously. I will be pure."

Max put the tin on one of the front seats, sliding the orange peeler into his back pocket. "How're you feeling now?"

"Like I'm pure-ing," Zachary said before breathing deeply.

"Good, I've got a story to tell you," Maxwell said. He picked a cup up and drew water from a barrel strapped into one of the rearmost long seats. "Feeling like some water?"

"I don't trust you, Max," Zack said calmly.

"All right, Bernie can give it to you, but you've got to drink something, mate."

Bernie took the plastic cup of water and handed it to Zack, who grinned at him and slurped it loudly.

"You remember that nutter we met in Rockland? Wouldn't come out of his room?"

"Jeeeeeeves," Zachary said. "I thought it was funny because he sounded more British than you."

"Right," Maxwell said, smiling a little – a good sign. "Did anyone tell you why he wouldn't come out?"

"No, but I tried," Zack said, drooling a little water.

Bernie remembered it, they were at the Nyack Motor Inn, and the desk clerk made the mistake of telling them not to bother the only other person at that end of the building, he was a resident named Jeeves who rarely left his room. He remembered her saying that, *rarely*, not never, but Zack was sure she said never, so later that night, after their gig down the road, Zack got away from the band and started pounding on his door, drunkenly inviting poor Jeeves to party at three in the morning.

They were ejected from the Nyack Motor Inn, and ended up sleeping in the bus that night. What Max was going to do with that story, Bernie had no idea.

"So, I had some time to chat with the desk clerk, and she told me all about Jeeves," Max said calmly, taking a seat on the bunk across from Zachary.

"She didn't," Zack said. He looked to Miranda and held his glass out. "Refill! Water, it makes me alive!"

Miranda smiled kindly at him and refilled his glass. Zachary watched her every movement.

Maxwell waited until the plastic cup was back in his hand before gently continuing with his story. He had to start twice to get Zachary's attention back, repeating; "The desk clerk was very nice to me because she thought I had an interesting accent," clearly and slowly, leaning on his English accent.

"I heard you, Max," Zachary said.

"All right," Max said, smiling. "She said Jeeves had a rare condition, where his skin was turning orange."

"No," Zachary said skeptically.

"It's true," Bernie said. "I was there."

"No shit?" Zachary asked.

"Absolutely," Bernie reassured.

"But poor Jeeves," Max continued. "It didn't stop at a little orange. Soon, he started looking about as orange as you do," he said, nodding at Zack's bare chest, where the reflection from the old yellow paint on the ceiling was tinting his skin bright orange thanks to a mild sunburn.

Zack looked down at his chest and seemed a little concerned. "Nope," he said quietly to himself. "Nope," he repeated in an urgent, hushed whisper.

"In fact, everything he saw started to look orangey-yellow," Max said. "So I have to ask, are we looking a little off color to you?"

Zack's eyes darted to Miranda and Bernie then back to Max, alarmed.

"See, Jeeves went to see his doctor, and he told him that he's fine, but there was only one solution for his condition," Max said as though he was breaking the most serious of news, but gently. "You have to sleep a whole night through to the dawn. There's no other way. Oh, and stay well watered if you can, because your skin needs the water to recover."

"You're lying, you're, there's no way," Zack said, looking at his chest, poking it.

"You can't pick it! That's the worst thing for this condition," Max said. "Because there's people out there who don't understand, they don't like people who see everything in orange, who *look* orange."

"Oh, my God," Miranda whispered, hiding her face in Bernie's back, trying as hard as she could not to laugh.

"There are people who walk around, watching for the orange skinned." Max whipped the orange peeler out of his pocket and brandished it between them like a deadly weapon. "Who will want to peel you!"

Zachary shrieked, tossed the plastic cup, retreated into the back corner of the bunk and pulled the sheet up between him and Maxwell. "Stay away!"

"Do you want to get better?" Maxwell asked.

"Yes!"

"Good! Then sleep, drink water! Stay on the bus where you're safe," he said, standing up and slowly backing towards the front of the bus. "There are a lot of people out there."

"You're such a fucker, Max! Don't peel me!" Zachary cried.

"I'm going to leave this with whoever guards that door, and if you try to leave, they're going to peel you like an orange," Max said in a matter-of-fact manner.

"I won't leave," Zachary whimpered.

"Good, you know the rules: no picking, drink water, no leaving the bus, and sleep."

"I know the rules," Zachary repeated.

They made it off the bus, and Miranda buried her face in Max's T-Shirt and laughed so hard she could barely breathe. "I can't believe that worked," she whispered after the hysterics passed, and she leaned on Max with an arm around his waist.

Max pointed at their backup guitarist and crooked his finger. The guitarist walked over. "You got the acid for him, you guard the bus." Max planted the orange peeler firmly in his hand.

"I didn't buy it," he replied.

"I know you're lying," Maxwell said. "Zack there is too spazzy to deal with bikers when he's sober, and I know no one else would get it for him, so it's you. You stay here 'till Zack's back and don't let him out."

"What do I do with this?" Darren asked, holding up the orange peeler.

"Threaten him with it if he tries to get out," Maxwell said, causing Miranda to snicker. "Trust me, should keep him under control for a couple hours if you just let him keep believing what I told him. He hasn't peaked yet. Oh, and did you get the shit back from him?"

"Yeah, but," the guitarist started to explain.

Max gently pushed Miranda away, then turned to Darren and jammed his hands down both his pockets and forcefully fished out a clear vial with an eyedropper. "None of this, thanks," he said as he uncapped it and dumped the contents onto the grass. "Lots of older teens looking to make new mistakes here this weekend, and I'm not going to have you selling or doing this shit here," Max recapped it and carefully put it in his pocket. "Not even leaving you with residue."

"Man, I wasn't going to share, that'd be so stupid," Darren said.

"Now the only stupid thing you have to avoid is letting Zachary off the bus for about six more hours. This isn't the kind of thing where you let stoned morons like him walk around."

"Fine," Darren said. "Anything you say, Master, swell."

Maxwell put his arm around Miranda's shoulders, she put his arm around his waist and they started towards the main house. "Beach," she said.

"I'm knackered," Max retorted. "You can go swim though."

"Nope, beach," Miranda said, pulling at him. "You can sleep on a towel down there. Catch a nap before dinner with me."

"Just make sure nothing falls on my head," Max replied, changing his direction towards the road leading through the farm, down towards the shore, the cabins and the beach.

Bernie couldn't help but notice the faint smile on Susanne's face as she started to follow them. He caught up to walk beside her.

"There are sparks above them, and trailing behind them," Susanne said so only Bernie could hear. "He is a good man though, isn't he? The destiny does not guarantee that."

"He's my best friend," Bernie answered, it was the most honest response he could give.

V

Maxwell was faced with a choice, try out his new guitar, or to get to know Miranda that afternoon. The guitar lost by a surprisingly large margin.

The cabins on the way to the beach were well kept, despite Bernie and Max's absence for most of the previous three summers. Allen had a lot of helpful neighbors who traded days at the cabin during the summer for services, and their work was better than anything Maxwell, Bernie or Scott could do.

The year round and summer cabins were arranged in two large half circles. Most of the smaller summer cabins were in the outer ring with tree and foliage coverage between. The larger, year round cabins were in the inner circle, and some of them were large enough to have a small yard.

The largest of the cabins, number fourteen, stood apart entirely, closest to the lake. It had two full storeys, and Max was still surprised that he and the band would be staying there with their guests. "Is there a bathroom down here, or is it all still outhouses?" Miranda asked as they passed through the heavy front door. It was made of thickly varnished medium sized logs, Max remembered putting it in with the help of Bernie and Scott while Allen put the hinges on.

"This cabin's more a house," Max said. "The john's just down there at the end." He pointed down the hallway past the kitchen.

"Okay," Miranda said, walking towards the hall. "I remember getting into big trouble when we were kids for getting caught in the cabins. Whatever they thought we were doing must have been so much worse than the truth, I couldn't visit for a week."

"High cost for hanging out away from the parents," Maxwell agreed. He remembered stealing keys in the off-season and sneaking off to a cabin with all his friends. It was the first time they really got time away from their parents without supervision, close by, but no one knew where they were. Nothing really changed, Maxwell still had an acoustic guitar, Miranda still played flute back then, and that was taken into the cabin, and Bernie and Scott were right behind. If anything, they were too young and too interested in being together as a group to get into any serious trouble.

The real rascal business took place when Maxwell and Bernie were thirteen. Scott and Miranda were twelve. They snuck into a cabin and discovered a mostly full jumbo bottle of peach schnapps. Everyone got into that precious supply, by the time they got through half of it, Miranda was sound asleep, Bernie was stumbling drunk and worried that his father would discover them. Scott and Maxwell were taking turns on the bottle, both of them were desperately ill later, leaving vomit deposits behind the cabin, but their drunken sleepover was never discovered. Maxwell still couldn't smell peach schnapps without feeling a little ill, however.

The ceilings in cabin fourteen were tall, made of split logs with heavy beams for support. The main hearth was an oddity, it actually had a cast iron screen that could close it in, and heat pipes leading to other parts of the house. He always thought it looked like it was grinning at him, when the iron mask was brought together. During the summer the hearth doors were open, it was clean and empty. A half circle of stones from the lake surrounded the front of it, and hard wood floors with broad, varnished boards surfaced the rest of the large room. There were three large sofas against the walls, two six foot long hand made side tables, and still enough room in the middle for a couple dozen people to gather. Towards the kitchen there was another large room, where a hand carved table and chairs for twenty-one people.

The cabin was rented for receptions, special parties, and many other occasions, but the cost to outsiders was so prohibitive, they almost always decided against it. Locals knew that they could offer trade in services and some cash, Allen's preferred method of bargaining to use the space. When it wasn't rented Allen and the staff prepared meals for the other cabin guests. The food was plentiful, filling and cheap, while the atmosphere was always social. What Allen and his family had in their cabin business and the lake the Three Families shared was just short of magical to Maxwell. It was a wonderful place to grow up.

Max paid little attention to the space then, except to acknowledge that it was spotless. He took the key out of the second largest room's door and went inside. It was furnished with a broad, low dresser with a triple panel mirror, a queen-sized bed with a wrought iron frame, and a door leading out to a balcony. He took the key from the trunk at the end of the bed, opened it and dropped his saddlebags inside. There was just enough room for his new guitar behind it, so he put it on top and opened the case. It was the kind of instrument he pictured himself earning with a hit record. Their debut only seemed to resonate with audiences after they saw Road Craft live. They needed the album after that, but the album itself didn't draw much attention unless the listener was already a fan of darker music.

He another took a look at the glossy black guitar, followed the trim with his eyes to the dark rosewood fret board and shook his head. The dream of making the band work, getting in front of large audiences as Black Sabbath and Cream had done seemed to go hand in hand with a guitar of that class, one didn't seem to make sense without the other. He would still play his new instrument, despite the strings he felt were attached to it, and he would do so as if there were thousands in the audience. He closed and latched the case then slipped it behind his saddlebags in the trunk.

There were some improvised jean shorts that would work for something to swim in, that is if she got him in the water at all, in his saddlebags, and he immediately got to opening and digging. After a moment he found them, and was half way out of his clothes – the bottom half – when he heard Miranda coming up the stairs. "This place is amazing, I love how the stairs are all split logs. This main house was run down when I was a kid, I remember-" He turned his backside towards the door, being between jeans and shorts, and continued to change.

"Hello," she said with a giggle.

"Sorry, been in close quarters for too long, not used to having a door to close," Maxwell said as he buttoned the jean shorts. "Not many secrets on that bus."

"No complaints," Miranda said. "You didn't tell me to stay downstairs, either. Oh, I found towels."

He turned to see her framed by the doorway, down to her dark swimsuit, having left her dress behind somewhere along the way. She was holding up a pair of large folded towels. "That's good," Max said, closing the trunk and locking it. He put the key under the leg of the bedframe. "As long as I don't have to use the towel I stole from a hotel a month ago. It hasn't been washed since."

He stepped outside and locked the bedroom door, wedging the key in a tiny space where the wall met the floor on the other side of the hallway. "Worried about people getting into your room?" Miranda asked. "Here?"

"No, luv," Max said, accepting a towel from her. He felt a strange lump in his pocket and realized then that he'd taken the shard with him. "Just making sure I get the nicest bed in the house. Never know who'll try to take the room."

"Do you still have a room in the main house?" Miranda asked as they headed down the stairs.

"I cleared out by June," Maxwell said. "Thought this would be our summer, you know? Coming back from tour early wasn't the plan, there's just not much booking out there. Too many disco stages. Looks like I'll be moving back in."

"Well I'm happy you're back," Miranda said.

"That's a silver lining," Maxwell replied as they passed through the front door. "A shiny one."

They made their way out of the cabin. Miranda was about to go towards the main beach. Maxwell could hear the murmur of the crowd and sounds of children at play. He put his arm around her waist and said; "You remember when you were here, there was the big beach, and the other beach?" He slowly guided her in the other direction, watching a smile grow across her face.

"We were never allowed to go there," she replied.

"Now it's our turn," Maxwell said. "Thought that's where you meant to take me when you tried to drag me off to the beach." He led the way down a nearly grown in path behind the cabin. It was clear enough to walk down at night, but straying would get anyone lost in the dark. During the day, it was dim, hot and the air felt thick.

A natural cave leading through a rock face awaited them, it had been cleaned up and a thick boardwalk was built to lead through it. The cool air in the dark passage was a momentary relief. As soon as they reached the other side, a waft of pot smoke drifted past the entrance. "I'm no prude," Miranda said. "But I'm not going to smoke, or take anything this weekend, except for maybe a few beers. I'm not going to do anything I know I'll regret either," she said.

Maxwell looked back at her and she avoided his gaze, obviously wary. "I just don't want that loud beach," he said. "I'm not dragging you off to get you high, luv. Feels like I've been on the road years, seen more people half-mad on that stuff. Just dealt with one of them." He had her full attention, her expression had already turned from one of trepidation to a soft smile and in the golden light of the afternoon as it was screened by leaves overhead, she was prettier than any women he'd ever seen. He wanted to do what his well-tested instincts told him to, to take advantage of the situation and get closer, but he decided to trust her instead. "In all that time, after all those parties and strange places, what I think I saw today has done my head in worse than anything." He stepped in closer to her. "If the first thing you said when you came through there was that you'd be getting lost on an acid trip, or even lost in some smoke, I'd have found my way off alone somewhere."

"I can help you with whatever's going on, Max," she whispered, taking his hand. "We'll have an afternoon, some quiet."

She took the lead then, slowly following the last twenty feet of the trail down to a secluded beach, located in the nook of a bend on the relatively small, spring fed lake. The beach shore wasn't sandy, but made of tiny, fine grey pebble stone gathered from a nearby streambed.

There was a large fire pit and a smaller one off to the side. With trees bending down overhead, encroaching ferns and other undergrowth all around, the sounds of the larger beach were absent, and there was room for twenty people, their towels, coolers, and any other basic beach supplies. The pot smokers who Max and Miranda caught a whiff of earlier were near the trail entrance sitting on lawn chairs in the nude. "Two beards, can you take that down the beach a bit?" Max asked politely of the trio. "Breeze is carrying that right into the cave."

"Sure, man," the nearest one said as he passed the pipe to a young woman to his right.

"Two beards," she chuckled and pointing at his long beard and his crotch.

"Oh, that's right on," the glassy-eyed young man to her right said. "That's it, man, that's making it all the way back to San-Fran. You're Two Beards from now on." He started standing and picking up his lawn chair. "You're all-right, dude," he said to Max as he held his thumb up and shook it at him before moving on.

"The other way, mate," Max said, pointing towards the edge of the beach furthest from the more public, all ages site. "No one cares if you smoke, we just don't want to send a cloud over to the uptight beach."

"Oh, right, man," he replied. The trio made their way to the other end, and Maxwell got his first look at the space since the previous summer. There were people at all three of the unlit fire pits, and nudity seemed to be the craze that afternoon. He could see at least fifteen people, and he counted four swimsuits, his and Miranda's included.

She seemed unaffected by the scene as they walked closer to the water and spread their towels out onto the fine pebbles. "Do you know any of these people?" she asked quietly.

"Don't recognize anyone," Maxwell replied. It was unusual, the Gathering had brought young people from around the world, enough to outnumber the locals many times over. It was still early for them yet. On a Friday many of them would still be working that early in the afternoon. Miranda curled up with her arm across his chest as soon as he settled in, and rolled up against him for only a moment before saying; "way too hot for that," and rolling away so air was passing between their bodies. "You come here a lot when you're home?" she asked.

"All the time, usually with my acoustic, but that's been smashed," Maxwell said. "Normally there's only two or so people here, five people is busy."

"What happened to your guitar?" Miranda asked.

"Zachary," Maxwell said. "Last year's been bad, especially for him and Darren."

"Why especially them?"

"Started on a high with the record out all winter, sold a couple thousand around, then we get on the road to find it's not in record stores. The company bought most of those copies to boost numbers, shipped most of them to radio stations and a few hundred to us. Sent us the bill for the ones we got too. Bernie,

Scott and I had to take turns running ahead of the tour as soon as we started, trying to get a few shop keeps to buy them, put them out. We're down to what's in the house, sold everything we brought with us, but we worked our asses off, sold most of them at gigs, really."

"And that's what's been hard for them?" Miranda asked. "What about you?"

"Zack and Darren expected more out of this summer than anyone, I think, starting on that kind of high, and getting out there to see disco taking over everywhere, getting as many cancellations as we did gigs, it brought them way down."

"What about you?" Miranda said, rolling over so she could look at him with her chin on his chest. "I know I've only been around today, but I can feel how tense you are."

"And you're a relaxing sort to be with," Maxwell said with a raised eyebrow. "I must be a bunch of rods and nuts 'round everyone else."

"I'm serious," Miranda said. "I have your record, it's really good, especially the parts without Zack, you must have been on a high when you started the tour too."

"I was too busy earning," Max said, stroking her cheek instinctively. He'd never had close, comfortable moments with anyone like he was having with Miranda. He could see her sweating as much as he was, though, and the water was looking more inviting by the second. "I picked up where my father left off when the money ran out a week into the tour. Started looking for that damned book, too. Didn't have time to wallow about all our misfortunes."

Maxwell caught sight of Two Beards and his lady friend, her long blonde hair hanging limp past her shoulders in the still air, approaching with a plastic bag in her hand. He recognized the shape of what was inside from twenty feet away, two beer bottles. Their gentle jingling confirmed it.

Miranda turned to see what Maxwell was smiling at. "Hello again," Miranda called out.

Two Beards smiled at them both as his blonde friend gave Miranda the bag. "We thought, since you two don't smoke, maybe we could bring you some beers instead. The lady down there said you're kind of the King and Queen this Gathering, so it's probably good for our energy here. I'm Candace, and this is Peter, but I think he'll be Two Beards for the rest of the week. Our friend is Gavin."

"I'm Max, this is Miranda," he replied. "King and Queen?"

"You've got this aura around you, man," Two Beards said. "You can't see it, you're inside it, I dig, but it's like this golden green thing, letting the shadows out in little pieces. Burnt leaves, floating away on the wind."

"You are very high," Maxwell said with a smirk.

A sharp elbow in the ribs was Miranda's response to his remark. "Thank you very much, we're all equal this week," she said.

"Why don't you get down to your real skin, man," Two Beards said innocently. "It's nothing to anyone here, but it's going to make your flow go so much better. Helps get the air at you too, feelin' free."

"Maybe I can get some of what you're smoking later?" Max asked. "I'm in the main cabin, I'm sure I'll have something to trade."

"Sure, man," Two Beards said. "Yeah, I'll get around there tonight. You think on what I say though, dig?"

"Get naked, won't be able to stop thinking about it now," Max replied.

Two Beards seemed satisfied with the exchange and turned back towards the group his trio joined at the outer edge of he beach. His girlfriend leaned down low. "You're right, he's really high, but he's right too," she whispered before turning and catching up to him.

"Paying respect to the King and Queen of auras," Maxwell said, shaking his head. "Going to be a week to remember."

"Could be," Miranda said. "Something to think about though, I don't see anyone else wearing a stitch."

Maxwell raised his head and glanced down the beach long enough to get an eyeful of young to middle aged nude loungers and bathers then put his head back down. Even the people who were wearing suits before had left them behind somewhere. "Funny how suits disappear here."

Miranda's face made another appearance in front of his, her chin resting on the top of his chest. Her brown eyes stared into his. "Never gone nude on a beach before."

"Who, me?" Maxwell asked. "Maybe when I was a wee thing, two or three."

"No, me," Miranda said. She was blushing from her full lips to her sweat-covered forehead. "There was a lot of topless going on in Spain, but I never went nude. I don't know…"

"Ignore 'em, we don't have to if you don't want to," Maxwell said. "I'll take one of those beers in a minute though."

"Good," Miranda said, putting her head down. Maxwell felt her sigh against him as he traced his fingers along the arm she had across his chest. "This is nice," she whispered after a few passes of his hand. "I feel a little out of place though."

Maxwell didn't have patience to listen to her go back and forth on the decision to take her one-piece suit off, or much modesty, and as much as he liked being close to Miranda, he could feel sweat pooling on him. "Time for a dip then," he said, extracting himself from her, standing up and dropping the little clothing he had on his way into the water.

He could not ignore how aggressively cold it was. Spring fed lakes were frigid regardless of the weather, but he did manage to outwardly pretend it was no problem at all as he ran to diving depth and leapt forward. It was just as much a shock as it was relief.

He managed to face away from the beach as he resurfaced, gasping once. A few long strokes took him to neck depth waters on the beach's slight grade. The curve and peninsula in the shape of the lake provided a natural divide complete with tall, thick trees between the two beaches. The quiet of the calm, cool water was always a comfort to him. Maxwell couldn't deny that he was a creature most suited to summer.

His bravado was rewarded as he looked back towards the beach from where he was almost neck deep in water. Miranda was running towards the water, her swimsuit left behind. He was quietly thrilled at the sight, she was more beautiful than he would have guessed. An instant later she splashed into the water up to her knees, shrieked, tried to stop and fell in. Miranda came up sputtering. She recovered with a little more grace, flinging her wet hair back and beginning her wading journey towards him.

Maxwell began walking towards her. She noticed him when he was waist deep. "Oh, no," she said, sloshing a couple steps down the bank.

"You're already wet," he chided. "May as well come the rest of the way in."

"Was it always this cold here? It's August, I mean-" she didn't have a chance to finish before Maxwell surged towards her. He caught one of her hands in his and held it lightly.

"It was always this cold, luv," he said, slowly teasing her deeper into the water. "You were just too young to care for long the last time you were here."

"Lemmie go," she said cringing as she was guided at arms-length to mid thigh depth.

"I'm not holdin' you, luv," Max said, letting her hand go for a moment, then touching only her fingers. He took two steps into deeper water, letting her hand go entirely. "Here goes," she said, dipping under completely.

She came up with a gasp. "Wow! That's not what I remember." She bent forward, then whipped her hair back overhead so it fell behind her, flicking water into the blue sky. She closed the distance between them, and drifted into his arms so her back leaned against his chest. She gasped again as Maxwell brought her into neck deep waters. He let his hands rest across her belly and didn't say a word. There wasn't a single thought in his head to share anyway.

Miranda rested against him, her hands on his. They had started something. More sons and daughters of the sixties were coming to the beach, and Max counted six who were chasing each other into the water. As much as holding Miranda in his arms was thrilling, it felt as though they'd fallen back into an innocent time, when people could simply play.

"Do you want me to let you go?" he asked quietly, his chin nearly resting on her shoulder. It was his way of checking on her happiness, her comfort, and making sure he wasn't misreading her ease with him.

Miranda entwined her fingers between his and turned her head, meeting his lips. Maxwell held her close as their kiss continued on from the first electric touch of their lips into an intimate and eager exploration that felt like it was only minutes long. They drifted lazily in the cool water, the kiss an extension of their close embrace. Being with Miranda was exciting and easy at the same time. His arms remained around her, gently holding her and she fit against him comfortably. Miranda and Maxwell's kiss was serious at first, a statement of want that felt like it had been building for much longer than a day. It was as though he'd missed the woman she'd become for years, and finally found her.

Time, their closeness, and their kiss continued on, but it was at times needy, then slow, and finally a little playful, celebratory. Neither of them knew how long they were together, left alone in the calm water.

They were finally interrupted when Maxwell and Miranda heard Scott's voice drifting over the water. "Max! We're going to barbeque here, we've got some coolers! We'll be by the fire pit."

Miranda groaned her disappointment and slowly turned her face away from the kiss, Max letting her lips leave, and shouted. "Thanks!" before whispering; "he always had bad timing."

Max kissed her behind the ear and gave her a squeeze. "They're going to expect us to get out sometime."

"Listen, um," Miranda said. "I've fallen in with someone for a night before, but I didn't know him well, and it was sort of a free love thing." She took a breath and sighed. "I don't want that, you know, right? I want us to be a thing, a good thing. I'm not easy that way."

"Never thought you were," Maxwell said. He'd had one-night stands before, there was a feeling of something fleeting whenever one was happening. An unspoken contract that stated simply: expect nothing past the morning. He did not have that feeling with Miranda. "This goes on and on, luv."

"What's that supposed to mean?" Miranda asked with a soft chuckle.

"Just saying I've never wanted just the one, forsaking all others kind of thing. Never wanted an old lady," Maxwell said.

"Don't strain yourself trying to talk about your feelings," Miranda said. "Good thing I speak caveman." She turned around and shook her head at him. "One day and I'm naked in a lake with you."

"Not what your aunts would want?" Maxwell asked.

"Not a good time to bring my aunts up," Miranda replied. "But if they did catch us like this, they'd try to have us married by the end of the week. They're a bit weird, very woman's liberation, believe it's all right for us to have fun too, but they still want me married off to you as fast as they can arrange it. I'd wonder if we were under a spell, but I've got a ward tattooed. Can't happen."

"I don't remember seeing a tattoo," he said.

"It's very small, you'll have to look for it later," Miranda replied with a wink.

"So, you haven't cast a spell on me?" Maxwell asked, his hands moving lower.

"Didn't say that," Miranda said, kissing him on the nose then pulling away. "We should go in."

"I'll be out in a minute," he said as he watched her walk away, emerging from the water. "Need to simmer down."

"I'm sure no one would care. Nothing to be ashamed of down there either," she added with a smirk.

"If it's just the same," Maxwell said.

"I could wait with you," she replied.

"May as well wait for dinner while you're outside having a smoke with him," he whispered.

"I'm the cook in this analogy," Miranda said, amused.

"Well, I suppose I could walk out with you, grinnin' and boasting," Maxwell replied.

Miranda laughed. "Now that's something I wouldn't want my aunts to see. All right, I'll leave if you agree never to call me your Old Lady again," Miranda said. "I get what it means, but I don't have the years."

"Done, promised."

Miranda turned in time to see Bernie and Scott taking the last of their clothes off. "Oh, wow, Bernie's like a blonde sasquatch."

He looked at what prompted her comment, and a moment

later, his problem was gone. "That did it, ready to come out," Maxwell said.

A curvy blonde woman ran up between them, untying her two-piece. "And there's the trouble I saw for Bernie or Scott."

"What? April? She's barely ever here," Bernie said.

"You don't think she's pretty? She's a knockout." Miranda said, taking Maxwell's hand as they started making their way out of the water. "Like Marilyn Monroe."

"Too fair haired and demanding," Maxwell said. "She's one of the rich daughters in town."

When she was more than half way out, he looked at Miranda's bottom caught sight of a small, circular tattoo. "There it is!"

"There's what?" Scott asked as he took slow strides into the cold water.

"Oh, Exponentia Silentium seal on her bum," Maxwell said, patting her cheek with just enough vigor for three light slaps to echo across the water.

"Hey!" Miranda said, laughing and covering. "Let's not start that."

They moved their towels closer to the main fire pit, settling in beside the coolers Scott and Bernie brought with them. The sun and heat dried them as they laid out enjoying the beer Two Beards had brought. It was just cold enough, having been out of his cooler less than an hour.

"I forget you know about that stuff," Miranda said as she lay beside him.

"More than I'd like to," Maxwell said. He couldn't help but think about the boy who asked that his family be brought to the water. He followed an urge to look towards the shore and saw them standing there. They were filthy, their clothing was old and weather worn. Maxwell looked at them calmly. "I know I'm the only one who can see an immigrant family on the edge of the water." He whispered. "If you take my hand right now, and look where I'm staring, you'll see them too."

Their pleading eyes reminded him of one of his father's lessons. *The living only have a duty to the dead if they are chosen to speak for them.* Miranda took his hand and gasped. "It's as though the sunlight can't touch them, they're in a shadow."

"How many?" Maxwell asked.

"Six. Four children, two parents. They look like they've been bound," she replied.

"Fuck, I'm not crazy," Maxwell said. "They're standing over my shorts with the shard." He stood up and walked over, not worried that the family disappeared the moment he was on his feet.

Miranda hurried behind him. "Are you okay? What are you going to do?"

"I'm fine, I need you though. You can take the place of a Summoner in a circle?" he asked.

"I was trained since I was little," Miranda replied. "How did you know?"

"I remember you and Bernie talking about it." He pointed to Bernie, whose head was just coming out of the water. April was sneaking up on him, about to push him back down but was interrupted by Max's pointing finger. "Need your help, mate."

Without a moment's hesitation, Bernie started sloshing out of the water. "What's up?"

"Have to release an immigrant family who was murdered here about a hundred twenty or hundred forty years ago by a corrupt priest," Maxwell said as he picked up his shorts and started fishing for the shard. He tried not to think on how he was picking up more details about them as seconds passed.

"I know this story," Bernie said. "There was a con-man who came into the town pretending to be a priest. He hung a family as thieves after tricking the constable into believing they stole the Sunday offerings."

"Well, I've got the family in hand," Maxwell said. "Need a Guardian to finish the circle so I can release them over the water here."

Bernie stopped and stared at him for a moment, unbelieving. "What? What's going on, Max? When did you decide to believe what people have been trying to tell you?"

"Since I just saw them, the little ones eyes begging like, well, beggars, for help."

"What are you going to do?" Bernie asked.

"I'm going to conduct them on, just the simple way, just the direct way. This water is the most pure and often blessed body in the whole province," Maxwell said as he looked at the shard. There was nothing special about the thick sliver of petrified wood. "I'll do my turn as weaver."

"Are you sure?" Bernie asked. "You don't need to read anything or prepare?"

"Or get initiated?" Scott called out as he approached. April's wary blue eyes searched the scene as she emerged from the water with him, her arm linked with his.

"The Sun Callers weren't initiated," Maxwell said. "First hunters who could speak and hold a spear weren't initiated, but they were praying and casting spells, what? When we first started stringing syllables together ten thousand years ago, probably even further back?."

"Are you sure you want to weave this?" Miranda asked gently.

"A weaver needs three things: knowledge, conviction, and clarity of purpose. I'm going to use an old translated British ditty to send these spirits away from their worldly prison by using the surface of the water as the sacred space where they can get out and move on." He took Miranda's hand and kissed the back of it. "Hundreds of hours of lectures and training from my father and a sudden belief in the other side are enough." He looked to Bernie, who nodded.

Scott got behind them, guiding April along at his side. "Do you have enough room, or do you want me to get everyone else out of the water?"

Maxwell looked to the left, where there were four people in the water fifty feet or more away. "We're all right here. Guardian, protect us."

Taking his cue from Maxwell, Bernie stepped to the edge of the water so Miranda and Maxwell were behind him. "I call the Guardians, our Ancestors and the Ancient Spirits who would protect the circle we cast from interference and those within it from harm. Honor our purpose as we honor you, and guide us through our rite."

Maxwell could immediately feel as though he, Miranda and Bernie had been separated from the rest of the world. When Bernie turned back towards the water and nodded, he took a deep breath and let it out slowly. "You'd better know what you're doing, Max, there's power here."

Miranda didn't wait for her cue. "I am the Summoner, and call the ones our weaver has brought us here to protect into the circle. Let him guide you in, and trust that he means you no harm."

Maxwell felt the dark pastor before he saw him. His form, more shadow than man, stood on the water behind Bernie. "I recognize you, malicious spirit, and have no fear."

Bernie turned around and, judging by his sudden head jerk, Maxwell guessed he was surprised to see the glowering shade three feet away. "I ask that our defenders conduct this intruder away from our sacred space."

"Holy shit," Scott said from outside the circle, several feet behind Maxwell.

The tall shade dissipated suddenly, as though he were smoke caught in a gust of wind. Bernie remained facing the outside of the circle, looking across the water. "Go ahead, Max," he said.

"I have called my Guardian and Summoner into this circle to open a passage across the turbulent waters between the living and the dead. He could hear a young girl's voice whisper; "Ablesmith," into his right ear. A lesson his father drilled into him over and over again reminded him to examine the voice that uttered the word, not take for granted that it was the one he was looking for.

"Max," Miranda whispered. "They're here again."

He opened his eyes and saw the family, appearing as though they were in better days. They stood in the middle of the circle, clean, healthy and in brighter moods. The little girl who tried to be heard looked up at him with bright blue eyes, smiling, nodding. "Ablesmith, that's us," she said with a British accent. "Who are you?"

The beach was silent, people were carefully, slowly approaching the circle, and stopping to watch no less than ten feet away from the edge. "I'm Maxwell," he replied. "Are you and your family free?"

"He can't get us if we stand between you three," answered her young brother.

"I call the spirits that guard us and this sacred space to break the bond between this," Maxwell caught himself mid sentence and corrected. "The Ablesmith family and whatever may wish it harm. They are to be conducted across the waters, beyond the physical world."

The four children beamed up at him, grinning, but Maxwell felt something else from the parents, and had to make a conscious effort to look them in the eye. Even though their pain seemed to have eased, he could feel their anger, and he knew what he had to do to release them. "I promise you justice," he said, looking from Henrietta Ablesmith to Cole Ablesmith. "Go in peace and be free from hate." The entire family turned towards the water then. "Bernie," Max whispered. "You know what to do."

For the first time Bernie saw the family as they passed through him and the second to youngest, a little boy who clung on to his sister's hand, looked over his shoulder at him. "Thank you, Sir," he said in a near singsong tone.

Maxwell could see Bernie staring at the family as they continued across the lake's still waters, but was not delayed in his duty. "I call to our defenders and keepers: It is time for you to take our charges into your care and deliver them. We focus our will with you with clear purpose. Protect these souls as they are freed. As it is right in light, so may it be."

"May it be right in light, so let it be," repeated the crowd reverently.

Golden light surrounded the family as they walked out of the circle and onto the lake. To them, it was solid ground, and the water was a path of glittering, liquid gold. By the time they were over twenty feet away, the family and the light faded.

"I bring this rite to a close, with thanks to all those who wished us well, who stood in our defense, and to our guides," Maxwell said. "This circle is ended as it began, in light and peace."

The crowd of over thirty who were on the beach and were witnesses to everything looked at Maxwell, Miranda and Bernie in wonder, a spell that was broken when someone clapped once. The people there followed the example, breaking the peace with applause. It didn't suit Maxwell at all, he'd done something that had to be done. He felt he would have to deal with consequences very soon. Everything he'd just done and experienced made it plain that he was wrong to doubt for so long. When the noise started to abate, Miranda gave him a hug and a brief kiss.

Maxwell turned his face to the crowd and asked; "Anyone got a smoke, a beer and a burger?" which caused a wave of laughter. "Maybe a tattoo gun too," he whispered to Miranda. "I'm going to need some protection." He pinched the cheek where he knew Miranda's protection tattoo was hidden and was rewarded with a surprised squeak, then a punch in the arm. It was enough to get him smiling again.

VI

As the sun kissed the calm lake waters in yellow-red hues, clothes went back on, more beer was brought out, and there was no escaping that a fairly low-key party was beginning on the beach that was reserved for more adult fun. Maxwell and Miranda changed at the big cabin then returned to the beach in time for barbeque.

She was quiet, but so was he. He knew he wouldn't last in front of the fire pit after he'd had something to eat. Scott was one of the greatest grill masters Maxwell had ever seen. He could turn a cut of meat fit for dog food into a moist, mouthwatering morsel with the assistance of a hibachi. The funniest thing about it was that the short drummer had better luck with cooking while smoking pot, which there was no shortage of around that fire pit.

Maxwell passed, knowing that he'd be out like a light shortly after his first puff. Miranda returned from Bernie's big cooler beside the fire pit with two beers, and sat down with him on the sand. "Thanks, luv."

"I've never seen anything like that," she said quietly. "Never felt peace like that. After they left, I mean."

The shadows cast by the tall trees around them grew longer, the sunlight was fading, and the fire crackled to life under Bernie and Scott's attention. "Bernie hasn't so much as looked at me since," Maxwell said. "He always wanted to be a weaver. I remember hearing it when my father was alive. I think the jealousy went away when he realized I'd never be initiated, can't blame him."

"I've never heard of a releasing ritual going like that," Miranda said. "The feeling that you've helped spirits find peace can be very strong, but I've never heard of anyone actually seeing it happen."

"It's all the same in the end," Maxwell said. He took a long pull on his beer. He took his time swallowing, knowing that Miranda and the few people nearby who were overhearing were waiting on his next word. "I saw innocent people being trapped by something, and I sent them off in the right direction because I knew how. If you and Bernie weren't there, I probably would have tried to do it alone, but I know well enough how dangerous that is. I had a persistent teacher."

"You're powerful, Max," Miranda whispered. "If that's even the word."

"I don't know," Max told her, looking her right in the eye. "That was the first time I've ever put what I know to use." He pulled her close, drawing her back against his chest. She settled in and smiled, still paying close attention to him. "Never felt peace like this either. You, me and Bernie getting into a rhythm and performing, same as music. Now I just wish I knew what the big bloke was thinking."

"Max!" called Allen from the path leading onto the beach. He was with Darren, and judging from his bearing it was serious.

"No rest for the wicked," Maxwell said as he got up. "Stick around here and meet some people, I'll have this chat with Allen alone, it's a long time coming."

"See you later," Miranda said. "Take it easy," she added with a smirk.

Bernie started walking towards Allen as well, leaving the fire pit in Scott's capable hands. The large grill they had laid atop the fire was already being plied with sizzling meat, and Max's stomach growled its farewell. "Time to pay the piper," Maxwell said under his breath as Bernie drew close enough.

"Don't worry, man, I've got your back. Nothing we did back there was wrong," Bernie replied.

"Where is the book?" Allen asked, turning around and leading the way down the path to the cave passage. "Where'd you leave it?"

Maxwell realized then that he didn't have his jacket with him, and the book was most likely on a lawn chair beside the bus. "Back at the bus, should be fine."

"Why isn't it in your room in the cabin? Or in your father's safe? Or in the library cabinet?" Allen asked.

Maxwell could feel a strange tension in the air as they came through the other side of the cave. He knew it was coming from the bus. "What's happened?"

"Man," Darren began to explain, looking spooked. "Everything was cool for a few hours, Zack was trying to sleep, you know how that goes, can't sleep on LSD, but he was quiet, you know? Looked out the window a few times to make sure no one was coming to the bus, but everything was cool. Then he got restless, and while I was talking to a few people who were hanging out close by, he got out one of the windows. I didn't think he could fit, you know? Before I could even chase him, he ran around, messing with us I guess, then grabbed your jacket and went back on the bus. I locked him back up and held up the peeler like you told me, and he didn't get out again. Then, maybe fifteen minutes ago, I hear him yelling and shit, just ignored it at first thinking he was peaking pretty hard, but he starts screaming about being immortal and praising-"

"Don't say the name," Allen said.

"What passage was it?" Maxwell asked Allen.

"Anyone who knows better won't touch that book," Allen replied. "What about that didn't sink in?"

"Better you get your hands on it and get it away from Zack than let him mess around with whatever he likes. He believes he's half Ozzy Ozbourne and half David Bowie for Christ's sake, and he's got an ego that makes them both look like meek choir boys."

"He's your band mate, your guest, and it's your book," Allen said, turning to face Maxwell. "This is a problem that is going to last, I'm guessing, but I won't know until someone who has read the book, an expert on it like you can tell me how bad it is."

The cab lights of the bus were on, and Max could see Zachary sitting calmly in the front seat. His head was bowed and his shoulders were hunched in such a way that told Maxwell that there was something wrong with him. He barely noticed the crowd of people around the bus. Many of them clutched religious symbols or quietly watched what was going on.

Max and Bernie ran the last of the distance between, Allen barely keeping up behind. They were on the bus quickly, but Maxwell slowed himself down in those last steps, stopping to kneel beside the seat so he was just below eye level with Zack. He was bare chested, with a little blood on his arm. It was immediately evident that he was coming down fast. "I did it, man, the Aurora Trial, I'm immortal now," Zachary said wearily.

Max glanced at the symbols drawn on most of the bus's ceiling, relieved that almost all of it was done using the black markers they used to make flyers. There was one scrawled in blood, but it looked like getting enough on the metal surface was a real struggle. "That's cool, are you all right, mate?"

"Yeah, I'm tired, but I don't feel high anymore, like that shit was just drained out of my system," Zachary said.

"Can you show me what you did in here?" Max did, picking the old book up from the floor at Zack's feet. "You said the Aurora Trial?" he tried to remember roughly where it was, what it was.

Zachary gently pulled at a page in the middle of the book and Maxwell found what he was looking for there. It was a rite that was supposed to give a spirit the ability to hide in living bodies and appear in reflective surfaces. He sighed in relief and patted Zach's cheek. "You're all right, mate. I'm sorry I left you here with your thoughts and an orange peeler."

"Pretty funny, that was your best," Zachary said as though fighting to stay awake. "I know how I can get. You take care of us. We fight, I pull shit on stage, get fucked up, but you keep the wheels turning, make sure there's someone there when I finish sleeping it off. I know, man, I know. You're an older brother, a bitchy British older brother, but the food's on the table. I know."

"Thanks, mate," Maxwell said soothingly. "Just, no more acid for a while, especially so bloody much. Hendrix keeled over because of that stuff, remember?"

"Yeah, don't have to worry about that though, do I?"

"You know none of this works, right?" Max said, holding the book up. "It's all chicanery, theater for the religious."

"I don't know, Max," Zachary said, his dark, tired eyes fixing on his. "Feel like something got me for a while there, it was hard to finish."

"I see you did a little blood work there, too," Maxwell said, nodding at a small prick on his lead singer's arm. If it weren't for the smears around it, he wouldn't have noticed it at all. "Going to have to start calling you Ozzy."

Zachary laughed quietly. "Man, that hurts, like a lot. They make it look so easy in the movies, you know? Just cut with a knife, and out it flows, but it kept on clotting, had to keep picking myself."

"Well, no more of that, and fake blood on stage if you're going to go all Alice Cooper on us, right?"

"Yeah, man, definitely."

Allen patted Max on the shoulder. "The Southern Circle want to take care of him. They'll get him hydrated and bless him, they have two nurses in their group too."

"You all right with that, Zack? A bunch of granola munchers are going to take care of you tonight, sound good, mate?" Maxwell asked.

"Yeah, I'm hungry," Zack said.

Maxwell took a good look at his friend, who was slack jawed and pale. "Yeah, let's get you off the bus," he said as he helped his friend up and off the bus into the waiting crowd of middle aged and younger women.

"Feel like a bloody asshole," Maxwell said as he climbed back aboard and dropped into the front passenger seat. He held the book on his lap and rubbed his forehead with his free hand.

"I don't know much about LSD, but he didn't look high," Allen said. "More like he was tired."

"Whatever's left in his system is just kicking his ass while he's coming down," Bernie said. "When you're on that much, your heart races for hours, then you come down and it doesn't necessarily slow down for a long time, it just burns off whatever energy you have left."

"You don't do that, do you?" Bernie's father asked.

"Twice," Bernie said, not looking at Allen. "Just a microdot, about a hundredth of what he was on. It's not my thing."

Maxwell picked up the thick black marker that Zachary had been using and stood up. He began putting a line through all the symbols on the ceiling.

"Well, glad you're not into that at least," Allen said. "What's all this? I don't recognize most of it." He said, gesturing to the symbols on the ceiling.

"We'll have to sand all this down later," Maxwell said. "He turned the bus into a chamber for giving spirits the ability to hop from one living body to another, appear in mirrors too. It's a spell for people who don't want to let go of their dead. He thought he was making himself immortal, but this isn't made for the living."

"So he didn't give a spirit that gift?" Allen asked.

"There's no summoning component to it, you have to summon

a spirit once you're finished," Maxwell answered. "Zack barely knows enough about this stuff to pretend he's a novice, so I doubt he could remember a summoning to use."

"So he didn't invoke a major spirit?" Bernie said.

Maxwell pointed to one of the circular symbols at the back of the bus. "Three there," Maxwell said. "All in one seal. Old enough so no one knows what the language sounds like aloud, Sumerian. They're household Gods though, so not Old Ones."

"Any idea what they were Gods of?" Bernie asked.

"None," Maxwell said. "I listened to my dad, but not well enough to memorize that whole tribe of minor Gods."

"Max," Allen said, picking up a marker, shaking it and joining in on the striking of symbols. "You led a ceremony a while ago. The people who told me about it say it went well, miraculously."

"I wouldn't say miraculously," Maxwell said. "Did what it was supposed to."

"So, I'm already getting pressure from the Circle to initiate you, and I think my son should stand with you during the ceremony as your brother," Allen said. "There are things you should know, and I can't tell you unless you're initiated."

"Like?" Maxwell said. He was already tired of the topic.

"Where your father is really buried," Allen said. "That graveyard hasn't been used to bury anyone in a long time."

"I want Miranda to stand with me as Summoner," Maxwell replied, watching Bernie smile a little as he looked for a marker that worked.

"I think that can be arranged," Allen said. "Welcome to the fold, Max."

"There goes the neighborhood," Maxwell said.

***

Maxwell could no longer assume anything he saw or felt was all in his head, a defense he'd used most of his life. The book was securely in Max's jacket again, but he felt absolutely nothing from it. The shard was a different story. He suspected that it was why the Ablesmith family was dislodged from the crossroads, why they were able to follow him, and why their tormentor was following him. If he kept the stone, they would be the first of many.

When he finished working on the bus he quietly left when no one was looking. There were campfires with people gathered around them dotting the field between him and his bike, and he was ignored as another shape passing through the humid darkness between.

He made his way to the main house, ignoring the people who were inside – a crowd of older visitors playing cards at the kitchen table, another at the long dining table doing the same, a few older gentlemen in the den having a drink and a cigar, and then he was in the library. Three older fellows, one of whom Maxwell recognized as someone who used to visit his father, were sitting in the large armchairs. The sofa and table were empty. "Sorry, gents, time for you to find another room to have your evening brandy," Maxwell said, opening the French doors, bowing and gesturing towards the hall. "Lots of room in the house."

"Pardon me, son," one of them said, a tall man with a full head of grey hair.

Maxwell noticed that the locked cabinet where many valuable old tomes were kept was open, and the man sitting next to it had an old book bag in his lap. "You're fucking leaving in an orderly, expedient fashion, library's off limits," Maxwell said with crystal clear enunciation, staring the grey haired man in the eye unwaveringly.

The trio took their bottle, one took his book bag, and they all took their glasses out of the room. "I fear for today's generation," one said as he passed Maxwell.

"Fear's the problem, not today's generation, grandpa," Max grabbed the book bag from one of the gentlemen, opened it and retrieved a book he knew his father brought to the collection – Jackal's Book Of Practices – he held the black bound tome up and threw the gentleman's book bag back at him. "Not yours, you bloody thieving geezer. Hammond, right?"

"I used to do business with your father, young man," he replied. "That was-"

"His," Maxwell said. He opened the roughly cut pages to the middle where he knew he'd find a note from his father. The yellowed flipbook page said: *$2,800.00 owing – Gregory Hammond*, and Maxwell held it up. "Don't suppose you have this on you?"

"Twenty-eight hundred dollars?" the shorter of the elderly fellows scoffed. "I should tell you a truth about your father, he always overcharged."

Maxwell may have not loved his father as well as some sons did, but hearing him slighted in the least raised his ire. "Oh, you think he overcharged, do you? Wait 'till you're beggin' me to fetch something for you, lazy thief. This is mine now, and forever," Maxwell said, snapping the large book shut and brandishing it for a moment. "This, all this here's off limits, get along ye geezers," Maxwell said. He closed the twin doors behind the older men then locked them.

Maxwell waited a moment as he waited for the elderly fellows to move down the hallway. The pressure he felt from the shard, though it was ever so slight, was gone, and Maxwell remembered that the main house was blessed and warded in countless ways. He hadn't realized the pressure was there until it was gone, like a stone weighing all his moods down.

The library wasn't a place he spent time in since his father passed. He had forgotten how impressive it was, with an old hearth made from river stones nearest to the fire and blue quartz on the far sides. It was the second hearth built in the house. The walls were covered with heavy shelving filled with books. The old armchairs and sofa in the space had been reupholstered numerous times, the last rebuild had one of them in brown, and two in black leather. The sofa was redone in a gaudy fabric with twisting tree limbs and birds printed across a field of green.

The thickly varnished study table had three old wood chairs around it, even though it was made for six. His handiwork was still carved on one of the corners, the Cantonese symbol for *RESIST FOOLS,* an act of vandalism that did not impress his father back in the day.

The old candle and oil sconces had yellow bulbs in them, and all the lights were on. Maxwell turned off three of the four switches, leaving only the two small lights by the door on, and he checked to make sure the old trio had gone. When he was sure they were down the hall and most likely complaining to the card players in the kitchen and dining room about their rough treatment, Maxwell walked to the bookshelves at the rear of the room.

He knelt down and reached into one of the shelves, behind the books where there was a knothole in the backing of the shelf. He pressed his index finger into the knothole and reached up, pushing hard on an old, narrow steel plate. The plate moved and Maxwell felt a click underfoot.

A narrow section of floorboards came up with a slight pull, the latch unlocked using the mechanism in the bookcase, and Max lowered himself down. He reached for his zippo lighter and remembered that he'd thrown it at Panos weeks before. The house's second basement was a relic, and only had a few electric lights strung up. He pulled the trap door closed above his head and made careful steps down.

He felt the stony wall for the old light switch and found it. The single light in the narrow hallway flickered, it was on its last minutes. The concrete walls left behind by Bernie's grandfather were bone dry, the ceiling was made out of the same material, skills the man took back to Canada with him from his service in World War Two were put to use on the rebuilding of an old cellar into a secret set of rooms.

Maxwell pulled his key ring from his inside jacket pocket and found the old two-tine key right away. There were five steel banded doors ahead before a ninety-degree bend in the narrow hallway. He headed for the second one on the left. The key slid into the bolt smoothly, but it took some effort to turn before he heard the bolts slide on the other side.

"You got me, you old bugger," Maxwell said as he pushed the heavy door open. The steel hinges creaked loudly. The floor was marked with wards of protection, interlocking circles and symbols in white, red, black and green. The ceiling had more marks on it, but these were meant to turn prying eyes away.

Whatever was brought down into the surprisingly large space, a fourteen by fourteen foot room, had to be moved through the narrow, secret passage in the basement, the only other way to get into the hidden bunker. There was a worktable in the middle of the room, square, laden with his father's scrying tools and many other objects. Maxwell took a quick inventory of the scrying tools first, there was a fine copper bowl, a brazier with a wrought-iron stand, copper incense burners of varying age and ornamentation, as well as a silver plate and a fiercely sharp, narrow dagger. He knew he'd find knucklebones and river stone runes in the old leather bags on the silver plate as well.

On the other side of the table his father's ceremonial tools were laid out, including an athame that was made by his great grandfather. The dish, bowl, simple working blade, three seals – one of iron, one of wood, and one of silver, all round and ornate – and the hanging bell were all where they ought to be. There were small, clear vials, one of blessed virgin oil, another of blessed water, and the last was blessed alcohol. If he didn't know which order they were to be placed in, he wouldn't know which was which, but it had been drilled into him. The wand, a simple branch, was not there, nor should it be – Maxwell knew that it was buried with his father, wherever he lay.

With bated breath, Maxwell drew the oldest thing on the table out of a folded cloth. The athame had a finely carved bone handle, featuring a doe's head on the hilt, and a silver-plated cross guard. The blade was finely crafted iron, and the oiled cloth was meant to keep it from air and rust. He held it up in the light and inspected it closely. The seven-inch blade was still as fine and rust-free as it should be, evenly coated in oil. He picked up an old machine oil tin and slowly re-coated the blade over the cloth, then sheathed it in the scabbard beside.

"Now, let's see what condition your big brother is in," Maxwell said. He turned to the shelf behind him and opened a lacquer black, long case. Red velvet padding held a long sabre with a silvered basket in its fine black scabbard. It was a Weaver's sword, and it had been used to defend the Circle from Purifiers once in England. He picked it up gingerly, even though the scabbard was heavy, a quality made to be carried into battle with the sword. "All right, killer, let's see how you are," Maxwell said, shuddering at the memory of fencing lessons, something he managed to get out of after two years. The thick blade gleamed in the light of the bare bulb, the oil coating on the metal adding to the shine. "Your coat is good for another year, I'll fix you up later." He slipped it back into the scabbard and closed the case.

Kneeling down, Maxwell opened another black box, this one was made of stained wood, not nearly as precious, and looked at the amulets beneath. A few were in velvet bags, the rest were made of cheaper, sturdier stuff – old iron or heavily varnished carved wood. He pulled the dark blue bag he was looking for up and shook his head. "Never thought they'd get this on me," he said to himself, drawing a two inch wide silver circle out of the bag. He could still recall his bitter disappointment at receiving it for his sixteenth birthday. Bernie was promised car insurance, and the opportunity to drive, but Maxwell got a fine silver amulet instead.

The pentagram was the main feature of the piece, with carefully crafted protection symbols, two of which were marks passed down through his family, the serpent on the left side of the amulet and the doe head on the other.

"Here we go, almost wish the old man was here to see this," Maxwell said, standing with the silver chain in his hand, the small amulet dangling from his fist.

> *"We are the wardens,*
> *walk without fear.*
> *We are the weavers,*
> *act with knowledge.*
>
> *I am young and proud,*
> *wisdom will come.*
> *Humbled by this token,*
> *service is my lot.*
>
> *Ancestors,*
> *lead me through wilderness.*
> *Light ones,*
> *guide your instrument.*
>
> *As it is right in light,*
> *so may it be."*

Maxwell put the chain on, pulled his hair out from under it and looked at how it fell on his chest. "No adjustment necessary," he muttered. "Like he knew." He pulled an iron symbol, a circle with three roughly made hands coming together in the middle, out of the box and closed it.

"Time for the rest," Maxwell said, scarcely glancing at the books on shelves that stood a few inches from the walls. There were five trunks at the back, all locked. He unlocked the middle one, a giant made from thick wooden slats and heavy metal strapping with his two-tined key and pushed the heavy lid open. It creaked on its hinges, the inside stopped at ninety degrees so it served as a surface to affix knives and an old German Luger pistol to the top. The trunk smelled of oil and frankincense.

He took a well-used leather scabbard from inside the trunk, and unstrapped a blade with fine serrations across the back and a slightly curved edge. He tested it against the cuff of his jacket, and the leather parted with the merest touch. There was a hollowed out section in the middle of the blade's body with a silver insert inside. Symbols made to ward off dark spirits and turn the eye of the enemy were etched into the insert, and the hilt was decorated with the same symbol he wore around his neck.

He slipped it into the scabbard, buttoned it shut, then tied the knife to the scabbard again with a leather thong. He took a small collapsible shovel from the trunk then closed and locked it. Maxwell looked along the books, all neatly sorted on the shelves. So many were hand-written, bound with care. He could remember many of the family grimoires, all uniquely bound to last centuries, that his father used to teach him history, spells and old languages. Most of what was on the thick shelves were from families whose lines came to an end, those were of great interest to collectors. Maxwell found a space for the one he'd taken back from Hammond and carefully slipped it in. That particular grimoire belonged to an individual practitioner who claimed to summon spirits to do his bidding. His descendants were alive, but refused to admit any attachment to the man, so the grimoire had value, but family to search for it.

He found what he was looking for, the grimoire belonging to the Lamonts. Maxwell brought it down and opened it on the far end of the table, away from the altar objects. He looked for the ceremony he needed quickly, but was careful with the parchment just the same. They were a good family, and became very powerful in France because every generation there struggled to have sons. Each eventually did, until the last generation was killed when their ship was sunk. They had plenty of daughters, however, and the alliances that they made through them over hundreds of years gave them great wealth and power. He was happy to see that his father had finished translating most of the pages: Maxwell's French was terrible. Each of the translated pages were sandwiched on archival paper between parchment leaves in the book, with a full English version of what was on the page.

Maxwell compared the iron symbol in his pocket with the drawing in the book and nodded with satisfaction. "Might just be able to get rid of this shard after all," he said. "High milk? This requires high milk? What is high milk?" he asked himself as he read the next paragraph. "Hope I don't have to fight something for it," he muttered as he reached over for a book published in the modern style, with a square glued binding, and flipped through the pages. "Oh, that's easy," he said after reading the description of high milk. "Guess milk that pure was harder to make in the Lamonts' day."

Maxwell returned the Lamonts Grimoire to the shelf and used the basement exit, a narrow door that moved out of the wall entirely and into the hidden hallway on tracks to allow a person to pass, to leave. The door could only open from the inside, from the outside it sealed into a paneled wall, a finished part of the main house's basement that served as an extra bedroom.

The basement was quiet, even though there were cots set up for children down there for a sleepover that would be an epic event for anyone under thirteen. He made sure the storage room at the other end was locked, as was one of the bedrooms where they kept antiques when there were more visitors than they could keep track of.

Maxwell continued upstairs and ignored two older people,

one in a baseball hat who looked irritated, and another in a suit who matched the trio he kicked out of the library. The latter tried to stop him by repeating; "young man," over and over again, louder each time.

Max went to the fridge and took a couple single serving cups of cream, then turned on the taller, old man in the suit who was hounding him across the first floor of the house and stared him in the eye. "What?"

"You were very rude to some old friends of mine a moment ago, and I'd like you to apologize to them. It is only appropriate."

"Can you get Hammond to apologize for trying to steal one of my father's books? One of the last books he fetched for him?" Maxwell looked to the kitchen table, where Miranda's aunt Gladys had joined the Bridge game. She put her hand down slowly as she observed him. "Hammond owed my father twenty eight hundred dollars for the book, didn't happen to have it on him, so I took it back for safe keeping."

"He was a customer of your father's for a very long time," explained the older gentleman. "You didn't give him a chance to-"

"Hammond wasn't in my father's will, and the note he left didn't mention any payment, so he doesn't get his book. I'm wondering if he should ever get it, in fact. It happened to be a book filled with experiments no one here would like to see repeated, research into imprisoning spirits, creating barriers that Old Ones would be attracted to so a Summoner could try to communicate with them. What's an old car dealer like Hammond going to do with that? Imprison a few spirits so he can trade with an Old One? Bring a little good luck his way? A nice young wife, or good business?"

"You're accusing a pillar of the community with something that would get him expelled from the Circle, you're not even initiated," replied the old man, turning pale.

"You in on it?" Maxwell asked. "Interested in a little dark

trading? Did you ask him to steal the book? Go looking in the library?"

"What?"

"Don't get in my way, don't get involved with this, I'm going to make sure everyone knows there was a thief in the library, who he was, and what he tried to steal. I don't know your name yet, mate, but I could learn it easy enough. Start asking if you've had a run of good luck lately, wondering aloud if you've been fiddling with some darker business. That is, if you get in my way," Maxwell said, pushing past him, noticing Gladys' smile on his way through the kitchen door.

Before anyone knew what was going on, he was on his bike, kicking the starter so hard. It started on the second try and he was down the road, rolling towards the crossroads. No one was on the dirt roads in that darkness, where the starry sky could barely be seen between the trees above, and his headlamp revealed only a precious oval in front of him. He didn't want to take the time to retrieve his old edsel from the stand-to at the back of the barn, he wasn't even sure if it would start after he'd been away on tour for months.

He could feel the old remains of the chapel before they came into view, an old broken thing catching just enough light to stand out at the back of a field of graves. Maxwell got off his Harley, and kicked at the inner edge of a pothole forming in the middle of the crossroads. The sparse clouds obscuring the moon cleared momentarily, shedding silver light on his work before being obscured again.

He had the feeling that eyes were on him, and he turned to look at the broken chapel. For the first time in his adult life he suspected that that feeling may be caused by something other than his imagination, and he pulled the small collapsible shovel from the inside of his jacket, staring at the building down the overgrown road as he screwed it together.

He stabbed it into the hole, striking hard through gravel and piled the half shovel of gravel beside. He almost didn't hear the sound of shoes stepping on gravel behind him. He whirled around, shovel in both hands.

A smiling older gentleman held his hands up casually. Light seemed to cling to him just enough so Maxwell could make out all his features. "I come in peace," he said in a comforting baritone voice. He straightened the front of his black suit and continued. "Just a friend taking a stroll in the moonlight."

Maxwell looked the man up and down. His hair was cut sensibly, styled perfectly, his eyes were a piercing blue, and the gentleman smiled easily. He looked robust, but not overweight, and his shoes were freshly polished. All ominous feelings about where he was, what he was doing, and that he could have evil eyes on him were gone. "Long way from the farm, didn't hear a car roll up," Maxwell said, lowering the shovel.

"I've never ridden in one of those contraptions, my boy," he said. "Always wanted to ride along on one of those though." He gestured at the motorcycle. "I find it remarkable that someone like you, a man who spends most of his time doing things for other people rides on the back of a steel horse that can only carry one other person. The bus is more your kind of beast, or at least that's what I would think."

"What do you know?" Maxwell asked, shoveling another load of dirt out of the hole and piling it to the side.

"I know your father was afraid of this," the gentleman said. "He had visions of you, making the ultimate sacrifice after a very short life of servitude. He wanted you to be powerful, to be reasonably self-serving. This one for all business you have with your band, he doesn't like that, that's not the path he wanted for you."

"Who are you?" Maxwell asked. "What could you know?"

"I'm the one who can take your burden, Maxwell. I have made

pretenders into masters, paupers into politicians, and musicians into masters. Samuel may have said something about me coming to make you an offer," he replied.

Maxwell stared at him for a moment, recalling the warning Samuel gave him about a demon, perhaps an Old One attached to the shard he was about to bury who could offer bargains. He reached out with the tip of his shovel and touched the man's suit jacket, it moved like normal cloth. "Nope, you're having me on, mate. Good one, almost had me with the whole 'deal with the devil at the crossroads' story coming true."

"You can touch me because I am manifest," the gentleman said. "Not many people get to see this kind of power, some spend their entire lives trying to summon a spirit, or a demon who can appear in the flesh and they never get the privilege. Not so much as an eerie wisp of mist. You should see their faces when they die and make it to the other side, how they wish they didn't waste so much time trying to get that kind of attention. I never get tired of their reaction." He brushed the dirt off his suit jacket. "This is a miracle, boy."

Maxwell shook his head and dug a few more shovel loads of dirt out of his little hole, leaving them in a neat pile around it. The shovel was dropped to the side as he withdrew the shard from his coat pocket. He couldn't help but notice his companion's eyes widen at the sight of it. "Trying to trick me into giving you this by pulling the crossroads prank," Maxwell said, holding the shard up. "Not even a fair attempt."

"I can prove that I am what I claim to be, Max," the gentleman said.

Maxwell dropped the shard into the hole and pulled the iron seal with three hands reaching towards the center on it from his pocket. He tried to begin the incantation, to pull a cream cup from his pocket, but could not move.

"Let me show you a piece of your future, just a little piece of what awaits," the gentleman said. He snapped his fingers.

Bernie was at his side, a grin on his face. The sound of his band filled his ears, with the exception of the singer, they were playing Proud Mary. It was easy, they were having a good time playing a cover they'd done a hundred or more times. The lights heated the right side of his face, and there was no doubt that he was on a stage, filled with that incredible feeling that only came with the cheers of a full club and good band chemistry. A gunshot rang out, and the back of Bernie's head exploded in a spray of blood, bone and other soft matter.

By the time Bernie fell to the ground, Maxwell was somewhere else, the screams of the club goers far behind in terms of both time and distance. He was sitting in a diner, older. It had been eleven years since Bernie and Darren were gunned down, he hadn't seen Miranda in just as long, and there was a sadness that went beyond a love lost or dead friends. There was something he could not do, or somewhere he could not go that haunted him, and that sorrow had grown old, become a thick crust atop everything he was like ill-fitted armor. Three old silver rings adorned his right hand, one was a sigil he knew, but the other two were alien to him.

This was only a short stop, a break for a coffee and breakfast before he moved on down the road with no destination. The waitress, an older woman who offered him a smile as though she was trying to brighten his morning. "Here you go," she said as she placed his plate of eggs, pancakes and bacon in front of him.

"Thanks, luv," he replied. His voice was lower, it sounded as though he had aged thirty years, not eleven. He caught his reflection in the napkin dispenser as he reached for the syrup and stopped. There was a thick scar from his top lip just past the bottom of his nose, and another crossing his right eyebrow onto his forehead. Those eyes were barely his, aged, sorrowful. A gaze that was a vibrant deep brown had become hollow and faded.

He was about to turn the dispenser so he didn't have to face himself looking back, when a blur of red and blue crossed behind him. Maxwell was on his feet and spinning on his heel in a second, facing a young woman in a gas station windbreaker. She slashed towards his throat with a steak knife, the strike coming so close that it nicked the collar of Maxwell's leather jacket. He effortlessly picked up a chair, took several quick steps around his table and threw it at her.

The four legs tangled her long enough for him to step around then lunge forward, grabbing the forearm holding the knife. He ripped it from her hand. Maxwell put his hand on her forehead and said; "I command this spirit to depart. I invoke Sagiras, Keeper Of Tombs, Watcher On The Path, aid me in freeing this girl from the spirit possessing her. Protect her from intruders and keep her from harm. I call upon you to become her liberator, become her guardian."

By the time he finished, the young blonde gas attendant was on her knees, thrashing so wildly that it took both of Max's hands to hold her head. "You can't run forever, you whoreson! Everything you touch is tainted, the further you travel, the more you taint!" she screeched in her own voice and two others that did not belong to her.

"Not her," Maxwell said, feeling as though his chest and head was filling with energy, a kind of pressure that he recognized as the power Sagiras had given him more than once. He released it through his hands, bathing the young woman in light and illuminating the diner for several seconds.

"I don't know what I was doing," the young woman said, tears beginning to run down her stunned face. "I'm sorry, Sir."

Maxwell picked her up off the floor and was about to comfort her when he saw a torrent of blood running down her inner thigh. The spirit knew its attempt would most likely fail like so many others, and cut her just so she'd be dead by the time it was finished. He'd failed to notice the blood on the floor during the fight, and while he concentrated to cleanse the girl. She fell back down, pale.

"Rest easy, luv," Maxwell said. The blood pooled around her. "Look at me."

"I'm light headed," she said, her eyes closing.

"I've called the police!" the waitress said.

"Call an ambulance," Maxwell said. "Stay here, luv. Try to keep those eyes open for me." It was no use, the artery her possessor had cut spilled her lifeblood out onto the floor by the pint, and no amount of pressure could help.

He knew they wouldn't make it in time, judging from the trail of blood to the door, she was already bleeding before she came in. He had to leave. The spirits that followed him would not be kind to her soul if he was still there when it left her body. "Losun, I summon thee, and request you attend this soul. Take her in your hand, and take up your sword against those who would obstruct her on her journey to the Glade."

He rose and strode from the diner, aware that the girl was dead. The car he'd been nursing since Chicago, a rusty Oldsmobile, waited in the car lot. He'd have to buy another junker, steal another set of plates.

The parking lot was gone in another step replaced by gravel under foot, and a dark night in the woods all around. He wasn't back at the crossroads, he was older, it was another Gathering, twenty-one years later to the day, and there were only twenty-eight people in attendance. The lake that was once pure was stagnant and black. A great evil lurked there, and Maxwell stood on the shore with his great grandfather's blade in one hand, and a lantern held high in the other. "I have no fear for you," he said as a shadow as substantial and deadly as a lion rose from the still water. It was almost shapeless, drinking the yellow lantern light into its dark form.

Maxwell's throat was dry, his head pounded, and his heart was beating so fast it felt like it was trying to escape his ribcage. "You have called me, Weaver, and come to greet me alone," it stated, rising to tower over Maxwell. Its words were expressed through a voice that sounded like the wet, slow ripping of flesh. "What is your offering?"

"I offer my body as your vessel for seven days," Maxwell said. "In trade for the soul you hold captive. Surrender her and I will allow you to use me then leave in peace."

"Peace is not my nature," the thing replied.

"Seven days, I get my meat back in working order, and Vanessa."

"No," the Old One replied, its shadow form jerking as though taking amusement in the denial. "I get your body, your soul remains inside, I keep Vanessa while I own you, and then I leave you. You can have her and your body back in one cycle of the moon."

Maxwell dropped the sword on the sand, pulled one side of his jacket open to reveal a chest full of protective tattoos, and said; "Done." He brought the hot iron lantern to his chest, braced himself, then touched the metal to two of the tattoos, scarring through the pigment.

The summoned beast seized him the moment the seal on his chest was broken. It was as though he was being crushed and ripped through from the inside out at the same time, but his screams did not make it to his throat. Maxwell was no longer in control of his voice, or his body.

VII

Maxwell was on his knees back at the crossroads. He could still feel the echo of the previous moment's anguish and his heart was racing. The hole was in front of him, the shard was back in his hand, and the dark woods were in front of him. The humid air of the night and reality of his bashed knees made him certain that he was back where he belonged, whether he had been mentally transported to three horrors or was somehow there in body, he couldn't tell, but he was sure he'd returned.

The gentleman helped him to his feet. "I'm often the bearer of bad news, but I've got to tell you: I've seen some hard roads ahead of people, but few have so many stops for pain and suffering as yours. It was hard to choose which horrific events to warn you about, I don't envy you."

"Summoner rule number one," Maxwell said, catching his breath and stepping away from the gentleman. "Dead things lie. Rule number two: Demons lie."

"I've never liked those. It's not fair to us honest, hard working beings. I keep my business clean, Max. Don't you want to hear my offer?"

"That's your thing," Maxwell said. "You have to make the offer, then you let me decide and leave me be for a while."

"Exactly," the gentleman said. "Hey, you're good at this, have a real sense for what things from the other world want."

"So, out with it."

"All right. Road Craft, the way it is, is done. I can't touch Zachary thanks to a little experimentation he did on the bus, so this part of the deal is contingent on you dropping him from the lineup. So, picture this. Miranda joins the band, you two fall in love – that has nothing to do with me, you just can't change some things – and make music unlike anyone has ever heard. Cream meets Joan Jett, only even better. You go play that farewell gig, change none of your intentions, and that's where your dream is made reality. Picture it, the disco era hold-outs, those big rock n' roller suits, have a man in Sudbury, you know, visiting an aged Uncle, and he sees you as their savior. He doesn't want the old Road Craft, he wants the new one with your firecracker of a lead singer, Miranda on the mic, and you leading with your guitar. One year later, you're playing stadiums, and somehow you guys avoid the pitfalls of drugs and over doing it on alcohol. That's not a promise I have made anyone else, but it's easy with you lot, because you and your band will get along like the family you are, life on the road will be bliss, and everyone wants to work for you. Legends in just three albums and four years on the road. Everyone in Road Craft gets what they want, stardom, riches, a long career, and I ask that you brace yourself for what comes next. Miranda gets pregnant with a firecracker of a daughter, a beautiful creature with big brown eyes. The best of both of you in a bassinet. I'll give her prodigious talent and creativity, just to sweeten the pot. Then, after you've seen her first steps, heard her first words, and you've known the real love of a family with Miranda, your road ends. You are fulfilled, Maxwell, spared the hellish life you are headed towards now, and all the people you love are spared the kind of suffering and death that makes even me shudder. Your clock stops at twenty-seven, and then your soul serves me for a century plus thirty-five years. It'll be over like that," the gentleman said, snapping his fingers. "Seven years of heaven on earth starting this Saturday night, and then a quick death, a short service, and you're free again."

Maxwell could not help but stop and consider it. If he was willing to offer that much, there was more, he could press and get something else, but there were always long strings attached to such offers. The trade seemed too heavily in his favor. Maxwell looked to the gentleman, held up his silver amulet and asked;

"Would my soul bear your mark forever?"

"Well," the gentleman said. "That's an unavoidable consequence of selling your soul, yes, but you'd have full visitation privileges."

"I would serve for a hundred thirty five years, but never truly be free. I could not leave your sight without suffering and anguish."

"Now you're just quoting your father's second Grimoire, dirty. I would dismiss you when your time was up."

Maxwell steeled himself and pressed his hand to the gentleman's cheek. It felt like moving stone, cold, and nothing like the flesh it appeared to be. "I seek only truth, the light of my ancestors illuminates you."

"You don't have that kind of power," the gentleman said.

"I call Charles Foster to the crossroads," Maxwell said with determination.

His father stepped out from behind the gentleman, tall, in his long dark trench coat, loading his pipe. "You'll answer his questions," he said to the gentleman, who turned towards him slowly. He had a sharp British accent that was far more aristocratic than his son's. "You'll answer three of his questions honestly, then he'll make the deal, or turn it down."

"I will," the gentleman said, surprised, looking the specter of Maxwell's father over carefully.

Maxwell had difficulty pulling his gaze free of his father, who was calmly lighting his pipe. The smell of cedar tobacco smoke filled the air, a scent that followed his father around while he was alive. The mannerisms of the gentleman had changed completely, he was more interested in inspecting the ghost of his father than what Maxwell was saying, bending low to look at him from the bottom up, standing back to get a fuller look, and occasionally waving his hand through the apparition. This was an enchantment his father's spirit was weaving to trap the gentleman in a distraction. Maxwell had read about it in stories that read more like fairy tales when he was young. "Ask your questions, Max, remember the rules."

The rules, Maxwell remembered, were the most important thing. The first he remembered was what a demon could not change. They could not change what gifts someone was born with. If Miranda and he had a daughter, the gentleman had no power to imbue her with great talent. They were also incapable of ensuring the birth of a child, that was something left to more powerful things and biology. "What are the lies in your offer?" Maxwell asked.

"Riches, success, opportunities are all things I can guarantee, but happiness, a child and alteration of free will, I can't," the gentleman answered.

"Good," Charles said, puffing on his pipe. "You've always been able to make a meal out of a mud pie, Max, you don't need his limited help. There are better questions, more important questions, think harder."

Maxwell watched the gentleman puzzle at the image of his father. It seemed like his spirit was distracting the demon nearly to the point of madness. It couldn't last much longer. The next question came to him. "Can you guarantee the safety of everyone I love, and do so without making other people suffer?"

"No, that is not possible. The disaster you'll experience will happen no matter what you do, only I can prevent it if you take my offer. By preventing that, five people will die, two will be forever changed, but you will not know them," replied the gentleman as he carefully measured Charles' height with his hand then compared it to his own.

The last question was easy for Maxwell. "Tell me about the end of my deal, all the plans you have for me at the end of one hundred thirty five years, what does that look like?"

"You are still imprisoned, but you don't feel that way: You will have been the master of other souls I command, teaching them how to wield magic in the spirit world. This will undoubtedly twist you into something you barely recognize, but you will still be valuable. I will entice you to stay after your term of service by making deals with your friends, your loved ones, and your children if you have any. You will never leave."

"There, was that so hard?" Charles asked the gentleman. "What do you say, Max? Do you take his deal? Yea or nay."

"Nay," Maxwell said. "I'll take my chances, thanks for the warnings."

The gentleman seemed to clear his head, and looked at Maxwell. He seemed genuinely saddened. "I do not envy your path, boy. Believe me when I say that I truly hope it is not as dark as it seems, and coming from someone like me, that is a statement worth worrying over." He froze in place, losing color. In a small cloud of dust he crumbled into gravel and sand.

"Wish I could stay, boy," Charles said, "but there's nothing holding me here, not even that trinket in your hand. One thing, mind you: There are some serious consequences to leaving that shard here. It's the best place, you're right with your choice, but leaving it in one place will cause trouble you're going to answer for."

"Dad, wait," Maxwell said he had no idea what he wanted to say next, but he was relieved when his father stopped and fixed him with a mildly amused expression.

"I love you boy, wish I said so a lot more, proud of you too. Just don't let anyone else pick that shard up. You'll hate yourself for what it does to them. Do what feels right, watch your back, and you'll be as strong as you need to be," his father said.

"Is it going to be as bad as he said?" Maxwell asked, feeling as young and as frustrated as he did during his lessons.

"Refuse to embrace sorrow as your companion," his father replied, emptying his pipe. "Farewell, my good boy." He turned, began walking down the road whistling Strangers in the Night, and disappeared.

Maxwell fell to his knees and stared down the empty road. A tear rolled down his cheek, and he brushed it off with the back of his hand. It was followed by a torrent. He could not remember wanting the company of his father before that moment, and as the smell of his cedar scented tobacco dissipated, there was nothing he wanted more.

He forced himself to bear up, and wiped his tears away. "Bloody hell, what good is it if you're right and dead?" Maxwell said, dropping the shard into his inside jacket pocket. He immediately retrieved it. "Sorry, dad, I've got to try to get rid of this anyway." He turned, dropped it into the hole, put the iron symbol he'd brought with him on top of it, and burst the cream cup on top, so the white dripped on the shard and the iron icon. "This cream I bless in the name of the Goddess, life giving milk from a mother for sacred purpose." He could feel the rite working, a calm, peaceful sensation washed over him. "I commit these things to the earth, where they will cause no strife if they are recovered by any person ignorant to their purpose. Be reclaimed by the world and made as one with it once more."

He pushed gravel atop the hole until it was flat. "I seal thee under the crossing of roads, to be gone within one generation, hidden beneath a symbol of goodness until your power is gone."

He turned towards his motorcycle and felt something rough and thick against his neck, the fibers scratching at his skin. He reached up to fight the noose under his chin as it tightened, and he was pulled slowly upwards. Before his hand could get under the rough rope, he was on his toes, struggling to breathe.

Panic seized him as his feet left the ground and he began to gently swing and turn until he could see the twisted face of the pastor. "You won't reveal me," he rasped.

VIII

"Why is he getting rid of it there?" Miranda asked. "That's worse, isn't it?"

"It's where his father would put it," Allen said as he drove his pickup truck down the dirt road. Miranda sat between Bernie and his father. "The graveyard has been a cursed place since my grandfather was your age. There's no consecrating it again, not without accounting for everything that's there, so the Circle uses it as a place to trap things that we want to limit in the ground. It works, but there are so many things there now, it's become dangerous. Charles used it, but he was the last. We keep it up so the uninitiated don't suspect it's true nature, and so we have a place to put our public headstones up."

"It's like a toxic dump," Miranda said. She looked over her shoulder to make sure her aunts were still following. "Max was never told because he wasn't initiated?"

"That's right. When he's initiated we're going to be sharing a lot of things with him, things that will explain a lot about his life, about his father too." Rock n' Roll band came on the radio, and his father turned it down, he was more of an Elvis man. "That's about right," he said. "I never liked the graveyard, to be honest, glad no one I knew is buried there."

"No one has honestly been buried there for over a century," Allen said. "We use the same five graves over and over again whenever an initiated dies to fake burials, so we can perform our ritual somewhere else. Keep our graves from being desecrated."

"Is that what happened at this graveyard?" Miranda asked.

"Nevil Sands used it to gather power in the early eighteen hundreds," Bernie said. "He turned it into a spirit trap, and started getting rich. I never found out what happened after that."

"His family is still running on that money," Allen said. "Ask April, she's related. I was surprised to see her at the gathering."

The sting of Scott getting on with April, the curvy blonde who they barely knew from high school, instead of him at the beach was eased. "I had no idea," he replied.

"I had a dream where you two were seriously involved," Miranda said. "I mean, seriously, highway to marriage and kids. That's why I had you promise you wouldn't forget all about me."

"You're going to have to warn Scott instead," Bernie said. "He intercepted."

"Thank the ancestors," Allen sighed. "A Webb and a Sands, that's not going to wash with my brother."

"What do you think Uncle Desmond will do?" Bernie asked.

"Have a heart attack, maybe nothing though. April's the bright spot in that family, I think."

Miranda looked to Bernie, an eyebrow raised. "Are the Sands still a problem? I know my aunt Gladys looks like she's about to spit every time they come up, but she won't talk about why."

"Dad?" Bernie asked.

"Long story," Allen said. "That's his bike, I think."

"Samuel was right," Bernie managed to say before Maxwell was caught in the headlights, struggling in mid air, hanging by a black noose tied somewhere in the blackness above.

"Hang on," Allen said, pressing the accelerator to the floor, then slowing down at the last moment so Maxwell could get his legs up on the hood. They piled out of the truck in a rush, Bernie was half on the hood, trying to get a grip on Maxwell's legs to push him up. "Cut the rope!" he shouted.

"It's not a normal rope," Allen said.

Bernie felt hands gripping his pant legs, pulling him away from the truck with firm, forceful tugs. "Something's trying to get me," he said as he looked over his shoulder and saw nothing. He pulled himself all the way up onto the hood, shaking the unseen hands off, and stood with Maxwell's legs in his arms.

Maxwell gasped his relief, then rasped; "My boot knife!"

"I am the purifying fire," Allen started to declare into the night, standing in front of the hood of the truck. "Guardian against that which shrinks from light. I call on all the Guardians that have come before-" he was interrupted as an unseen force pulled him away from the truck then out of the headlight's beams.

"Allen!" Miranda shouted, running after him. "Get Max, I'll get your dad!"

Bernie found the long bladed, horn handled knife strapped to Maxwell's calf and began pulling at the leather strap that tied it there. "I'll have it in a sec, you breathing?"

"Yeah, rope's tightening again," Maxwell said as he struggled to expand the noose, trying to push his fingers between it and the rope.

He felt cold fingers trying to interrupt his work, they were cold, small, children's digits. Bernie pulled a small vial of holy oil from his pocket and pulled the cork off with his teeth. "I reclaim this space for the living, for the light and command all souls with ill-intent to depart!" he shouted, splashing his hands with it, standing up, then rubbing the oil on Maxwell's neck. The pressure on his neck was gone, and the black noose let go. Maxwell fell onto the hood of the truck, dragging Bernie with him, and they rolled off into the gravel road.

Susanne's voice cut through the night as she approached, her arms wide. "I am the Seer of Atrani, I call my Goddess through the door, Luna grant me the cleansing light."

Bernie looked up in time to see a broad shaft of moonlight illuminate the road. Gladys ran to his father, who was still half in shadow on the roadside. Miranda fought to pull him all the way into the light. The sounds of cloth tearing and his father's muffled voice prompted him to run to him as well.

"Proserpine, I call on your life-giving nature to press these dead things away," Susanne continued.

Bernie got to the road side, where the light met the darkness as though he were looking from one world into another, and locked gazes with dim grey eyed man who led his congregation in pulling at his father's arms, the shades of children pressed their small hands into Allen's mouth, pried at his eyes and pulled on his hair. Miranda was barely holding on.

With a flick of his wrist, and all the conviction he had, Bernie sent the last drops of his holy oil at them. He grabbed his father's belt and hauled back with all his strength, with all his weight. The shadows retreated, and his father was brought into the silver moonlight. "Are you all right, Dad?"

"I'll be fine," he said. "Leaving the bike here," he stood shakily and walked to the truck.

"I pray thee watch over us during our retreat," Susanne said. "And thank you for coming to our aid." Gladys joined her, retreating as she made signs of protection towards the crossroads.

Miranda was at Maxwell's side before Bernie could get there. "Is he all right?"

"Breathing, he hit his head, but it doesn't look bad."

"Bloody hell," Maxwell groaned as he struggled to his feet holding his head. He looked around and nodded. "Past time to clear out." He started for his motorcycle and Bernie got in his way.

"Tomorrow," he said. "You pick that thing up tomorrow, it's off to the side, it'll be fine."

"Not a bad idea," Maxwell said.

"Max will ride with Allen and Bernie, Miranda with us,"

Gladys said. "Come!"

Miranda gave Maxwell a brief kiss and ran back to their car.

They were on their way back to the farm in a hurry, Maxwell sitting between Bernie and Allen. He wanted to get a good look at his father, but couldn't in the dim cab light. He could tell there was something wrong, his father was being too quiet, and driving too quickly.

Maxwell knew there was something seriously wrong when Allen drove his pickup truck up the lawn of the main house, almost to the front door. "Dad?" Bernie asked as his father opened the driver side door and slid out this side, staggering to his knees.

Maxwell and Bernie were out and at his side in a rush. He was still awake, and groaned when Max and Bernie got under his arms and dragged him up to the porch and into the house. "First floor bedroom," Maxwell said to Bernie, who looked too stunned to think.

In the clear light of the kitchen everyone could see his torn, blood soaked shirt. There were scratches on Allen's neck, face, and the tear in his bottom lip. The darkness hid most of the bleeding while they were driving back, but some of Allen's wounds, not nearly all, still seeped red. The fight with the Pastor's spiritual congregation had taken a greater toll than Allen let anyone see until he couldn't stay upright anymore.

They passed through the adjacent kitchen, busy with night owls still up playing cards, talking and drinking. "Oh my God!" or "What happened?" were the general cries of surprise as they moved him through. Maxwell couldn't help but bitterly note at how completely unhelpful most of them were. Only two people seemed to know what to do as they passed.

They put him down on the double bed and were immediately pushed aside by one of the card players. "I'm a nurse," said the tall, middle-aged woman. "What happened?"

"Animal attack," Bernie said as though by reflex. "He found a raccoon den."

She turned around, regarding Bernie and Max. "No, what really happened? There are scratches in your father's mouth and throat, like someone tried to pull him inside out." She looked to a younger woman beside her. "Go get my medical bag, Tammy, and the extra kit in the trunk." She handed her a set of keys and the younger woman with a perm that matched the nurse's and she ran from the room.

Maxwell stepped in close enough so he could quietly tell her and not share with the rest of the first floor dwellers. "A shadow haunt got him, we got him away as quick as we could."

"Good," she returned her full attention to Allen. "Can you hear me, Allen?"

He nodded, his eyes focusing on her, half open. "Glad you could make it, Dianna," he said.

"I bet you are," she said with mild amusement, but her serious manner returned quickly. "Try not to talk, we're going to take care of you. Do you feel any pressure on your chest? Squeeze my hand twice for no, once for yes." She waited a moment then nodded. "Good, are you having any difficulty breathing?" Maxwell could see the two squeezes of Allen's hand. "Okay, any trouble seeing?" Two squeezes again. "Any ringing in your ears, or difficulty hearing?" Two more squeezes. "All right, you're clear for possession and a whole bunch of terrible injuries you don't want, probably thanks to these brands on your chest. That had to hurt. I'm going to check you over. I'm going to have to cut your shirt and pants off. Don't worry about helping me, I've done this more times than I can count. Sonny, you stay," she said, looking at Bernie. Tammy arrived with a large red and brown tackle box and a large shoulder bag. "You go let Jerry check you out then send him in. Everyone else, out."

Maxwell took one more look at the scene. Most of the bleeding was stopped, from what he could see, the rest looked slow, and Allen didn't look like he was in any danger. He opened his scratched eyelids a little and nodded at Maxwell, so he left. He was met at the door by a powerful looking, tall man with an easy smile. "Max, I'm Jerry, have a seat."

Maxwell was shown to a chair at the kitchen table where Jerry began prodding his neck. "I'll have some of that, if you don't mind," Maxwell said, pointing at a bottle of Wild Turkey bourbon.

"Pot would be better," Jerry said, feeling his way down Maxwell's sore neck. "Go ahead though, if that's your poison."

Miranda came in, her aunts heading directly for the bedroom where Allen was being taken care of. "What are you lookie-loo's doing?" Gladys said to the dozen people hanging about in the kitchen and the hall. "It's almost midnight, the kitchen's closed. Shoo!"

Miranda poured Maxwell a glass of Wild Turkey and handed it to him, taking a seat behind Jerry. "How is he?" she asked, flashing a smile at Max.

"I don't think the rope burns are bad enough to leave any scarring, bruising on the neck is going to be annoying for a week, maybe a little longer. You were really hung up, but the discs are all right. You've got a good goose egg on your forehead here, but if you're going to hit your head, that's where you want to do it. A nice thick part of the skull." He touched the bump, and Maxwell flashed him a dangerous glance. It was throbbing hard already.

Maxwell took a belt of the amber drink in his hand and winced. "God, that's awful stuff," he muttered.

"Here," Jerry said, putting a joint in Maxwell's hand. "I grew it myself." Maxwell finished the glass of bourbon and put it back on the table.

Miranda stole the neatly rolled pot joint from him. "I'll light this for you," she said.

"Sure," Maxwell smirked. Jerry finished checking Maxwell and sighed. "Any other injuries?"

"I'm a little sore on the left, think I hit the truck there somehow," Maxwell said.

"Shirt off," Jerry told him.

He pressed on Maxwell's ribs, causing a little wincing when he got under his left arm. "You're going be all right, but don't be surprised if your shoulders and back are sore. I recommend you finish this," he said, extending his hand out to Miranda, who took a drag from the joint and passed it to him. It was rolled using three or four papers, slightly large compared to what Maxwell typically smoked with the band when weed was around. "Share it with this one, because it's always better with two," Jeff said as he handed the smoldering joint to Maxwell. "Then right to bed, no sugar tonight though, got it?" he said, looking to Miranda.

"He wasn't getting lucky tonight anyway," Miranda said, exhaling a small cloud.

Maxwell took a deep pull on the joint. The throbbing pain of his head and bruised neck began to fade immediately. "Thanks, doc, this beats a lollipop."

"Anesthesiologist," Jeff said. "Training to be a doc though. Take that thing, and her back to the big cabin. Sleep."

Susanne came out of the bedroom, sniffing, her eyes found the joint in Maxwell's hand just as he was starting to hand it back to Miranda and he froze. "I thought that's what I smelled."

"He's an anesthesi-man," Maxwell said, trying to hold his breath and pointing at Jeff with a ring-bedecked finger. "It's on the up-and-up. And I'm up and up." Maxwell exhaled, Miranda took the joint from his fingers. "Allen going to be all right?" he asked.

Susanne let Jeff into the room and nodded. "He's going to be fine. If you two plan on smoking that whole thing yourselves, you should start walking now." She looked to Miranda, who was taking a more conservative drag than before, as though behaving a little for her aunt. "And you're not injured at all, so take it easy on it, yes?"

Miranda nodded and handed the joint back to Maxwell, who was standing up. The fog descending on his senses made it clear that he really didn't have much time to get back to the main cabin and his bedroom gracefully.

The farm and the cabins a short way down the road felt safe, and the night air was finally cooling. Miranda and Maxwell didn't have trouble finding their way together.

IX

The heat of the day was just starting to creep in through the windows of Maxwell's room. He watched Miranda sleep as he woke up slowly. She'd borrowed one of his t-shirts late the night before, it bunched up overnight, riding half way up her back. She spared him questions, didn't try to hold him accountable for what he tried to do, or the trouble he caused. For her, it seemed that it was enough that everyone made it back, and she was surprisingly unshaken by the events.

Instead of giving him the tongue-lashing he deserved, she offered companionship and comfort. Most remarkable of all, he was sure he fell asleep first, and his ease with Miranda was partly to blame.

With great care he slipped out of bed, immediately regretting the act of moving at all. His back, his shoulders and especially his neck were stiff and sore. He didn't bother dressing, but crept from his room in his boxer shorts, picking up his pants, a shirt and his guitar case on his way out.

The door creaked as he opened it and he cringed, Scott was right outside in the hall, staring at him with an amused grin with a cigarette dangling from his lips. "Good morning," he said.

"Quiet," Maxwell whispered.

Scott peeked over Max's shoulder and smiled. "You guys had a good night after all," he whispered, taking Max's guitar case.

Max carefully closed the door and started putting his jeans on. "We were too tired and stoned, nodded right off," he said.

"I got it on with April, man she's a handful in all the right ways," Scott said. "She must be adopted, can't be from the Sands family. How they could make an angel like that, I can't see it, she's a pure sweetheart. A dirty minded, playful sweetheart. I love her laugh, maybe more than anything. It's hard to think she's from that family. I don't think her dad knows she's come here though. She takes off when the sun comes up."

"Careful there," Maxwell said. "Steven Sands is dangerous, her whole family is worth their reputation." He took Scott's pack of cigarettes out of his shirt pocket and popped one into his mouth. His band mate offered a flame with his lighter, and Maxwell nodded his thanks. They moved down the hall to a bench and sat down.

"I'm telling you, Max," Scott said. "April knows all about that stuff, we talked about it. She wants to be initiated here, but it breaks her heart to know that there's no way. Samuel would probably allow it, maybe encourage it, but her dad and the rest would make a huge stink, or try to wedge themselves back in."

"They'll never get back in," Maxwell said. "Tell her to stick around, get to know people, try to make it right with her brother at least so she doesn't have to walk away from her whole clan. She'll get her initiation," Maxwell said. "It'll take time, but if her heart's in it, it'll be worth it. I feel like I've survived the gallows, then got knocked out with a bat," Maxwell groaned, massaging the back of his neck.

The sounds of plates, voices and other breakfast activity drifted up from the first floor. Maxwell's stomach grumbled. He craved a hot shower more, and from the slant of the sunlight, he could tell he had gotten up early enough to catch the hot water tank before it was empty.

"What happened last night? No one's talking, but I caught a look at Uncle Allen, he's got two stitches on his lip and scratches all over." Scott said.

"I tried to dump something I found on the road," Maxwell said. "I think it's been the cause of what people have been seeing, the good and the bad."

"Yeah, that's another thing, I've never heard of what happened at the lake yesterday with that family. Not outside of fairy tales and old stories about spirits in the night and shit. You know, from when people thought they could still meet their Gods in person and get up after being dead a few days."

"That's what I'm saying," Maxwell said. "The Dawn Shard, I think it throws gasoline on the fire whenever spirits were around, or when someone's performing a ritual. It definitely has some big blokes attached to it already. I was afraid that someone would get an enlightening surprise during their morning prayers if I kept it around here. We do have some people here who pray to the holy trinity, and I'm all for them getting a visitation from one of their high spirits, or even the Man himself, but the Dawn Shard seems to attract as many charlatans, and those souls love a believer. I dumped it and sealed it in the ground."

"But, if that's really what brought the spirit world into Technicolor, then it made what we saw on the beach happen, right? I mean, sure, if you felt there were spirits in need of release, and you performed that ritual without the shard around, then maybe you'd get the same result without seeing the spirits, but what we saw was like a miracle or something. That was all good, right?"

Maxwell looked down the hall at the sound of the shower flow stopping. He would prefer to take a shower in the main cabin as opposed to having to use the public ones in the bathroom building outside. "Check this out," Maxwell said, raising his chin and showing the rope-shaped bruises around his neck. "That shard is definitely a bad news, good news situation. You saw the good news, and when I went to bury the thing, I got the bad news. Bugger who was holding that family we released tried to hang me. Bloody hell, he did hang me. Bernie, his dad, and Miranda's Aunts got there just in time to save my ass. Didn't end there though. The bad pastor and his whole congregation got a hold of Allen. Felt like I stepped into one of those old medieval paintings with the demons inflicting torment on a trapped soul. I'll never look at one of those the same way again."

"That's why you're wearing your medallion, and why you've got that weaver's blade," Scott said, saddened a little. "Yeah, maybe it's not worth it, glad everyone came out okay though, really. Uncle Allen looked beat up when I saw him downstairs, he was helping out in the kitchen."

"That's a relief," Maxwell said. "Any idea how Zack's doing?"

"He passed out with a bunch of hippies late last night," Scott said. "I think he found a few fans who took care of him after he came down and Southern Circle let him out of sight."

"Good, we need to start playing, our last gig is coming up," Maxwell said.

"So we're setting up in the barn today?" Scott asked, his mood visibly improving.

"Yeah, going to see if Miranda will join in. Get some of the other musical folk up on stage too, maybe we can make our last show our biggest. Backup singers, tambourines, keyboards, I'll take horns if there are good players around. Everything but the kazoo."

"My cousin brought his accordion," Scott said.

"Maybe we can get him on the old Hammond organ if Darrel doesn't want to," Maxwell said.

The door to the bathroom opened, a puff of steam rolling out and just far enough down the hall to precede Bernie. "Good morning," he said to Scott and Maxwell. "Better get in there before someone jumps in. They're already out of hot water in the main house."

"Done, and done," Maxwell said, butting his cigarette out in the freestanding tray beside the bench.

"Oh, did Scott tell you that we went out and got your bike this morning? I was afraid to leave it so close to the road."

"No, he didn't," Maxwell said. "Thanks, I owe you one."

"De nada," Bernie replied. "I'm going to start setting the barn up. My dad's already told me I'd get a list of chores to do if I hovered around him."

"Cool," Scott said. "I'll give you a hand."

"Oh, who rode my bike back?" Maxwell asked.

"Scotty," Bernie said. "I hate riding two wheels on gravel, remember?"

"Thanks again," Maxwell told Scott. There was something wrong there, maybe he scratched his Harley, or something worse, but Scott had a guilty look about him.

"No problem, Max."

The bathroom was still steamed up while he took care of his morning needs, and it didn't have a chance to clear before he got into the shower with a disposable razor he found in the cupboard. He shaved, then turned and let the hot water massage his sore neck and shoulders. The day before had left him with more questions than he could handle. Three of them nagged heavily.

Why were he and Miranda separated when they were young? He understood that her aunts didn't live in the country, but he'd heard there was more to it. Everyone seemed afraid of the book, but from his experience, the shard was far more dangerous. The biggest question on his mind was one that he was sure other people shared: why was the spirit world interacting with him and people around him so much more clearly, so aggressively.

These questions, and thoughts of Miranda took turns occupying his mind as he selfishly, guiltlessly used up almost all the hot water left in the main cabin's tank. He felt the water begin to cool, and hurriedly finished washing. By the time he was finished, the water was getting colder by the second. If he stayed in another minute, he may as well be bathing in the lake.

There was a line of five people with towels in the hallway when he finished, and the fragrance of freshly fried bacon was in the air. "Sorry folks, you'll have better luck finding hot water in the public bathroom," he said as he passed, causing groans and shaking heads all down the line. None of them should be trying to use the main cabin's bathroom, as far as he was concerned, they weren't staying there.

He carried his guitar case downstairs into the main room, which had two old, wooden folding tables set up so more people could sit and eat from platters of eggs, bacon, toast, sausages, waffles, English muffins, and a yellow-orange casserole. Maxwell headed to the dining room, and the main table, where a plate was put into his hands by Gladys who said; "Mangiare a sazietà," gesturing to the table.

Amongst a full table with children in high chairs and people moving in and out of a crammed kitchen, there were several older people there who Maxwell recognized, including Scott's mother and father, Nadia and Desmond. They both smiled at him from their seats, and Maxwell shook Desmond's hand. "How'd our boy do out there?"

"Best drummer on the circuit, and he didn't fall into any trouble. He spent most of our time chasing after Zack and Darren," Maxwell said as someone spooned a helping of the deep-dish egg and cheese casserole onto his plate.

"I wish he'd shave more," Nadia said. "He has such a nice face."

"I'll remind him," Maxwell said. "I'm sure that compliment will get his attention if it comes from me, that's if I can get him away from April when she gets back," Maxwell said, forgetting that she was from a family not well liked by the Webb's. It was difficult to think of the smiling blonde girl as a Sands, daughter to the only family that had been exiled from Circle events and ceremonies.

Nadia changed the subject right away. Her husband's mood darkened as he continued to pick at his eggs. "I hear you're getting initiated this week?"

"Can't fight it any longer," Maxwell said with a slightly forced smile. "Time to step into the circle."

"Good, it's about time."

Maxwell's plate gained weight again as an older woman speaking a language he did not recognize stepped out of the kitchen, dropped two steaming waffles onto his plate, grabbed a big spoon and then added scrambled eggs and a few sausages. She flashed him a smile, dropped a half dozen strips of bacon on top of everything then gestured for him to move along. "I'm being directed," Maxwell said to Nadia and Desmond.

"Where's my son right now?" Desmond asked.

"Scott's setting his kit up in the barn, he'll be there a while."

"Thank you, Max," he said.

Feeling as though there was a reckoning coming for his friend, Maxwell decided that it was none of his business. Whatever happened with Scott, April and their parents would be too complicated for him to get into, especially considering the little he knew about the feud. He spotted Samuel in the corner, sitting alone at a card table, treating a plate of yellow casserole as though it was chocolate cake. Maxwell stopped to stand beside a chair there, and Samuel said; "Please, have a seat, boy. It's a good day, and I have this," he gestured to his plate. "I keep asking what it is every year when I come here, and that Gunnering woman says some name I could never pronounce, and I know nine languages. Doesn't matter, best thing I eat all year."

"I remember it's yellow and filling," Maxwell said. "Don' think I've had any in a couple years. Need my coffee though, be right back." He stood and fetched himself a cup of coffee from one of the side tables and was reminded of the previous night's events as he dumped two creamers and a couple sugar into the steaming hot black. By the time he returned to Samuel, Allen was joining him, trying to keep his smile small so he didn't aggravate his stitched lip. "They kicked me out of the kitchen," he said.

"Ever since I was a lad, I've offered to help the ladies in the kitchen, and I have been shooed out almost every time. At my age, with my lungs, I've given up, they seem happy telling me what to eat and feeding me too much of it."

"Maybe I should stop offering too," Allen said.

Samuel's fork stopped half way to his mouth. "Oh no, not until you're wobbly kneed and wheezy like me. The offer is worth four times the favor." He shoved the forkful of egg casserole into his mouth and looked as though he'd eaten ambrosia.

"How are you this morning, old man?" Allen asked.

"Better than you," he said after finishing his mouth full. "Nice clear weather, it's not the heat that gets me, it's the humidity, none of that nonsense today. How are you? That looks painful from here," he said, gesturing towards Allen's face with his empty fork.

"Lip bothers me more than anything," Allen said. "Pretty good otherwise."

"I'm sorry about all that," Maxwell said. "I brought that on, should have been better prepared, handled it myself."

"You needed to cast a circle before what you tried last night," Allen said, trying not to move his lip too much. "Just don't work alone when you don't have to, and with everyone here, you don't have to. There're more folks around here willing to do something foolish than you'd guess. All's forgiven, boy. Just hold off on anything else until initiation."

"My last one, you're lucky," Samuel said. "You'll have this one leading it next year, or maybe we'll break tradition and finally have a Priestess running things?"

"That's more likely than me taking over. Susanne is our best weaver, and she's staying in Canada, so you'll see it happen," Allen said.

"Oh? That's going to be good."

Maxwell couldn't hold his questions any longer. "I sealed the Dawn Shard in the ground last night," he said quietly.

Samuel picked his watch out of his pocket, opened it, nodded, then snapped it shut. "I know," he replied. "We'll see where that leads, I'll say it's worth trying once."

"All right," Maxwell said, a little surprised that he wasn't subject to an epic lecture. "So why does it seem like that's the thing to watch out for, and the book is about as scary as harsh language."

"The shard is a heavy burden, as far as we can tell, that's true," Allen was interrupted as Gladys dropped a plate with casserole, bacon and hash browns onto the table in front of him.

"Stop talking when you don't have to," she told him, pinching a tuft of his short blonde hair and tugging it as she walked away.

"I'll talk for you," Samuel said. "Some pair we make, one with lips that have to stay still, the other who can't catch his breath in humid weather. Max, you know more about that book than anyone here, your father wrote three volumes on it."

"That's mostly the history, where it's been, who had it when, and what the legends say it was used for," Maxwell said. "I didn't even believe most of what he wrote on how these rites work. It's locked up in my room, by the way." He whispered.

"Good, may want to keep it on you though, it's made of rugged stuff, it'll stay together, but that'll do for now. Maxwell, the covenant is a touchy topic here because there are people well practiced enough to break it, powerful enough to make that work for them," Samuel said. "You break the covenant, and you take the balance of reality out of the divine's hands. We bend the rules as much as a mortal can as it is, but if you use the keys in that book to take divine power out of the situation, you can throw the rules away. Knowledge truly is power, and as my fifth wife can attest, strange things happen when a High Weaver talks in his sleep. I summoned her Uncle Zini one night, and we were in separate beds for the rest of our marriage."

"So the shard is like raw power with endless consequences, and the book is temptation and power," Maxwell said. He watched Allen carefully eat egg casserole and felt deep pangs of guilt. Eating was not pleasant for him judging from the sweat on his forehead, redness on his face and how slowly he chewed. The scratches on the inside of his mouth must have made it a misery.

"Endless consequences," Samuel said, nodding. "I like that. You must understand, the shard and the book were found together for a reason. Panos may have broken from the Purifiers if he had them. He must have had plans the two pieces are awful in concert. A thing that draws a powerful demon in it's wake and attracts spirits combined with a book containing the definitive text on breaking or restoring the cycle of life and death in many different ways? You are trained well enough to know how dangerous that is, how tempting that is. Even I know I could be born again through such magic, and it would break the covenant utterly."

"Fear," Allen said. "That's what drives people to the book."

"Good point," Samuel said. "I accept that I'll be moving on soon, there are a lot of people I'll see once I cross over, and I'll be able to send a few messages back." He checked his watch again, nodded, then snapped it shut. "There are plenty of people who not only fear death, but believe that there is a debt to be paid when they reach the other side. People who pray to Gods who yield obvious results are the worst of them. They'll do anything to stay in this existence, away from whatever cost they've incurred. No one at this table has anything to fear. I'm glad you turned the Gentleman down."

"How would you know that?" Maxwell asked.

"I can tell the time, boy," Samuel said with a wry grin. "And you wouldn't believe what the time tells me." Maxwell could hear the gears inside Samuel's pocket watch spinning, and the old man took it off the table then slipped it into his pocket. "Now there's something about you and Miranda being separated," Samuel said, looking up to the stairs where Miranda was coming down in blue jeans and blouse that laced up the front, its long sleeves were cut on a slant, so it was short above her thumb on one side, but drooped down past her fingertips on the other. Her hair was still wet from what Maxwell assumed must have been a cold shower. "Allen was actually there, but I know the why's and the who's, so I'll fill you in."

Miranda crossed the floor and kissed Maxwell briefly. "Good morning," she said before moving on, kissing Allen and Samuel on the cheek before sitting down.

Her aunt Susanne was out of the kitchen with a plate with an egg, two pieces of toast and two pieces of bacon on it, in one hand and a cup of black coffee in the other. She put it down in front of her, kissed the top of her head then whispered something in Italian.

"I'm fine, thank you," Miranda said sourly. "And good morning to you too."

"What was that about?" Samuel asked once Susanne was back in the kitchen.

"Telling me I'm watching my figure," Miranda said, stealing a waffle from Maxwell's plate, taking a bite and waving it at the kitchen.

"No complaints," Maxwell said. "Samuel was about to tell us why you were whisked across the world when we were young," he pressed in an attempt to change the topic.

"Oh?" Miranda said. "I always thought there was something more to it."

"There was," Allen said.

"I'll explain, keep that face of yours still, or you'll never be as handsome as me when you're my age," Samuel told him.

Maxwell took the opportunity to begin scarfing the contents of his plate down. There was so much talking during the breakfast so far, he'd spent more time staring at his food than eating it. The egg casserole was the best thing on the plate, firm and cheesy on the bottom, creamy and tart in the middle, with crunchy cheesy on top.

"When you were just becoming teens, you were already very close," Samuel explained. "We could see it in how you played music together, we caught Miranda often reaching out to hold hands with you, and while Bernie and Scott were welcome to tag along, you two were really each other's world by the end. It came to the point where we had to make sure your family trees didn't cross sometime in the past, and we were pretty relieved to find out that they didn't. There was an engagement three generations back, but it was short lived, and it produced no children."

Allen rolled his fork in the air, looking at Samuel.

"Right, getting on with it," Samuel said. "Your mother was already planning to take a few years in Italy and Spain with her sisters, so you could know your people on the other side of the world. She also wanted to get you two away from each other so you could find your own way into adulthood, into a life of practicing magic. Even more importantly, she didn't want Max's refusal to believe in any of it to rub off on you, and even I could see it already was. Max's refusal to believe, to live a simpler life was a strong notion, even Bernie and Scott were influenced for it for a while, but their parents forced them into initiation, so that put a stop to it." Samuel took his last bite of egg casserole as he spotted Gladys coming towards their table.

"More, then?" she asked.

"I wish I could, but thirds is my limit I'm afraid," Samuel said.

"There'll be more tomorrow," Gladys said, shaking her head as she walked away with his fork and plate.

Samuel looked at Miranda and smiled a little. "The day you arrived in Spain, after you had spent time learning and living in Italy, you found your way through the craft to Summoning. Yesterday, from what I hear, Maxwell took to Weaving like he was born to it, so that part of things worked. Your affinities showed through any distractions because they were removed from you as much as anyone could without making the two of you terribly miserable."

"There was more," Allen said.

"Right, your memories," Samuel said. "I'm sorry, Max, but this is the bit I don't agree on with your father, I mean, didn't agree with. He cast a spell on you specifically so you'd forget how much you cared about Miranda shortly after she left. I bet you don't remember your first kiss, either. It was with each other, and you were caught too, or at least your father was pretty sure that was your first kiss."

"I remember," Miranda said. "We were caught snogging in the first barn stall. That was the first time I heard that word, snogging."

"Well, I have no memory of it," Maxwell said.

"You never forget feelings entirely," Samuel said, smiling a little. "I knew that when you saw Miranda, you'd get them back. What would happen from there, well, that's for you two to control. Your Aunt Gladys there believes that you're destined to be together, but I can tell you that there are few destinies you can't change, either by sheer force of will, or by believing that you don't have to work for it to come true. You two ignore the destiny mumbo jumbo, and do what you want. You're young, but you're grown, so it's up to you."

"Six marriages," Allen said, shaking his fork at Samuel.

"Maybe he's right, I might not be the right one to give advice,"

Samuel said with a chuckle. "But I'll tell you something not many people can say for sure. Every time I got married there were good times, and I'm still hoping for just one more. Those good times are so precious."

Allen shook his head and laughed softly.

"But you first, mister widower," Samuel said.

Maxwell had almost finished everything on his plate, leaving the other waffle uneaten. Miranda only had to point at it to get his nod to go ahead. Her plate was empty, and the waffle seemed to fill in the last of the gaps. "That explains a lot," he told Samuel. "Too bad my father's not around so I could thank him or give him hell, not sure which."

"You're sure," Allen said.

"You're right," Maxwell said. "It would be a shouting match for the ages."

The sounds of drums echoed across the field, the sound of Scott finishing with the setup of his drum kit. "I hear the drums calling you," Samuel said.

"Right, glad I didn't eat those waffles, I'd be too full to sing," Maxwell said, He finished his coffee and stood with Miranda.

"Thank you, guys," Miranda said. "My aunts won't talk about taking me to Italy, or anything before. That is, unless it's about meeting Max again."

"I think your aunt Gladys lives through you a little, but let's not share that insight," Samuel said.

Allen nodded his agreement emphatically.

"Thank you again," Max said, putting his hand on Allen's shoulder. "I should be the one all scratched up this morning."

Allen waved it off, and when Maxwell didn't leave he nodded. "It happened, and I would do it again."

The barn was all set up with all of Road Craft's equipment, even the spare amplifier they kept in hand in case of break downs was on stage, along with all four of their microphones on stands. "You gonna sing for us, Miranda?" Scott asked with a big grin from behind the drums.

"I'll watch first," she said. "I've been looking forward to seeing Road Craft live since your record came out," she said, grinning back at him.

"Thanks for setting up, guys," Maxwell said. "Should have left something for me to do."

Bernie looked at Scott and a more somber mood descended on the pair. Scott came out from behind his drums and sat down on the edge of the stage beside Bernie, who was examining their longest microphone cable by pulling it through one hand foot by foot. "Listen, Max, we know how much you've sacrificed for this band, and Samuel had a talk with us this morning," Bernie said.

"Uncle Allen too," Scott said, "Not that Sam let him say much."

Maxwell reached out, put his arm around Miranda and pulled her to his side, prompting an 'oof' and a giggle from her. "Hold tight, luv, it's a serious band meeting."

"Well, yeah," Scott said.

"Samuel told us that you were planning on selling that book so you could give us money for college," Bernie said. "Man, I had no idea, I would have helped you get it if that was why you were working so hard to track that thing down. Hell, you got shot at. If I knew what it was all for, I would have been there."

"No worries," Maxwell said. "Buyers have dried up for it, and now I know it was a bad idea to track the book down in the first place."

"You're joking, right?" Bernie said quietly. "Panos had it, even by reputation I know that guy's crazy, and he's hooked up with some weird former Purifiers. Who the hell knows what they were going to do with it."

"You did everyone here a favor," Scott said, pointing out to the field across the road from the barn with thirty tents and many more campers. "I don't know everything you and Bernie do, but if crazies like Panos get that thing, who knows? Big problems for peace and love in the world, I'd say."

"Either way," Bernie said. "You kept this band together with the same lineup even though there were days when one half wanted to strangle the other. Sometimes that bus got pretty small. I guess what I'm saying is thank you, and we'll be all right."

"Never had a doubt," Maxwell said. "Couldn't have kept the peace without you two. It wouldn't have lasted as long as it did if I were with anyone else out there. I just thought you two had a right to a good start after following me out onto the road. Wish I could have done that."

"Oh, we didn't follow you out," Scott said. "Well, maybe the first time, but after that I couldn't wait to get on the stage, behind those drums. Man, I'm going to miss that." He could see the short drummer start to tear up. "Memories like I never thought I'd make. The things we saw, how far we got, like having a record together. I don't know anyone else in town that can say that, and to do it with you guys? You're my brothers." He wiped a tear away and laughed. "I'm out of words, man."

"Touring with you guys," Bernie shook his head, his eyes closed before continuing. "Best time, man. I'll forget most of the bullshit, but those good times will stick. I wouldn't change a thing."

"One last gig, then," Maxwell said.

"I hate to tell you this, but we got a call from the Nickel City, they cancelled our gig," Bernie said. "Looks like this will be Road Craft's last stage."

Maxwell didn't realize how much he was looking forward to playing to a crowded bar room one last time. The wear and tear from months on the road was just starting to clear, and he had distractions waiting for him when he got home, so he was just starting to feel like he was actually back on the farm. A week off from rolling wheels and weekend shows was what he needed before one last weekend on stage, he knew it would be a show the few there would never forget. To hear it wouldn't happen at all was emotionally gutting. Maxwell didn't want to talk about it. He gave Miranda a kiss then let her go and started up the narrow side stage stair. "Let's wake the dead," he said as he put his case down and opened it.

"We're not opening with that, are we?" Bernie asked quietly.

Maxwell strapped his new guitar on, accepted a lit cigarette from Scott and smiled crookedly with it in his mouth at Bernie. "La Grange then, yeah?"

Scott started the low-key, drum rim tapping beat right away, smiling at the prospect of doing one of his favorite cover songs. Maxwell tuned the guitar, plugged in, and turned up while Bernie put his bass on then adjusted their ancient, small soundboard.

There was a feeling about the song, La Grange, that Maxwell enjoyed, and it was one of the few he could sing well, with a low, gravelly tone that he'd practiced so much on the road that he could do it by reflex. He hummed into the microphone while he started playing the first riff in the song, repeating it until the microphone turned up.

The sound in the large barn was always nice and clear, with stalls to absorb extra sound waves, heavy wood that didn't rattle enough for anyone to notice, and a large interior in front of the stage.

La Grange was one of their warm up songs, chosen so Maxwell could entertain the crowd with his limited singing skills while Zachary made his way to the stage, an almost nightly occurrence. "All right," Maxwell sung, signaling that it was time to get past the quiet opening of the song. That, easy going, relaxed mood started to come over him, and then the drums and bass kicked in. He caught Miranda's eye and winked at her without thinking.

She danced at the foot of the stage, slowly raising her arms over her head as she moved to the music. By the time the first solo came along, people were walking in, dragging lawn chairs, and some were dancing their way into the barn. The morning was still cool, and many of them had been watching equipment move into the barn with interest, the promise of live music irresistible to so many.

"We jamming this?" Bernie asked.

Maxwell nodded, and they extended the song by several minutes, repeating the main vocal parts, but instead of repeating solos, Maxwell took the opportunity to perform his own in a melodic blues style. His new Gibson guitar played like nothing else he'd ever had on stage, inviting his fingers to dance along the fret board, and the tone had the kind of growl he struggled to get out of everything he'd owned until then.

He glanced out at the gathering audience and didn't see Zachary. With no worries about having to get back on the bus and deal with his pouting, he decided to sing the one song he could accomplish that they recorded on their album. He knew he would struggle with the chorus, it was too high to suit his voice, but he decided that he'd give it a try anyway, and irritate Zachary, wherever he may be in the field outside the barn. Their singer was territorial about his duties, especially since he was terrible at everything else, especially guitar.

Then a thought struck Maxwell as they brought their ten-minute version of La Grange to an end, and he leaned down towards Miranda at the edge of the stage. "Do you know Wake the Dead?" he asked her.

Her eyes lit up, "Guitar or vocals?"

He hadn't even considered that she could play rhythm guitar, and shrugged. "Both?" He pointed to a backup, an old Greco guitar, a good knockoff of the Gibson Maxwell was playing, on a stand beside the drums.

She nodded and ran up the stage side stairs, plugged into their backup amplifier and had the guitar tuned in seconds. Maxwell could see Bernie and Scott were happy with her addition at a glance, even though they seemed just as surprised at her familiarity with a guitar as he was.

"What parts am I singing?" she asked.

"The chorus is all yours, luv," Maxwell said, hoping she had a good sound. He cringed at the very thought of her having a voice that he wouldn't want to follow on stage. The last time he heard her she was thirteen years old, and her voice was positively angelic, but a lot could change.

He started playing the ominous opening riff, Bernie falling in step on the bass, and Scott pounding an almost tribal beat on the tom drums and was happy to hear Miranda join in on time with the rhythm guitar line. There was no doubt in his mind that their album was regular listening to her. She also had talent of her own, forgoing the pick for effortless finger picking, something he would have noticed before if he paid any attention to the callouses on her fingers.

They broke from the intro into the main song, keeping to ominous minor keys. He sang the verses to his best ability, sticking to his comfortable range, they had the audience's attention, and most of the younger people seemed to enjoy it.

When it came to the chorus, Miranda sang with a strong tone that wasn't harsh in the least, but it had a slight rasp that Maxwell enjoyed. The little girl was gone from her voice. It had been replaced with the powerful tone of a confident woman.

One More Party (Wake the Dead)

Abandon your slumber
Your lasting repose.
We ain't done with you yet,
Wake, shake, rattle those bones.

Master necromancer,
I stand on this hill
To bring you forth
You'll abide my will.

[CHORUS]
Rise for this night
Drink from death's cup.
Keepers of the light
Come at sun up.

Dance down the avenues
Make merry one last time
Your dead I return to you
Before I make them mine.

[CHORUS]
Rise for this night
Drink from death's cup.
Keepers of the light
Come at sun up.

Here comes the day
Find your headstone,
Return to your graves
I will not be known.

They finished the song. Maxwell smiled at Miranda, nodding.

"You love it?" she asked a little too close to the microphone with a cocksure smirk towards Maxwell.

He couldn't speak over the applause without a microphone, so he kept nodding, pointed at the main microphone and stepped aside. "What do you want to sing?" he mouthed as much as yelled. There were at least forty people filling the barn and spilling outside.

"Anything?" she asked.

Maxwell looked to Bernie, who nodded and shrugged. "We're a top forty hotel band, name it," he shouted over the calming crowd.

"Slow Ride?" she asked, smiling.

"Let's do some Foghat," Maxwell said into the microphone he used for backup vocals. More than half the audience knew who that band was, and applauded. He knew the rest would recognize the song as soon as Miranda started singing. He pulled his bottleneck from his pocket and slipped it onto his little finger, then nodded.

Scott started with the drum opening a second later. Road Craft did have original music, but they mixed the better songs from their album with rock songs from the late sixties and more recent radio hits. There was no way to fill eight sets a weekend with only their music, they just didn't have enough, and it wasn't what hotel or bar owners wanted. They wanted bands that played popular music, so playing covers was the price they paid to play their own work. It was one they usually played gladly.

Miranda hopped up and down on her toes. She was so excited that she missed the first bar, but the band repeated it and she picked it up. Maxwell and Bernie didn't take long to find the melody, and backed her up. He went low, Bernie sung higher. The overall sound of them together was good, as far as Maxwell could tell. The audience was the real indicator though, and they were thrilled.

They kept their chain of songs going for a set that took them into the early afternoon. By the time they were finished the barn felt like a furnace. They played covers of Rebel Rebel, Dream On, Heart for the first time, which had its difficult moments, but the vocals were spot on and the audience didn't seem to notice that Maxwell had to fake much of the solo, and they finished with a Beatles tune that felt more like a theme for the jam session, A Little Help From My Friends. There were many other songs, but they were a blur. He played most of them as though they were by reflex, his eyes were for Miranda, and he played to her.

"Break time, folks," Bernie said into the microphone, grinning at the groans of disappointment from the audience. "We'll be back, just need some beach, barbeque and beer time."

Maxwell knew trouble was coming when he spotted Zachary coming out of one of the few stalls that hadn't been cut out of the barn. He put his guitar back in the case as fast as he could and locked it. Miranda looked at him, then Zachary, whose face was stretched into hard, angry angles.

"I've got this, it's all right," Maxwell reassured her. "Are we on the way to the beach?" he asked.

"Sure," she replied.

"I'll see you down there," Maxwell said.

"So this is how it is?" Zachary started, screeching as loudly as Maxwell ever heard.

"Zack!" Maxwell said, holding up a finger and rushing down the stage stairs to meet him. "People are having a good time here, we'll talk outside."

"No more of this band leader shi-" Zachary started.

Maxwell grabbed him by the scruff and dragged him to the back of the barn, then through the door. He could barely hear

Scott say; "Oh, shit, this has been coming for three years."

Zachary tried to slap his hand away, and Maxwell let him go with a shove. "Now, this was just a bit of fun," he said, trying to keep his voice low and his head clear. "I thought you'd be on stage by the end of La Grange, like always," he said.

"But you got your new chick up there instead, I know when I've been replaced you thankless son-of-a-bitch. I was there, getting ready to go on stage when she was singing one of our songs with you. That's my shit! I helped write it!"

"No, you wrote some bullshit lyrics about your uncle's Mustang for one song, and Scott had something better the next day, so nothing tried to do for the album measured up. No surprise, either, you couldn't show up on time if your life depended on it."

"Don't you dare attack my art, man, no one can do what I do for you on that stage!"

"Looks like someone just did," Maxwell said, snickering. "And-"

Zachary swung at Maxwell, throwing himself off balance when it was easily sidestepped. He squared up again.

Maxwell wanted to teach Zachary a lesson, or at least end the fight quickly so his sore shoulders and neck wouldn't have to suffer. That wasn't the way to finish a relationship with a lead singer he'd played behind for years, he knew. There was a harder way, but a better way. His father may have taught Maxwell an incredible amount about the Occult, but his real father, Allen, taught him how to be a man. Bernie taught him how to be a brother, and he knew those lessons didn't allow him to do what he wanted, only to do what was best. Zachary was a scrawny, tall man. If Maxwell actually fought him, it would end with his lead singer bleeding on the ground.

"All right," Maxwell said, standing squarely in front of Zachary and putting his hands behind his back. "Take your shot. You think I fucked you over today, so go ahead. Take it out on me. If this is the fastest way to get you back with us, brother. Let's get it over with and have some fun this week."

Some of the anger drained from Zachary, and Maxwell decided to use the opportunity to get the rest out on the table. "Nickel City called, there's no gig this weekend. Whatever you've got in your pockets is what we end the tour with." He said calmly, his chin still held out for a punch Maxwell suspected may never come. Bernie, Scott, and Miranda came through the back door, and Bernie stopped the other two from going further.

"No way, they can't cancel," Zachary said.

"They did," Maxwell said calmly. "Call came in this morning." Maxwell cleared his throat and continued with his next bit of news. "We're not touring again either, I'm done, Scott's done, Bernie's done. Road Craft's just another rock band that was lucky enough to get a record made as a souvenir."

Zachary's hands dropped slowly, and his anger became sadness. "So, next summer's off."

"You didn't hear me the first twenty times?" Maxwell said, letting a little of his irritation come through. Everyone in the band started talking about what they would be doing after the tour weeks before. There had been no official band meeting about it, but Maxwell couldn't see how someone couldn't catch on. "You're about as smart as you are punctual."

"Fuck you!" Zachary shouted, his anger resurging. The sound of Scott's laughter from behind him didn't help, Maxwell guessed. "I bet we'd be hitting the road again next year if you said you wanted to."

"I'm sorry, Zach, I didn't mean it. Listen, it's been a great time, but it's just not good out there, we're not breaking through. The bars are becoming dance clubs; I don't think we could book enough to buy Kraft Dinner and keep fuel in the tank. Time to grow up, end things right," Maxwell said. He stepped forward, starting to extend his hand to offer it to Zachary.

Maxwell was not prepared when Zachary kicked as hard as he could, and thanks to Max's forward momentum, his shin impacted squarely between his legs. Maxwell fell to one knee and held up his middle finger, barely able to stay up. The pain in his middle seemed to throb and worsen, and he relented, falling over onto the grass.

"Fuck you, Max. You won't see me after this week," Zachary said as he walked away. "I want my share when you sell the bus, too."

"You didn't pitch in when we got it," Bernie said to Zachary as he passed. "So you're out, bye."

Scott was about to step in front of him, but Bernie stopped him with a hand on his shoulder. "Not worth it," he said. "If this is the exit he wants, then that's what he gets."

Miranda was at Maxwell's side, helping him up slowly. The pain was not lessening quickly, but he breathed deeply and forced himself to his feet anyway, refusing to stay down. "Oh, I wanted to pound that bastard until he was a stain," he said, exhaling. "Next time he puts his hands up, I'll cave his head in."

"Doesn't look like you'll get the chance," Miranda said. "I'm sorry, I feel like I was the cause of all that."

"No, been coming for a while. Bugger's just not the kind that gets along with anyone who doesn't worship him. Can't believe he cracked my nuts though," Maxwell groaned.

"Are you going to be okay?" Miranda asked, half smiling through her concern.

"Just need a few minutes, maybe a dip in the lake," he replied.

"I'll get your guitar, put it in your room," Bernie said. "Just in case he gets brave and stupid."

"Thanks, mate," Maxwell said. "We'll start making our way to the beach."

Scott handed Maxwell a smoke and offered him a light. "He got you really good, huh."

"Never been hit like that," Maxwell replied, shaking his head and exhaling a lung full of cigarette smoke. "Good riddance to him. Wish it could have ended better."

"I wonder where Darren is?" Scott asked. "He'll probably get all the news from Zack, I wouldn't be surprised if we never see him again."

"Afraid you're right," Maxwell said. "No way for a band to end."

"It's better than some," Miranda said. "At least three of you are still friends."

"Yeah, any time you want to play, Max, I'll get behind the drums," Scott said. "Bernie's the same, but on bass, of course."

"You've got me if you want me," Miranda said.

"I'll play guitar for any of you," Maxwell said. "It's good days again, music is fun again."

"Yeah, about time," Scott said.

X

The four of them returned to the main cabin for a late lunch, and April was waiting for them on the bottom floor, helping with cleanup. She pulled her apron off and greeted Scott with a kiss that made Gladys stifle a smile and a few of the older ladies coming from the kitchen shake their heads.

"She is not her father or her mother, this one," Susanne whispered to Miranda and Maxwell. "A light came from the Sands family, she is a sweet girl."

"I haven't seen her in ten years, probably more," Maxwell said. "She's the butter to Scott's bread when they're in sight of each other though."

"We left food out," Susanne said a little louder. "Barbeque on the beach again tonight." She looked to Miranda then and said; "The proper beach."

"I'll see you there," Miranda said. Suzanne was the last of the ladies who were working in the kitchen to leave, with the exception of April, who grabbed Scott by the hand and headed for the main stairs. "I left my bag in your room, I have to change into my swimsuit."

Maxwell popped a cherry tomato into his mouth and enjoyed the tart burst of juices. Miranda picked up a plate of cherry tomatoes, cut celery, carrot and quarter sandwiches and started following the pair. "I have to change too," she said.

Maxwell was reaching for another cherry tomato when she stopped and looked over her shoulder. "You comin'?"

They were in his room scant moments later, and he realized that none of Miranda's things were there. He turned in time to see her lock the door and put the tray down on the dresser. Maxwell smiled, "What's on your mind, luv?"

Miranda kicked her shoes off, ran two paces and leapt the last four steps. He caught her, turned and fell backwards onto the bed. The smell of her, vanilla, rose and something a little spicy, was all around him.

He held her as he enjoyed playing past her soft lips with his, Max's hands slipped under her loose shirt, his fingers pressing their way from her hips to shoulders. Her skin was soft, and her braless back was a smooth track for him to run his hands up and down.

Their lips remained locked until the sounds of their excited breathing calmed a little. His hands wandered down, under the hem of her jeans, and he kneaded the soft spot on her back there. She moved against him, groaning against his mouth. Maxwell noticed she was distracted, her kiss was slowing down, and he took advantage of the moment, plucking at her full lips for a moment before kissing her neck.

She sat up and pulled her blouse off, then looked down at him, biting her lip. Maxwell ran his hands up from her waist to her ribs and then pulled her down on the bed beside him. He sat up and pulled his shirt off, then lowered himself onto one elbow to look at her. His silver medallion dangled between them. He rested his hand on her smooth stomach, gently tracing his palm across her soft skin.

"It's like I only forgot I loved you, Max," she said. "I remember now."

Maxwell stroked her cheek with a feather light touch. "I don't have those memories," he said. "But you're it, luv, the light I've been looking for."

Miranda's widening eyes and little smile was a reward in itself, and he leaned down to kiss her. He felt a tug on his belt, looked down then back up at her. Her smile had become impish. She unbuttoned her jeans and began pulling them off. "I don't want to wait," she said.

Maxwell rolled towards the end of the bed then opened the trunk there so he could get to his saddlebags.

"Where ya goin'?" Miranda asked as her jeans hit the floor.

"I've got condoms in here somewhere," Maxwell replied, rifling through his bags with reckless abandon. "Think they're under these things," he said, pulling a pair of leather pants he'd only worn once out of the bag and dropping them beside the chest with a plop.

He felt her breasts press against his back as she embraced him from behind. "I'm on the pill," she whispered against his ear.

Maxwell didn't bother turning around, but undid his belt and started pulling his jeans off. She helped push them off with her feet as she kissed him on the cheek, behind the ear, and down his neck.

He turned around and fixed her with a devilish grin as soon as his jeans were off. Miranda was caught off guard; her expression of surprised amusement encouraged him. She had never been more beautiful, and he tackled her with an embrace that made her giggle as they rolled across the bed together.

Some time later, they sat up together in bed. The heat of the day was fully in the room, but Maxwell and Miranda were too hungry to leave yet. They sat on top of the sheets, nude, picking from the large plate of sandwiches and vegetables resting between them.

"You're full of surprises, luv," Maxwell said.

"Good ones, I hope," she said, munching through a carrot stick.

"I have to admit, I was bowled over when you picked up that guitar. I think you're better than I am."

"No way, mister. I have technical chops, maybe, but you have a feel for it that I never picked up," Miranda said. "It's like a part of you, like your voice when you're playing. It's still notes, and strings and technical stuff to me. I like it, but I'd rather sing."

"Where'd you learn?"

"Spain," Miranda said. "My father had an old guitar and he showed me a few things. I liked it enough to start lessons the next week, and they set me up with a classical guy who almost made my fingers bleed. I'll never forget those blisters."

Maxwell caught her left hand and looked at it. Her callouses weren't as thick as his, or as hard, but they were there, surprisingly small on the pads of her fingertips. "What's your father like?"

"He's a deadbeat," Miranda replied, absent vitriol. "I like him, don't get me wrong, but he's more a boy who got old than a man. Lives in a little house he and his family made for him behind my grandparents. He rides a bike around, delivering things in town, sells the odd thing he picks up here and there, it's more like having an older friend than a dad."

"You miss having him around?" Maxwell asked.

"You know, I had a big fight with my Aunt Susanne about seeing him after we were in Italy for a while, I wanted to go early because school was over. I think I screamed at her for a week and she finally gave in. She said something it took almost two years to realize – that I'd get tired of him just like my mom did. By the time I left I was used to him borrowing money, not being where he said he'd be, getting really down and drunk at random times, then popping up out of no where as though he's got sunshine in his pocket, like life couldn't get better. He was so up and down, but never someone you could depend on, always taking the lazy way through life. I think I was in New York a month before I realized I didn't miss him at all, is that terrible?"

"No," Maxwell said. "I don't think so, luv. People can only change so much, my dad never did. Most of my memories of him aren't good ones, if I'm honest, and I think I only miss him now that I'm starting to believe all his warnings. Even still, he was a strict teacher, don't think he treated me much like his son most of the time, just an unwilling student. Our dads weren't the same, I'll tell you, I think I'd trade for a while given the choice. From what you're telling me I think we both got the short end. I bet you'll miss him again in a few years."

"Probably," Miranda said. "Maybe I'll write him a letter, tell him I'm moving back into Mom's house. Or maybe not, he might want to come and mooch off me until Aunt Susanne kicks him out."

"What about your aunt Gladys?"

"She loves him, but she's somehow missing whenever he's looking to borrow money, feeling down or too drunk," Miranda said. "I don't know how she does it, but she did it for about two years. I think she pushed me to stick with my guitar lessons more than anyone though. Got me to play a little on the piano in Italy too, but we didn't have one, so it didn't stick."

"We'll have to get an acoustic in your hands tonight," he said. "I'd like to see you play,"

"Oh, no, you break out the guitar, I'll sing along. I'm not like that with the guitar, I'm not so good that it can speak for me. I'll use the spare, it's better than the electric I had in New York, keep playing with you guys, if that's all right."

Maxwell laughed and chose a cucumber sandwich from the plate. "I think everyone wants you on stage, luv. I know I don't want to play without you."

A knock on the door startled both of them. "We're headed down to the beach," April said through the door in a singsong tone.

"See you down there," Maxwell said with a shrug.

"Wait," Miranda said after swallowing a mouthful of tomato. "Which beach?"

"Normal one," Scott shouted through the door.

"See you there."

Maxwell took a bite of the last celery stick and hopped out of bed. "Wait," he said. He unlocked the door and poked his head through. "Anyone around?" he asked Scott.

"They just got the meat from the fridge and headed down," Scott said. "Been busy in there?"

Max ignored the grins on both of them and pressed on. "We're going to make a dash to the shower, guard the stairs?" He found a two-piece swimsuit swinging from the outside knob, so he grabbed it and tossed it behind him.

"Sure, sure," Scott said.

"Good for it?" Maxwell asked Miranda. "There are no towels in here."

Miranda hopped off the bed and picked up her dark red two-piece. "It's a short run, sure. Looks like one of my aunts know what we've been up to."

"Good thing it's destiny," Maxwell said sarcastically.

"All clear!" Scott shouted from down the stairs.

"Good thing I'm nineteen," Miranda said, kissing him briefly. "Let's go."

They ran from his room, down the hall and into the bathroom. Miranda closed the door behind them and walked into Maxwell's arms. "You know," she said, snuggling against him. "I would have never thought, but you're actually a lot of fun."

"I'm loads of laughs, luv," he said as he held her and waddled them both into the shower. He braced himself and turned the cold water on first. He laughed as she dug her nails into his back and squealed.

Both her aunts knew they'd disappeared earlier in the day, and to his surprise, neither of them took him aside or gave either of them any trouble. Gladys did pay a little more attention to him though, it was impossible not to notice.

The occasional pinch on the arm as she passed by, or mention during conversation while they were on the more populated normal beach during dinner was a clear indication to Maxwell that she had her eyes on him.

Susanne only seemed to smile at him and Miranda when she saw them together. He would have thought the reactions of the pair would be reversed, but that was definitely not the situation.

The stage was filled with enthusiastic friends that early evening. After several songs a giant blonde and grey haired man named Greg Serra, who approached the stage with a resonator guitar and asked to join them in an almost sheepish manner. Miranda waved him up before Maxwell could say anything because he was busy trying to remember where he recognized the weathered man from.

Three songs after he was on stage, he stepped forward and began singing instead of only playing along with Maxwell and Miranda on guitar. Greg Serra's voice was a clear, booming bass-baritone that seemed effortless. He played the lead in an eerie version of *I Put A Spell On You*. His presence was more youthful than his appearance, smiling on one side of his mouth through most of the lyrics. Maxwell remembered where he knew him from; his father had one of his blues records.

Maxwell almost stopped playing backup guitar when he recalled meeting him as a young boy, taking a lesson from Greg on a few minor chords. When it was time for him to leave, he opened his big hand and offered a few guitar picks before telling him to keep practicing. He couldn't help but wonder if that wasn't the first Gathering that his father brought him to, weeks after arriving in Canada, and he suspected that it was.

They backed him for two more songs, then he nodded at everyone and left the stage to large applause, especially from the older people there, who crowded in as soon as they heard his voice. They only played a few more songs after that before the band called it a night. Miranda and Maxwell left through the back door before anyone could drag them to a fireside.

Miranda and Maxwell returned to his room with a small bag of pot he traded the last six-pack from the bus to Two Beards for, and a bottle of cherry wine.

That candle lit evening was slow, caring, and filled with breaks for conversation, imbibing and connection. They drifted off to sleep sooner than either expected. Comfort, contentment and companionship led them into the cool dark.

Maxwell didn't know why he woke up, but he was completely alert by the time his eyes were open. He didn't move, but watched Miranda's back and looked through the lightly curtained balcony doors beyond.

A familiar scent rolled in with the cool breeze, like a type of fuel. He identified it a second later as lighter fluid, then winced at the strong aroma of burned hair. "Panos," Maxwell said to himself as he started to roll out of bed.

A strong hand grabbed his ankles and pulled him off the mattress then across the floor towards the door with such force that grabbing the sheets did nothing to slow it down. The bedroom door was flung open, the jamb burst into splinters as the locked latch tore through it. Maxwell caught the edge of the door as he was drawn through with both hands.

"I command you to leave this house! I name thee, Panos!" Maxwell shouted. To his surprise and dismay, he saw the shape of the fallen monk in the darkness, letting go of one of his ankles, and attempting to reach down with the free hand towards his chest. The shade's hand gripped the chain holding his silver amulet around his neck, and pulled hard.

"What would you do to me that is worse than how I have suffered?" he asked, blood oozing down across his lips from where half his nose once was. The burns on his face were still black and red.

Miranda was in the doorway then, arms raised, fierce. "I have no fear for you, specter. You are named, Panos, and you will depart."

Panos dropped Maxwell's leg and regarded Miranda. "No, little girl, I'll carve you too. Make pretty ribbons from your lips, and cut the temptation off you." He drew a short hooked blade from his robes.

"I summon Zorusi," Miranda pressed, lines of light crossed her chest, hips and face, filling the room with uncompromising light and reducing Panos to shadow.

Maxwell was on his feet and between Miranda and the shadow the instant before it lunged, and he felt the sting of steel against his chest, the feeling of rough cloth against his skin, and Panos' labored stinking breath against his face.

Miranda continued. "Zorusi the Purifier who comes in the name of the Old Ones, I feel your light and banish you from this house, Panos."

Panos screamed as he faded. The panels along the walls rattled, and the railing along the stairs fell down, then there was silence. Maxwell fell to the ground, unbalanced as his foe disappeared, and Miranda came down on her knees right beside him.

Bernie was there along with Scott a moment later, one of them turned the hall lights on. Maxwell checked his chest only to find a shallow cut and a notch in his amulet chain. "That felt like it hit a rib," he said, checking it. "I won't even need stitches."

"Are you all right, Miranda?" Bernie asked.

"I'm okay, just wiped. That was the most powerful invocation I know," she said. "Thankfully, that one doesn't stick around. He doesn't have to be dismissed."

Maxwell could tell that whatever Miranda did worked. There was a distinct sensation that the main cabin was clear of influence, just a building with no memories or impressions within it. It was only something he noticed once the warm, peaceful impression the building left on him before was gone. "Seems like your invocation got rid of everything," Maxwell said.

"You feel that too?" Scott said. "Or feel nothing, rather. It's almost cold."

April emerged from the room she and Scott shared with a blanket in hand, and wrapped Miranda in it. "You're going to feel a little chilly next, after bringing something that big in, then letting it go," she told her.

"Thank you, April," Miranda said.

"You're welcome." April's big blue eyes looked around then, noticing, maybe for the first time that everyone was watching her. Everyone was at least curious. "My Dad still has all my Mother's books and lesson notes from before he was kicked out. I read them over and over, kind of makes me feel like she's still around, like he never killed her."

Scott put his arm around her waist and gave her a supportive squeeze.

"Oh, no, it's all right now," April said reassuringly. "Well, it isn't, never will be, but I'm okay. I've never been happier to be anywhere, I think. I'm so glad I snuck in for the Gathering. Tell me what I can do to help, I want to help."

"All right," Bernie said. "There's holy water in the kitchen. We have to ward all four walls of the house from the inside, all the windows and doors, then we should get to bed. We'll be good for the night, at least."

"I'll just get something on first," Maxwell said, standing then helping Miranda up.

What followed was surreal for him. They moved in pairs, flinging droplets of holy water at every outer opening in the house, blessing the space in the name of their ancestors and attending guardians. He remembered his father's advice, that the blessing should carry belief and conviction, and for the first time, he was able to invest both into what he was doing. Time seemed to slip by as they worked, and when they were finished, faint pre-dawn light filled the world around them.

"Whose Panos?" Miranda asked once they were behind closed doors, back in their room. "You knew him by name, and I've heard the name before."

Maxwell dreaded the question, and was tired, but he felt the least he owed her before going to bed was an explanation. He could work on the rest when they had some sleep. "He was from an order that the Catholic Church denounces called the Purifiers."

"I know the Purifiers, they're more active in Europe," Miranda said, slipping into bed.

"He was kicked out because, and this is just what I heard, he began practicing magic. He stole the Libro de Puertas, holding a girl hostage in the states to get it. I met him before that, when we were on the road in Maine. He came after me when he heard I was buying a haunted kettle. Was supposed to belong to one of the witches burned there a couple centuries ago. That's not the first time I've seen his carving knife coming. He was still with the Purifiers then." Maxwell slipped into bed beside Miranda, and she curled up against him, resting her head on his shoulder.

"Is that where you lost your earlobe?" she asked.

"That was the second time I met him, after he had the book," Maxwell said.

"How did you get it from him?"

"I'll get to that," he replied with a tired chuckle. "It didn't end well for him, in Maine. He attacked me in front of this roadhouse, and I tossed him into traffic. It was better than fighting a man who looked like he knew how to use his knife. This station wagon bumped him, he wasn't hit too hard. I got away smiling then, bugger had to deal with three carloads of people who stopped to see if he was all right, and explain why his case was full of hooks, probes and knives. I made sure he was fine from a distance, and got out of there. Little more than a year later, I caught up with him when he had the book and shard on him. He had a gun, I had a tin of lighter fluid and my zippo."

"And you killed him?" Miranda asked, surprised.

"No, he was barely burned, enough to distract him, singe him a little, but he stopped, dropped and rolled well enough. Just smoking by the time I left. His nose was what probably hurt most, someone cut half of it off, and that's where I aimed my fluid. Bugger nearly took my head off with that gun of his, but a few seconds of fire was distraction enough for me to get the book. I'm still going to call every hospital in Montreal asking after him though, he died somehow, need to make sure it wasn't me."

"I've never seen a spirit like that, I've heard of strong spirits, but that was just beyond."

"I've never seen anyone channel like you did," Maxwell said. "It was like you became light for a moment, and this house was wiped clean. That was a Sumerian House God you brought in, and he came at your calling. That's power."

"First time," Miranda said. "I didn't see a point in holding back. Not with what was going on."

"You're an amazing woman, Miranda," Maxwell said, kissing her briefly.

"I love you, Max," she told him.

"Love you too," he replied. It took him a long time to find

sleep. He couldn't stop thinking about Panos, and how he was extinguished, not badly burned and breathing fine when he left him. Maxwell hoped that he hadn't earned the revenge Panos had come to exact.

XI

Maxwell woke early the next morning feeling like he had barely slept at all, which wasn't far from the truth. He was on the phone, calling hospitals in Montreal on the only phone in the main cabin. It was in the main room, but there was no one around yet. The sound of the radial dial's gear echoed in the empty main room as he turned ten numbers onto its face.

"Hello, I'm Panos Mitro's nephew, and I only just found out that he may have died in your hospital last night, maybe the night before. Can you help me? I just got in country and want to make sure someone is making arrangements," Maxwell told the receptionist at the hospital in a concerned tone. "He did not have an easy life, and he was just in an accident where his nose would be cut up badly."

"I haven't seen anyone meeting that description, but I can check for you, monsieur…"

"I'm Andrew Mitro."

"Give me your number and I'll call you if I find anything, Monsieur."

"Thank you so much," Maxwell said. "Please hurry if you don't mind, our tradition demands that we are buried within two days of dying."

"I'll see what I can do," the secretary replied, hanging up the instant she finished talking.

Muttering curses under his breath about Panos causing him as much work in death as he did in life, Maxwell made the first pot of coffee. With a cup in hand, he returned to the telephone, dialed Information again, asked to be connected to the Montreal Information line, then asked after the number for the next hospital.

The receptionist didn't respond the way he expected when he reprised his worried nephew routine. "s'il vous plaît tenir," was all she said before putting him on hold.

He sipped his coffee while listening to a repeating tone that was made to reassure callers that they were still on the line. By the time someone picked up again, his coffee was gone and his stomach was growling. "Bonjour, this is the nephew?" the voice of an older man asked.

"Yes, is my uncle there?"

"I'm afraid so, you are in Montreal?"

"I'm in Alberta, and I can't miss work, so I'll have to take the red-eye," Maxwell said. It was one of his father's tricks. If you only needed information, but wanted to keep your distance, you could sometimes get more information over the phone by pretending the inconvenience of going to the source in person was much higher than it actually was. "Why? Is there a problem?"

"No, no," he reassured. "I'm Doctor Hickey, I treated your Uncle when he came in. Did he have a history of mental illness?"

"Yes, going back as long as I can remember."

"I thought so. You must understand, I only recognized your uncle by the description you gave us, he never told me his name. He drew on the walls with his own, well, matter. Strange symbols. He had a pistol on him too, but that's been handled – the police came to pick it up while he was still alive. Your uncle assaulted one of them while he was being interviewed, but didn't speak English or French, it was something else. We thought it might be Greek, but one of my colleagues who spoke the language said it wasn't that either. The police are looking for a young man for questioning, but you'd have to call them for the details."

"Did the young man they're looking for do something to him?" Maxwell asked.

"He may have tried to light him on fire, but those injuries were superficial, so yes, but he didn't kill your uncle, if that's what you are thinking. Someone else did that weeks before he was brought in. Your uncle had injuries to his face, mostly his nose. I'm sorry you have to hear this, but if you're coming anyway, I should warn you. Half of his nose had been cut away. That wound got infected, and it worsened for at least two to three weeks. The infection spread, and by the time he got here, there wasn't much we could do. He died early yesterday evening, the antibiotics didn't have long enough to work, and he was very weak. I'm sorry, it's sad seeing family pass, I know, but in times like these-"

Maxwell hung the phone up and breathed a sigh of relief. "Looks like the right one killed you, asshole." He muttered as he headed for the kitchen in search of leftovers and more coffee. "You tortured a girl for this bloody book, and her father got to you before you could get away. Wish he finished the job though, because we have to deal with your soul."

That night Darren returned with his girlfriend. Unlike Zachary, he had no ire for Maxwell when he learned that their last gig had been cancelled, and hooked a rented tape recorder up to the soundboard, laying a few extra microphones around to catch the sound of the drums. He joined them, and Maxwell was reminded why Darren made such a good rhythm guitarist. He spent half of his time hopping around the stage and stoking the audience, drawing them into the show by leading them in clapping, or shouting repetitive parts of the lyrics.

The energy that had been drained during months of touring had returned, and it was good to see Darren enjoying himself. Having Miranda on guitar also freed him up to play their old Hammond organ, which led to Bernie singing the only things he had the bravery to deliver to an audience, Iron Butterfly and Doors covers.

The new lineup had their picture taken by someone from the Star, Miranda in Max's leather pants and a vest with guitar in hand, Maxwell bending low, concentrating on a guitar solo behind her. Bernie stood beside them, looking out from the stage, and Scott was behind and above them all, drumsticks raised high, about to smash the cymbals. Darren almost got cut off on the left, sitting on a milking stool nailed to a crate, head thrown back as his fingers pounded the keys of the Hammond. The organ was cut out of the picture, so to anyone who couldn't guess what he was doing, he just looked like a madman on a milking stool.

The next day they were on the front page below the fold with the headline:

GATHERING FESTIVAL GETS MUSICAL

Three days of playing music, spending afternoons at the beach, and getting to know the people who had come from five different countries to attend the Gathering passed. Maxwell and Miranda were inseparable. Scott and April were similarly attached.

As the evening reserved for initiations drew nearer, the number of people gathered swelled until the field nearest the main house was covered with tents, and the gravel lot beside it was filled with campers and motorhomes.

There was only going to be one show on initiation day, and it ended before noon. The heat and humidity fell on the Webb farm, and the barn was like a furnace before the morning was through.

Miranda's shirt was off, revealing a bikini top underneath before the set was half over. Scott and Maxwell made a joke out of it after they finished playing Radar Love by kicking their jeans off and finishing the morning in their boxers.

The large crowd, larger than the barn could hold, all broke up as they finished their last song for the day: Feel Like Making Love.

Maxwell and Scott put their pants back on, then followed Bernie and Darren through the small door at the back of the barn. Miranda was right behind them.

Maxwell patted the hood of his black and white 1958 Edsel on his way by. "We're going to have to take the boat out tomorrow, make sure everything's running."

"That's yours?" Miranda said.

"Every last foot of it," Maxwell said. "I can't keep riding my Harley on gravel," he said, taking Miranda's hand. "Can't keep testing my luck like that."

"About time," Bernie said. "I'll help you tune it up."

They only made it half way to the beach before a Mercedes tore into the circular parking area in front of the public bathroom building, nearly running several people in swim suits, carrying coolers and towels down. A tall, middle-aged dark haired man in a suit got out of the passenger side and zeroed right in on Scott. "Who's that?" Miranda asked.

It took a moment for Bernie to see it, he hadn't run into the man since he was a child, but he realized who it was as Bernie said his name. "Steven Sands, he's April's dad. Trouble."

"And the only family to be kicked out of the circle," Maxwell said. "We were kids when it happened, but that didn't stop my father from going on about it."

"Scott," he said, slamming the car door and pointing at Bernie. "Where's my daughter?"

Scott stepped forward and said; "you're looking for me. I haven't seen her since last night. She left late."

"We haven't seen her, not last night, not today," Steven said. "Did she say where she was going? Who she was getting a ride with?"

"I was asleep," Scott said. "When she left I was already

asleep."

"You're free to look around, I'll go with you, we'll get everyone looking," Bernie said.

"I'll hit the gravel lot, check the motorhomes," Scott said.

"You've done enough, thank you," Steven said, opening the car door.

"Wait," Bernie barked, striding towards Steven. "If you're going to cause trouble, you're going to leave. You're not welcome here. I'll go look with you and you're leaving your car here."

"I should have recognized you right away, you're as tall as your father, just as indignant too. That's not going to help you in the world, son," Steven said. He looked at Maxwell then. "April's not the real reason why I'm here anyway. You have something that belongs to me, boy."

Maxwell crossed to the car, Miranda stuck to his side, still holding his hand, but he let it go. He stopped to stand beside the front bumper of Steven's car. He could see Angelo inside, acting as chauffer. "What would a puffed up suit want from me?"

"The Libro de Puertas, the Book of Doors, I paid Angelo twenty thousand dollars to have an errand boy fetch that for me. I hear nothing for months, then that it's in town, and that he can't give it to me."

Maxwell felt the weight of his mistake then, and understood why the Elders did not want the book to find the man who paid for it's retrieval. Steven Sands was the last person he would trust with the book and shard, he'd rather give it back to Panos. "The money is between you and Angelo, and the rest is mine, bugger off."

With a quick, practiced hand, Steven slapped Maxwell across the face hard enough to turn his head and cut his inner cheek against his teeth. "Don't you dare speak to an elder that way, young ma-"

Maxwell stepped forward with a fast, straight jab with his left fist. Steven didn't have any warning or time to respond. His hands started to go up after the shocking strike to his mouth. Steven, easily half a head taller than Maxwell and broader shouldered, staggered back. "Seems you've mistaken me for one of your kids, geezer," Max said before slapping one of Steven's upraised hands away and hitting him in the nose so hard with his right hand that he felt the crush of cartilage under his knuckles.

Steven staggered backwards, and Maxwell pushed him to the ground with only the slightest effort. A quick fist struck upward, catching Maxwell in the cheek too lightly for him to care. He waved the hand away and swung as though he was trying to pound through Steven's head to hit the ground.

He got three shots in and stood up, straightening his bloody rings. "Dad told me all about you, cunt. Beats his kids, beats his wife, even smacked Bernie there once while visiting, but just once."

Angelo started to open the door and Maxwell shot him a furious glance, pointing a finger. "Back in the car! We'll roll this piece of shit back into the passenger seat, and then you can roll the fuck out of here."

Maxwell knelt down to pick Steven up by the front of his jacket and smirked at the sound of the large man whimpering. He had him on his feet, leaning against the back door, Bernie, stoic-faced, opened the passenger door and helped him in. Blood ran from his nose freely, his mouth was a bashed, broken mess. "New generation coming up," Maxwell said to Steven and Angelo. "We'll look for your daughter, but she'll decide whether or not she goes back to you."

"I'll give you fifty thousand," Steven struggled through his injuries, spitting blood at the dash as he spoke. "For book."

"You're going to want to keep your head up," Maxwell said before slamming the door.

"Holy shit," Scott said as the car began reversing.

"What was that?" Miranda asked as she picked up his right hand.

"Nothing good about that man, maybe his kids turned out different, but he's rich because he makes sacrifices, deals with dark things. I went too far though, way too far."

"I wanted to try to stop you, man, but he was a blood fountain on the ground before I had time to think," Scott said.

"I think you have a piece of his tooth here," Miranda said, picking a small white square from a cut on his finger, beside his ring.

"Da' told me never to punch for the mouth," Maxwell said. "Going to have to wash this up, get chunks of his cheeks out of my rings, too."

"About time he got his," Bernie said. "I don't like seeing anyone stomped, but he had that coming."

"What did he do?" Miranda asked.

"When I was young, maybe nine, I was visiting their house," Bernie said. "Playing with April and Trent, her older brother. April broke a vase when she was trying to give it to her father with a bunch of wild flowers she picked from the yard. There was broken glass all down the stairs, and she cut herself. She started balling, I think she was more scared that she was bleeding than badly hurt, so he came down, gave April shit, and when her brother tried to help, Steve gave him shit for not watching his sister. Then he slapped him. He bumped into me and I fell down the stairs. When my father and Maxwell's dad came to get me, I had a cut on my forehead, and they could sense something was wrong in the house, even past an abusive dad."

"As if that wasn't enough. The Circle demanded to get a look at the house, and I don't know what they found, but he was cast out a few days later. I still went too far," Maxwell said, looking down at the small patch of blood on the gravel.

"I've never seen anyone move that fast," Miranda said. She seemed stunned, still holding his bloody hand.

"I'm sorry you saw that. I've got an impatient side that only comes out when I'm about my father's business and I know I'm standing in front of a killer."

"We don't know that, Max," Bernie said, a warning in his tone. "April can say it, she's his daughter, but no one has proof."

"I'm starting to believe it," Maxwell said. "But you're right. Head down to the beach, I'm going to clean up in the main cabin."

"I'll clean you up, but no more of that," Miranda said. "I get that sometimes it's easier to just lose it, but you don't have to. You're not alone here, no one can corner you."

"You're right," Maxwell said. "I get that way, and I worry I could be like him."

"Okay, that's not what I'm worried about," Miranda said. "I just don't want you to do something you can't live with someday, or get thrown in jail."

"One drunk tank was enough," Maxwell said.

"Story there?"

"Got drunk, wandered off, got caught pissing against a wall, ended up in custody until the morning," he replied.

"Detroit," Scott said, laughing.

"Not my proudest moment," Maxwell said.

"Good weekend, though," Bernie said. "Detroit was fun, we got to see the Stooges, met Iggy Pop."

"You met Iggy Pop?" Miranda asked.

"Yeah, nice enough fellow, too," Maxwell said. "Give you the shirt off his back if he's happening to be wearing one."

"I'm going to go look for April," Scott said as they got to the veranda of the main cabin.

"I'll get out there too," Bernie said.

"What just happened?" Gladys said as she came through the door with Samuel. "We were just on our way out and someone said you were in a fight with a man in a suit?"

"Steven Sands paid us a visit. Pulled up, started asking about the book and his daughter. We'll have to keep an eye out for her, make sure she turns up sometime today."

"What about this fight?" Samuel asked, his voice not as strong. The air was becoming more difficult for him.

"He gave me a slap, so I put him down, put him in his car and they got out of here." Maxwell pointed at his slightly reddened cheek and Miranda's eyes went wide.

"He got you," she said, "Looks like one of his rings cut you."

"Still bleeding?" Maxwell asked.

"No, it's small," Miranda said.

"You know that's going to come back on us somehow," Gladys said. "You should have come to us."

"I was afraid he would turn the whole place upside down, don't blame him, mind you, but he didn't want one of us to take him around. He wanted to go on his own. He was more interested in the book anyhow. Then things turned when he tried to treat me like one of his kids."

"I understand, Maxwell, there's history," Samuel said before taking a labored breath. "Just let us take care of Sands, all right?"

"Absolutely," Maxwell said.

Gladys shook her head. "We're going to Sam's trailer to play some cards in the air conditioning."

"Maybe have a little wine," Samuel said with a mischievous smile.

"Behave, you two," Miranda said.

"Oh, I can handle him," Gladys said as they passed them on the stairs.

After Maxwell's right hand was cleaned up and his rings were washed, he joined Scott and Bernie as they searched for April. Word went out that there could be someone lost on the farm, and before the sun set, every tent, camper, motorhome, both beaches, the nearby woods and all the cabins were searched. There was no sign of her.

XII

Morley Parker retired from the Ontario Provincial Police three years before he set foot on the Webb Farm on that humid day. When word reached Archer Hardware that there was a missing girl, and the police decided not to look for her because she had habit of going off on her own, he rallied his oldest friends, Patrick and Richard Young, to join him in helping with the search. They followed him in their pickup truck without hesitation.

Seeing the Webb Main House on the top of the hill almost made him smile. He was always invited to the smaller holiday parties there, and the few he attended were lighthearted, enjoyable affairs.

His wife, Carrie, didn't like the place much though. She believed there were rituals performed on the farm, that the family was involved with paganism. Morley knew it was true, but he didn't share her dark impression. To him the Webbs and their friends were naturalists who brought some old, different religions to Ontario from Europe, and they were always helpful when called on in the community. They kept their beliefs out of any public activity too, so if you didn't know better, you'd assume they were just down to earth, good people. Their absence in church was the most noticeable difference.

The spread of tents in the broad field nearest to the road was bigger than anything Morley had ever seen. He was a little happy his wife hadn't lived to see such a large gathering of pagans, she would have crossed herself, got back in her car and driven as though the devil were on her heels. "I'm going to the main house, Rick," he told his long time friend. "You mind finding Allen or his son, Bernie for me? They're probably directing the search."

"No problem, we'll stay close just in case you find Allan first."

Morley walked up the main path to the house, noting that most of the visitors seemed busy, they wore serious expressions that told him that everyone had taken up the cause. April may be a rich girl, but she seems well liked, was his first thought. The sun was getting low, there were two hours of daylight left at the most.

He returned his attention to the path, favoring an ache in his knee he hadn't felt since he was still an Officer. He remembered the last time it acted up; he reported to an address where a family had discovered a box of old dynamite in a basement crawlspace. Walking that greasy wooden crate up the stairs and out of their home was the most nerve-wracking minute of his entire career.

"Pardon, Officer," said a tall priest coming down the path. He had a half dozen young children following him silently.

"Sorry, I didn't see you there," Morley replied, startled. "How are you, Pastor?" He asked, fishing for a name.

"We're doing well, kind of you to ask," the Priest replied, smiling broadly.

"What brings you and this little flock to the Webbs?"

"Just taking my orphans for a stroll, they've been cooped up for a while, I'm afraid. I'm glad I did. It gave me the opportunity to offer the little support we can for April."

"God giving you any advice on where I might find the girl?" Morley asked.

"Oh, you won't need his help to find her. A good thing, since I haven't heard from him in a while. He is mysterious in his way."

"Sure. I haven't seen you around, are you new to the Parish?"

"I was here some time ago, and am just returning. It is good to be back though. So much has changed," the Priest said, looking across the field at the bottom of the hill. The sunlight came out from behind a cloud then, and he seemed to grow pale. "We should be getting back, I don't want to tire the little ones."

"Have a good day, Pastor," Morley said. The clothes and especially the little black shoes the children wore reminded him of old silver plate photos of his grandparents. Everything about the pastor and his orphans seemed a little off.

He was only feet away from the veranda when the screen door banged open and a vision appeared that moved him to remove his Blue Jays baseball hat. A raven-haired woman who flashed him a smile descended and gave him a warm hug. "You don't remember, do you?"

"I'm afraid not, Miss," he replied.

"Susanne," she said. "It is good to see you, Morley."

"I'm sorry, it's been, what? Thirty years?" he said, remembering her as a senior in high school. "Where did you get off to?"

"I returned to Italy after I graduated," she said, leading him up the steps into the kitchen of the main house. "I moved to Spain for my husband then. He passed away a few years later, so I took turns living with different sisters."

"What brings you back?"

"My niece, Miranda," she replied. "I'll be moving in with her for a while to see if I enjoy Canada enough to stay. I think I will, but it's too soon to say. Who were you talking to on the path? I only heard your voice."

"New Pastor coming back to town," Morley replied. "He seemed a little strange, maybe from the old country too?"

"Only one Pastor has been here for cards this week," she looked to a stout woman.

"Pastor Villaro," the stout woman answered.

"Oh, it wasn't him. He baptized all three of my kids, I'd know him," Morley said. "This fellow looked like he'd just spent a month on a boat, pale, pretty thin."

"He wasn't invited," said Allen as he came in through the side door. "Nothing to worry about though." He had scratches on his face, and a well-stitched rip on his lip.

"What happened there?" Morley said.

"Nothing to worry about," Allen said. "Here to help look for April?"

"Sure am, brought a couple friends with me, and Terry's offered to bring everyone from the hardware store here to help if we need more people. Is Mister Sands here?"

"No," Allen replied. "He's not as worried as we are about this. We're just about to head off to the Erikson farm. We bought their place four years ago when Old Yves passed away. You're just in time."

A young, well-built man with blonde hair came to the door, he looked anxious. "Ready to go?"

"Looks like we have enough volunteers, Scottie," Allen said with a nod. "Thank your guys for me. I'll ride in your pickup, I'm still not driving."

"Wait," Morley said. "The Erikson farm has been abandoned for what, twenty, thirty years? It's got to be nine miles from here, why would she be there?"

"I don't know, but I've got one of those hunches," Allen said.

Morley knew not to question it. Allen and his father had helped him and other police officers more than once when people went missing, and the grave expression on his face told him that they would definitely find something.

They were joined on the road by a massive 1958 Edsel four door, its pointed rear fins only topped by the front – an oval front grill feature with paired headlamps. They arrived at the Erikson farm and Morley wasted no time in directing Patrick and Rick to check the few structures still standing. The barn had fallen down long before, leaving only a few small storage sheds and outhouses in various states of disrepair. That was, other than the main farmhouse.

Allen looked across the overgrown fields. The forest had been encroaching on the abandoned farm for at least two decades, and tall grass had grown in everywhere else. The farmhouse was a husk. Old and dilapidated when the Webbs bought the land, they had since removed glass and any fixtures from the inside. What was left overlooked the overgrown fields with hollow, dark windows.

"We should start there?" Morley said, pointing at the house and the two ramshackle sheds beside it.

"We'll find that a car has come through behind the house," Allen said, moving with long strides.

Morley followed him, a chill running down his spine as he glanced back towards a dark second floor window. The boards over the first floor windows and door looked intact, and he didn't see evidence that anyone had gone towards the house at a glance. There was no trail pushed through the grass, or other signs. He still could have sworn that something moved in that upper floor window. "We should check the house," he said.

"No," Allen told him firmly. "Stick with the group."

He stared at the pair of open windows in the dilapidated house for a moment then nodded. His eyes never stopped scanning the way ahead, and as they came around the rear, he saw what Allen predicted. The grass overgrowing an old tractor trail had recently been pressed down. "Pat, Rick, over here."

They rushed up to flank them on the left, looking through the grass and nearby tree line. Experience had taught Morley that it was easy to miss things in nearly hip-high grass. They followed the path of the car, and Morley shook his head. "Come and gone. It looks like whoever went in took the same path out, going a little off trail here," he pointed to a length of the trail where the grass had been pressed down by tires in a half loop running off and on again. "By that old coal chute."

"She's up ahead," Allen said, pointing to the end of the path, where the gutted husks of farm equipment occupied a yard with tall grass. His pace grew faster until he was running.

"Slow and careful," Morley said as he struggled to keep up with the tall man and his younger companions. The words would fall on deaf ears, he knew, but he had to try. He also had a feeling that he was leaving something important behind at the rear of the old house.

"You guys see something up there?" asked Patrick, his speech slurred thanks to his missing top teeth.

"Nothing yet," Morley replied, shouting over his shoulder. "Can you watch the house?"

"On it, Morley," Rick said.

"I can hear her," Scott, Allen's nephew said, redoubling his pace into a reckless run.

The blonde youth disappeared behind an old rust covered tractor and immediately shouted something Morley couldn't make out, then he screamed; "help!"

The world blurred past as Morley and the entire group, suddenly led by the longhaired, stocky Maxwell, broke into the circle of broken down farm machinery. Scott was cradling a girl in a filthy summer dress in his arms on the ground. Her fair hair was caked with crimson, the fingers on her left hand had been bashed into awkward angles, and Morley could not see her face.

His limited emergency medical training told him that he had to check her vitals, and keep her still, and that Scott had broken the second rule by pulling her partially into his lap.

He knelt down and could immediately see that she was still breathing. One of her eyes was closed, the lid and cheek caked in blood. Her other was open, a beautiful blue eye staring out of a ravaged face. Her lips had been cut away, and someone had sawed at her nose with a rough blade or unsteady hand from the bottom. Her smile had been replaced by a grimace of bloody teeth and gums.

Weak, raspy but sweet sounds came from her that were more animal than human. He interpreted them as expressions of relief, and sometimes she seemed to be trying to reassure Scottie, who kept telling her; "I've got you, you're going to be okay." She raised a still perfect hand and touched Scott's face as though she was making sure he was really there.

He moved in, catching a fearful glance from her. "You remember me? I'm Mister Dell. You used to play with my girls, Celeste and Mary."

She nodded at him and struggled to swallow.

"Don't say anything, just let us take care of you," he said. "I'm going to pick you up and carry you to the car now. He's going to stay right beside you, aren't you, Son?"

"I'll never leave you," Scottie said. "I'm right here."

He gently picked her up, a task that required so little effort, and couldn't help but think of his children as he gently cradled her against his chest. It was his girl Celeste, who was born with blonde, almost white hair that became a thick mane of fair curls that kept coming to mind. Years on the police force allowed him to push those thoughts aside. He concentrated on every stride moving forward, watching the path ahead, supporting her head properly.

She stared up at him with the blue eye that wasn't forced closed with blood and swelling. Everyone followed close behind, and Scottie kept up. As they drew close to the Edsel, April began to weep quietly. "Am I hurting you?" Morley asked.

She shook her head a little, her blue eye closed. He decided that whatever she was crying about wasn't something he could act on there. He had to get her into a car and on the way to the hospital, where he was sure there would be many more tears.

Maxwell opened the back door, Scottie hurried inside and Morley gently put her onto the back seat, laying her head in his lap. "Keep her steady, don't let her head roll from side to side, but don't touch her injuries."

Scottie nodded, clearing a lock of blood caked hair out of her face. "Yeah, I've got her."

A young brunette woman carefully joined the pair in the back seat, sliding under April's legs. "We'll take care of her, thank you."

He remembered delivering the news of Miranda's mother's fatal car accident then, and nodded at her, momentarily at a loss for words. Maxwell carefully closed the door and got into the middle passenger seat. He was squeezed in by Bernie in the driver's seat and his father Allen on the passenger side.

"Be careful," Morely said.

"Thank you for your help," Allen said before closing the passenger door.

"Don't worry about calling the police," Morley said. "I'll call from your place, it's the nearest phone." He watched the Edsel carefully turn around then head off down the road at a fair pace.

"That's the girl we're here to find," Rick said as he caught up with him. "Who did that? All I see is blood from here, what did they do?"

"That's her, that's little April," Morley said. "Someone cut on her, bad. We have a crazy in town, probably brought in with that Gathering."

"Do you think she'll make it?"

"From the clotting, and how long she's probably been here like that, I give her fifty-fifty. Whoever did that to her knows how to cut and not kill."

The three of them stood there, surrounded by the encroaching woodland and the sounds of crickets, buzzing creatures of summer for long moments before anyone spoke.

"Ever see anything like that?" Patrick asked quietly. He looked utterly dumbfounded, his stubble covered face a stunned mask.

"No," Morley said. "Go back up the road and call the department. I have to check something out here."

"What?"

"Don't worry about it," Morley said, heading back to his truck. "I'll just hold down the fort here, make sure no lookie-loos come around messing up the crime scene. You go call."

"All right," Rick said.

Moments later his childhood friends were gone, and he was returning to the rear of the farmhouse with a crowbar in one hand and a handgun in the other. It was difficult to keep his daughters out of his mind while he checked his revolver, then approached the coal chute.

His mind played tricks on him. Instead of little April, he kept seeing his daughter Celeste on the ground. He moved the grass surrounding the trap door covering the coal chute with his crowbar and found what he suspected he would, a broken padlock.

He holstered his gun then pulled his flashlight from his pocket before kicking the door up and open. There were scratches on the inside of the chute, it looked as though someone had recently slid down the four-foot shaft. Morley turned his light off and allowed himself a moment's hesitation. He had the distinct feeling that the man who carved into April was still there.

Those windows above had eyes, and they enjoyed watching other people clean up. He would not let the perpetrator get away. The grade of the blackened chute wasn't severe, so he carefully lowered himself down.

A moment's pause allowed his eyes to adjust to the light. Somewhere above there was a breach in a wall that was letting a little light through some of the floorboards. He had just enough to make out the furnace room.

The pot-bellied furnace for the house, made to burn coal or wood, dominated the room. With great care, Morley put his crowbar down at his feet and drew his pistol.

With the flashlight in one hand, and his pistol pointing forward, he moved on. There was nothing in the furnace room to see, he kept his light off until he came to the doorway. The next room was pitch black, there was no light getting in.

"Help me," someone said, struggling to say the words as though there was a heavy weight on their chest.

Morley turned his flashlight on and saw a young man, perhaps twenty years of age with long dark hair. His breathing was labored, his chin rested on his chest as he stood. "He's got me," the boy said.

A slow sweep of his light revealed that he was standing beside a bare boards bench with an old ballpein hammer, pliers and some mismatched cutlery.

"Don't move, Son," Morley said, training his gun on the young man. He did his best to look around the basement to make sure there were no other threats while he kept his eye on his subject. "What's your name?"

"Darren," he wheezed.

"Are you alone here? Is there anyone else in the house?"

The young man struggled to say something but his voice was choked off as though someone was pulling on his vocal chords, turning his words into choking and gurgling. The noise continued as he started grinding his teeth so hard that it made Morley cringe. He could see the young man was struggling, in pain, but the grinding continued.

"I can see that you're having some kind of trouble, Son. If it's drugs, if you took something, we can take care of you. Just step away from there. Come towards me slowly." The sounds of Darren's hoarse breathing and the loud grinding of teeth filled the room as the young man rocked slightly, his chin still down on his chest.

The smell of lighter fluid and burned hair came on a breeze from the darkness, and Morley did a quick scan of the rest of the room with his light. There was nothing but piled furniture to his right, all crammed against the wall. Up the middle was a path of blood leading to a closed door opposite. A table had been set beside the door, with some old jars on it.

The grinding and heavy breathing stopped suddenly, and Morley twitched his light back to focus on Darren, who was staring back at him, terrified. "Help me! He made me help him with my hands, but I couldn't stop him. Neither of us could stop him!"

"Calm down, Son," Morley said. "Is he still in the house?"

The flashlight went out, and fell out of his hand as though all the strength in his left arm was gone. His ribs felt as though someone was kneeling on them from the inside, and his heart began to race.

As though summoned from the memory of walking in on his first corpse, the stench of rot filled his nostrils. His feet felt heavy, and his arms slowly lowered down to his sides as though he was incapable of holding them up any longer. The pressure in his head continued to build, and then he felt someone else behind his own eyes.

It was worse than someone breathing down his neck, it was the feeling of being at the mercy of a thing that could remember April's screams. The struggle of trying to keep her still after carving her lips away so he could tear out those beautiful blue eyes.

"Fight him!" Darren screamed. "Don't let him all the way in!"

"Run," Morley said as he felt his feet begin to scrape across the floor, under someone else's control.

"He's too powerful, he can take us both, he still has my friend," Darren wept. "He doesn't kill, I wish he'd kill, but he doesn't kill."

With a clumsy hand, Morley shoved his pistol back into its holster at his waist. His slowly steadying gait brought him to the bench. Even his eyes were out of his control. His memory was invaded by the sensation of cutting April with a practiced hand. They'd find that she was missing an ear, and that every knuckle on one hand was carefully bashed, while the other was left untouched. It was in case she turned, and became a servant.

There had been more women than the thing in his body could remember, and he had his favorites. A tear rolled down Morley's cheek as the beast that had taken him recollected several of his favorites. "Monster," he managed to grind out of his throat.

"I am what Maxwell and people like him made me," Darren said, his voice one part the young man's, and one part a higher pitched, near frantic sound. The voices were in disharmony with each other, grating on the ear. "I was a man on a mission, to purify, to teach the ignorant few who peer into the veil and quest for its unnatural power, then I found a book while teaching an old man." Morley could see the memory, Vernor Gold, a collector of rare books who had a selection of volumes that the Purifiers did not approve of. Death was his sentence, and it was carried out by Panos himself. An expertly held hook knife opened his belly, and old Vernor was forced to watch as his small intestine was drawn out, then he was left to bleed to death. "You see?" Darren continued. "A man about his business, then the Book of Doors told me that the real power is not in this life, that heaven is only open to those who are recognized in the next life by those they've done good for. I have been cheated, but the book had power that I could carry past the living flesh. Tricks. Tricks for cheating and correcting that my old family of Purifiers cannot understand."

"Tossed you out," Morley managed as he watched his hands grow more graceful by the moment.

"You aren't supposed to see that," Panos said from Darren's mouth.

His right hand closed around the handle of the ballpein hammer and raised it. His left splayed itself out on the bench. "I will tell you why you're going to die, because my young thrall is right: I do not kill unless you give me a reason. I am still a Purifier," Panos said through Darren's lips. The grin there had grown so large that the scant light was glinting off his teeth. "Maxwell must die, he knows more about the book than I do. His power is manifesting. It is unnatural. It is an offense to the order of life. You make it easy now. They will find your body here. Hang the cutting on you since it will be days before April will be able to speak again, a week at least before the others are found. The other explanations for her will be too outlandish for their little minds to explain or believe."

The hammer came down in the center of his hand, breaking the skin and bone beneath. Morley made him miss his knuckles, but still felt every bit of the pain. He was receding; the pressure of Panos taking over was pushing him away from awareness despite his fight to remain in control.

"You have two daughters," Darren said with relish. "I will visit them if you don't let me take control. I'll do it in your flesh, so they can see their daddy's face grinning at them while I strip their belly flesh off layer by layer."

Morley rallied against Panos' presence and managed to get enough control back to drop the hammer. It didn't last. "You can't win." Panos said in his own face.

Darren immediately returned his chin to his chest, and began grinding his teeth. Panos was in full control. "I am going to kill you now, with your own weapon. The hammer was a test, a way to try to get you to take control one more time so I could crush your spirit. Your soul won't go far. The Dawn is near. You will shoot yourself in the head, and they will believe you slashed April until she can speak again."

With natural grace, Morley drew his sidearm, held it to his head, turned the safety off, and pulled the trigger. At the last instant Morley forced the hand to jerk, sending the barrel upwards. It was not enough. The bullet passed through his head high, but only high enough to leave him conscious and bleeding to death on the floor.

The pain was incredible, he could not move, and the ringing in his ears was as bad as or worse than anything. He didn't recall falling, but could feel the warm blood against the side of his face. Darren walked over, picked up the gun and looked at him, shaking his head. The young man wiped the tears from his face.

He could see it wasn't him. The thing that had ended him was inside Darren, he could see it in the boy's eyes. He desperately wanted to utter the only blessing he believed in at the young man, but instead of saying 'God help you,' he only managed to croak; "God."

"You'll see soon enough," Panos said with Darren's lips. "He has left us all here and there, like a child who has abandoned his ant farm in the back yard. Goodbye."

XIII

"She is ruined!" Maxwell heard Steven Sands howl. He was on his feet and out of the family waiting room before anyone else. He knew the nurses allowed Scott to visit April after she was stable, he didn't know her father had arrived. Maxwell didn't realize that everyone else in the waiting room were right behind him as he took the corner.

"Oi!" Maxwell said as he caught sight of Steven in a fresh suit, towering over Scott. They were right beside the door to April's hospital room. Trent, as equally fair as his sister but thick, a towering footballer, leaned against the wall opposite the door. He seemed calm, entirely unaffected. "Back up, quiet down!" Maxwell said, the harshness of his tone making up for his lack of volume. "She's right in there."

Steven quieted down, but was still so furious he was shaking. The bruises on his face reminded Maxwell that he was facing someone he had difficulty restraining himself with. The pair of officers down the hall reinforced his need to keep calm. "You should be inside, holding her hand, taking care of her, happy she's still with us," Maxwell said.

"Like any of you know anything about her or the future she's lost," Steven replied. "She was going to marry Revelationem Lux royalty, bridge my family back to our European ties, now no one will touch her. What am I supposed to do with what's in there?"

"Sir, I understand this is traumatic," said a nurse coming down the hallway. "But please keep your voice down."

"You see these people here?" Steven said, turning on the nurse and pointing at Scott. "Especially this one? They're her family now. I told her not to go near them, she went against me, and this is what happens." He looked to Scott. "You want her? You can have what's left."

"That's enough, Steven," Allen said, Bernie beside him. "If you want to leave, if you want to blame people, that's fine. We will take care of her, we'll answer all the questions you should be here for, and when she's well, she'll have a home."

Steven didn't say another word, but rubbed his hands together in the air as though he were washing them for a moment, then strode down the hallway. His son didn't make eye contact with anyone, but followed a few steps behind. Scott's father nearly bumped into him as he came around the corner. He was the opposite of Steven, the embodiment of compassion and concern.

"I'm sorry, Dad," Scott whispered as he accepted a brief but firm hug. "This wouldn't have happened if she wasn't hanging around."

"Don't worry about any of that. I doubt anyone could stop her from doing anything she wants to. Did I hear that right? Is Sands abandoning her?" Desmond asked Allen.

Allen nodded solemnly. "She'll never be alone. I know you don't have the room, so we'll move her into the main house if that's what she'd like."

"Thank you, Uncle Allen," Scott said.

The nurse, an older woman with three clipboards still under her arm, was watching everything. "I'll tell her doctor what's happened. Are any of you related to her?"

"No, but we have her father's number, so he can talk to him directly. If he doesn't change his mind about leaving her alone here, then we'll gladly make sure she has everything she needs." Desmond said.

"It's really up to her," the nurse said. "She's eighteen, and we can have her write her wishes down when she isn't so heavily sedated."

"Is she going to be all right?" Scott said.

"Well," the nurse looked at the group of them again before going on. "I will tell you what her doctor told mister Sands, but this didn't come from me, do you understand? I'm not supposed to, but I have a feeling he won't be coming back. Overall, April will be fine. Most of the damage was cosmetic. The damage to her left eye looks a lot worse than it is. She was able to fight off her attacker so he was only able to bruise and cut around the eye, so it'll look bad for a few days, but once the swelling goes down, she'll be able to open both her eyes again. The worry now is infection, so we have her on a course of antibiotics. Her hand will require several surgeries, the rest is a game of wait and see as healing begins. She's going to be heavily sedated for the next few days at least. That's as much as I can tell you though, the best you can do is make sure she's not alone. How do you know her?"

"My son is…" Desmond started.

"I'm her boyfriend," Scott finished. "I've known her since we were kids."

"I grew up with her," Bernie said. "We're all friends of hers, and she was taken from a party we were having."

"Well, the police cleared you all," the nurse said. "I'll tell the doctor to call her father, if he's really left her here alone, I'd appreciate it if someone could stay around."

"Funny, the police haven't spoken to us since we were first interviewed," Miranda said as she rejoined Maxwell. "They didn't say anything about who they're suspecting."

"I'm very nosy," the nurse said. "And I know Samuel, he called before she came in, told me to keep an eye on her and all of you."

"Valerie?" Allen asked.

"I was wondering when you'd recognize me," she said. "It looks like a lot of people have had a rough week. What happened to your lip there?"

"Farming accident," Allen said. "It's good to see you."

"I'm glad you're all here," she told them. "I couldn't imagine that girl having to recover alone."

"She'll never be alone," Allen said. "Don't worry."

"Thank you," Valerie said. "Tell Samuel I'm looking forward to his next batch of chokecherry wine."

"I haven't seen her in twenty years," Allen said as she walked out of earshot.

"About twenty three," his brother, Desmond said.

"Aunt Susanne said everything's almost ready," Miranda said.

"All right," Allen said. "I think Bernie can take your place, Desmond, that is if you'd rather stay here."

"Thank you, Allen."

"It's still going ahead?" Scott asked quietly. "Even with this?"

"The stars don't stop for anything, even tragedy," Desmond told his son. "They do it tonight or we wait another seven years."

"We're dedicating tonight's ceremony to her though," Miranda said. "We have everything we need, Samuel and my Aunts are already taking care of it."

"Okay, that'll help, thank you," Scott said.

"There's one thing, and it's not easy for me to say, Son," Desmond said to Scott. "We'll help her because that's what this family does, but you have to be sure of your commitment before you are the first face she sees when she wakes up. I remember what it was like to be young, and think that every girl was the greatest love of my life in the early days."

"I love her," Scott said. "We knew each other all through school, this is real."

"Are you sure, be sure, because I don't remember you talking about her for years."

"She's the Sands girl," Scott replied in a whisper. "I know what you think of that family, so of course-"

Maxwell didn't hear the rest of the conversation. Two police officers, one he went to high school with named Craig, a towering brown haired man, and an older one quietly tapped him on the shoulder. "Maxwell Foster?" asked the older one.

"That's me," Maxwell replied.

"We have a few questions, you're not in trouble, we're just trying to clear a few things up," the older officer said. "Let's have a word in the family room."

"Is he in any trouble?" Bernie asked.

"No, we just need information. He'll be back in ten minutes," Craig said.

"Be right back," Maxwell told everyone.

They all sat in the nearby family room, a space decorated with simple landscape paintings on the wall, brown sofas and chairs all around. John Travolta grinned from the cover of the Tiger Beat magazine on top of the stack in the middle of the coffee table. *John Travolta --- SHY? Unbelievable but true! His story inside!* The cover proclaimed.

Maxwell took a seat on one side of the room and the officers remained standing. "Questions?" he asked.

"We've come to understand that a band mate of yours, Zachary Ross, was just admitted an hour ago. He was found in his apartment downtown by a friend this morning. He's still in surgery, but we have been informed that his injuries are similar. It doesn't look good for him," the older Officer said. "The family has requested that you and the rest of your band stay away from him. They claim that you may have been responsible for providing him with psychedelic drugs that could be responsible."

"April was attacked and tortured, I can't see how drugs could factor in, and if I'm honest, I'm no dealer anyway," Maxwell said.

"Zachary's wounds are worse. It's early yet, but the doctor has already been able to tell us that most of the injuries were self-inflicted, except for the removal of his tongue."

Maxwell lowered his head into his hands, remembering the last conversation he had with Zachary. What made it worse was the nature of the injuries, they all seemed like the kind of work that Panos would do if he were alive. Maxwell knew for certain that the discarded monk had used ceremonies and spells from the book to empower himself in death. It was him, circling, possessing people who were not initiated or guarded. It made sense, Panos tried him first, visiting in the dead of night and trying to pull his amulet off him so he could get in. He failed, then he got into Zachary. "Does it look like Zack attacked April?" Maxwell asked.

"No, he almost bled out because he cut himself sometime early this morning," Craig said.

"Why would you ask that?" his older partner asked.

"If the two were similar, then," Max threw up his hands and shook his head. "I don't know, I'm trying to make sense of all this."

"Well, it looks like there is some kind of connection, judging from the wounds, but it's early yet. Zachary's condition is much more severe, there was extreme blood loss. Sir, could you stand for us and submit to a search?"

Maxwell did as instructed as Craig closed the door. "This'll just take a minute, Max."

"Need me to strip?" Maxwell asked.

"No, that won't be necessary. I'm Officer Rollins, that is Officer Gibbs," he said.

"I have a knife strapped to my calf under my pant leg," Maxwell said, putting his hands up. "It's peace-bonded."

Officer Rollins tugged his pant leg up and removed the scabbarded blade. He had the peace bonding off and was examining the blade in seconds. "Ever use this?"

"My father and grandfather used it for hunting a long time ago, but I just strapped it on for the first time a few days ago," Maxwell said.

"We'll keep this so it can be compared to the wounds."

"No, you won't," Maxwell said. "I'll have it back once you're done patting and prodding because I'm not under arrest and there's no sign it was used on anyone."

Officer Rollins put the knife down on the coffee table and began patting Maxwell down. It was the most thorough search he'd ever experienced, and by the end all the things in his pockets was on the table beside the knife. Even a crumpled napkin had been straightened and flattened out then draped like a poor man's doily over the table edge before he was done.

"I smell cannabis a little, are you a smoker, Maxwell?" Officer Rollins asked.

"I only smoke regular cigarettes, Officer," Maxwell replied.

"But you don't have a lighter or cigarettes on you?"

"I didn't say I bought them, I just smoke 'em."

"Right, okay, no drugs on you, get your things together and go on your way. You shouldn't come back to this wing, you should stay away from Mister Ross' family out of respect for him."

Maxwell found it extremely easy to resist the urge to ask what he'd done to deserve the banishment. Even though he didn't wield the knife that cut Zachary and April, he knew he'd brought the devil that did. The police wouldn't believe him if he told them both assaults were his fault, but if there was a hole he could have himself dropped into to stop any further damage, he would let them escort him to it. The first thing he picked up was the scabbard and knife, and under the watchful eye of Officer Rollins, he sheathed it then tied the leather strap around the hilt firmly.

"Zack going to survive?" Maxwell asked.

"It doesn't look good." Officer Rollins said. "Stay away from the family." He opened the door and led Craig from the room and down the hall.

Miranda was waiting outside, visibly worried. "All's well, love," Maxwell said to her. "They just wanted to pat and poke me a little, make sure I didn't give Zack something that made him cut himself. He's here in surgery they tell me."

"What happened? Is it bad?" Miranda asked, crossing the room and sitting down beside him on the sofa.

Maxwell pulled his pant leg up and started tying the scabbard there. "Those two don't think he'll make it, the family wants me and mine to stay away, so we'll have to hope Zack's too stubborn to die from here."

"I'm sorry," Miranda said.

"This is happening because Panos followed me back here," Maxwell whispered. "Anyone close to me is in danger. I think Zack was possessed, he's not initiated and he doesn't carry any protection like I do. When Panos attacked, he tried to get my amulet off me after separating us. That's why his blade didn't find a softer mark." He pulled the chain out from his chest so he could find the notch in the silvered steel. "He was trying to cut this off so he could get in."

"Okay, so Zachary, but why April?" Miranda asked.

"I'm not sure," Maxwell said before taking a moment to think. "It's known that he wants the Book of Doors, and she's close to Scott, everyone knows the Sands family too. Maybe she's just too close to it all? Zachary's wounds are self-inflicted, so Panos could have gotten in and done the work. I'm sure it was him, Purifiers don't do that anymore, especially not in Sudbury, there are too many people here who know how to catch them and make the bodies disappear."

"So Panos went after Zack to get to you?" Miranda asked. "Why? He's not a practitioner."

"But Panos doesn't know that. He's a member of my band without protection against possession, so he's the perfect target. Panos would assume that he knows something, as for April, the police say the timing is wrong for Panos to use Zack to get to April. I don't think they know enough to be sure about that though."

"So you think Panos went after Zack, possessed him, then took April, attacked her, and then returned him home so he could have his way with Zack then? That would leave him without a body."

"No," Maxwell said. "He had weeks to study the Book of Doors. That thing could teach him to do that and more. One of the most dangerous secrets that book breaks is the one about bringing power from the living world into the next as you die. It's one of the breaches of covenant, a ritual that helps break the division between worlds down. Panos is known for being glory hungry, I know it's something he'd do. He must have gotten into the secrets of possession too, I'll have to take another look at the book. I'm going to put initiation off."

"No, you're not," Miranda said. "You need to join us, especially now. You need our help."

"I need to get as far away from everyone as possible," Maxwell said. "I've brought misery and death home with me, and I don't want to see the worst happen."

"Oh, don't worry about me," Miranda said, picking up on his inference. "I'm not going anywhere, and I'm going to get you initiated tonight if it's the last thing I do."

Maxwell cocked his head and fixed her with a look.

"Poor choice of words," she said. "But you're coming, buster, and you're going to watch as we take you in and work you through all the trouble you've found."

"We'll see," Maxwell said.

"Max?" Scott said as he almost passed by the door. He stopped and turned into the room. "Everything okay?"

"I'm fine," Maxwell told him. "Cops just wanted to check my knife and ask if Zack had a history with drugs. They're moving their investigation on."

"Okay, good. Wait, why are they asking about Zack?"

"He cut himself a bit, they're taking care of him now. His family doesn't want us anywhere near him, so just stay near April's room when he gets out of surgery."

"It's that bad?" Scott asked.

"Looks like, but pay attention to April, she needs you more than Zack will," Maxwell said.

"Was it the same guy who got April?"

"They told me it looks like he did it himself," Maxwell said. "Wouldn't say anything else. We'll figure it out at the farm, all right?"

Scott looked stunned, his normally carefree visage etched with worry and an emotional weight he'd never carried before.

"Focus on April," Maxwell said. "Zachary has his people."

He nodded. "Yeah, I will. Listen, I have to tell you something," Scott said. "When I picked up your bike at the crossroads I felt something. Bernie had dropped me off and was on his way back, so I was alone for a minute. Before I knew it, I was kicking up dirt, and I saw the seal you left on top of the Dawn Shard. I didn't even know you left it there then. Man, I wanted to pick up the iron seal and get the Dawn Shard in my hand, I could hear my grandmother telling me to do it, but then there's the rule. Demons lie, so I reburied it. Thank the light you left the seal there, Max. If it wasn't covering the Shard, it would be in my pocket right now."

"Did you disturb the seal at all? Do you know if it moved?"

Maxwell asked.

"Maybe a little, but I didn't dig past it, just enough to see it."

"How many voices did you hear? Was it one that changed, or more than one?"

Scott thought for a moment, looking at his hands in his lap. "Definitely more than one. At first I thought I was gardening with my grandmother, she's been gone for ten years though."

"Okay," Maxwell said reassuringly. "Don't worry about it, everything's fine. I'll just make sure the seal is still there, maybe work a little harder in laying it down."

"I'm sorry, Max," Scott said. "I hope this isn't because I let something out." He stood up.

Maxwell hugged him. "In all this, I know one thing for sure: you're not the cause, you're part of the solution. Full stop, mate, you're the good sort, through and through."

XIV

The faces of his crying mother telling him; "We'll get you the help you need," and his stoic father at the edge of his bed barely penetrated the heavy haze Zachary Ross was in. His eyes needed drops, the nurse in white who put them in did so with terrifying speed and accuracy. She appeared with her applicator, the moisture dripped, then the pads went back in.

"We'll have to keep his eyes covered for the time being, you can hold his hand if you like," she told someone in the room.

A wet hand took his, squeezing a cross into the palm. It was a comfort in the thick darkness, except for the weeping. Across the murk in his mind, most likely the result of more drugs than he'd ever take on his own, expertly administered by the hospital staff, no doubt, that weeping rolled in like a sad mist over his calm.

The thick chunk of meat in his mouth would not move, his body was too heavy for any motion. "We're going to keep him sedated for a while," the white nurse-terror said an instant before all his mental pictures faded and he was embraced by the relief of sleep.

"Well, you're in a real spot, Zachary, I'm not going to lie," a warm, low voice said.

He opened his eyes to discover that the drugged haze was gone, and he was completely fine. The sheets were tucked in firmly around him in the hospital bed, and he was curtained into a space with a window overlooking Ramsay Lake. "I feel fine," Zachary said.

A glance at the gently grinning gentleman in a pristine suit standing two feet from his bed, and the memory of his own hands cutting his lips, his nose, his eyelids and more away came back. "I couldn't stop, I cut my own dick off."

"Now, let's take a moment away from the grisly details," the Gentleman said. "I'm here to help."

Zachary looked his perfect hands over, touched his intact face, then checked between his legs and sighed with relief. "Was it a dream?"

"I'd love to tell you that you took the brown acid, friend, and that it was all a bad trip, but I'm afraid I've taken you here. This is a space outside your mind, where I can help you create a space without distractions. You know, so we can have a little chat."

"Who are you?" Zachary said.

"One of my favorite questions," the gentleman replied. "I'm the man that's going to turn tragedy into opportunity for you. Oh, brother, this is your lucky day. You got caught by someone that your friend brought into your life, and there was no mercy in that crossfire. Then again, I shouldn't call him your friend at all, because friends don't let friends get possessed, now do they?"

"Panos, he took control, I, he, lured April away, and, oh my God!" Zachary said, remembering the torture of her, and being so afraid that he would start on Darren when he finished. He didn't, but went home instead, and then Panos forced him to begin cutting himself. "I'm so sorry," he said. "I tried to stop him, but he had me from the inside."

"I know," the Gentleman soothed. "It's Maxwell's fault. Panos wanted him, and couldn't find a way in, so he took you and made you do all the dirty work. I'm sorry this happened to you, Zachary, really, I am. It's time to move on, to make a decision about your future."

"What future?" Zachary burst. "Half my face is off and I don't even have a pecker!"

"Believe it or not, that's not the worst part. You're about to die without any guide to go by."

"I'm fucking Catholic! There's a heaven for people who get

murdered."

"Not only is there no guarantee of that, but everyone knows you could have fought Panos off if you really wanted to. He wore you down, took you unawares, sure, but something in you relished what you did to April. Taking power over someone else, making changes than no savvy surgeon could ever undo, and having your best friend, Darren, looking on because he didn't have a choice either. Bah! Choice, you both had it, you could have kept fighting, but I heard you. I heard you screaming inside at first, then you cried, weeping for your dear mother to save you, then your God, then you just watched. You gave up until the knife turned on you."

"I didn't like it!"

"The method, the bench in that old house, the audience, the tools, no, you didn't like any of that, but a part of you enjoyed the doing, the taking, the cutting. We're two spirits here, do you think there can be any lies?"

"April was beautiful!"

"But not memorable," the Gentleman countered, a twinkle in his eye. "Now anyone who sees her will remember, her face will follow them into nightmares, and that is remarkable, is it not?"

"Fuck you!"

"Oh, I'm here with the truth and that's what I get? Are you and Maxwell both made to be ungrateful? I suppose I'll find out when I visit you in hell and wonder why you both turned me down. There is too much doubt in your mind to prove to anyone at the gates of the Grove that part of you didn't like carving into poor April. I am the help you need, but no, both you and Maxwell slap my hand away."

"What? What help?"

"You're going to have to be more specific, because I approached Maxwell, and he could have prevented this," the Gentleman whipped the curtain behind him aside, revealing another bed where a young man was covered in bandages. His right hand, his face, and there was obviously padding around his middle under the blankets. "Now I'm approaching you, and I'm getting the same message."

Zachary stared at the bed and knew he was looking at himself. A tube in his throat was forcing him to breathe, and a monitor that displayed each beat of his heart. He was alone in the dim light. "We've matched shoe prints from your son to where we believe your son assaulted a young woman who was admitted with similar injuries." He heard an officer telling his mother and father in the hall. "We have to ask, does your son have a history of harming animals or keeping knives?"

"My son is not a monster," Zachary heard his father say. "How dare you insinuate that he could do this to anyone. This was drugs. He got high and did this to himself."

"I bet he hits Officer Tall-and-Handsome," the Gentleman said.

"I'm sorry, I interviewed and searched the young man you said provided your son with his supply, but there were no signs that he has engaged in trafficking. The doctors are telling us that there's no evidence of drugs in his system, but they aren't finished with their tests."

"Get out of here! Can't you just get out of here?" Zachary's mother wailed, slapping the shorter, older Officer.

The pair of policemen stepped away, turned and left. "Whoa, was I off," the Gentleman said, drawing the curtain. "Good thing I'm not a gambling man."

"If I never wake up, I'll never be able to tell them," Zachary said.

"I hate to tell you, but in a few minutes the first of a bunch of blood clots are going to start roaming around. The first will hit your brain, and then your heart. Those surgeons did the best they could, but they could only do so much. We're on the clock. Don't pass on what I'm offering like Maxwell did."

"You offered Max a deal? What could you do?"

"Oh, you could not imagine, so I'll give you a hand. What's the long note you like to hold on that song, Blazing High? Think you could sing it for me?"

"What?"

"Just indulge me," the Gentleman asked with an inviting smile. "Close your eyes, start singing that note, and open them before you're finished. It'll make you feel better, trust me."

It was the last thing he felt like doing, but he was hallucinating, so he had nothing to lose. "Blazing high!" he sung as he'd done so many times before. "Sooo Hiiiiiiii" he continued, closing his eyes and extending the note.

The world around him changed, he was standing, with a microphone in hand. The sounds of thousands cheering drifted up, and the band was playing that last note, Scott pounding a long drum roll, Bernie, Darren and Maxwell grinding the last note of the song. When he opened his eyes he was on stage, sweat running down his face, a full house in Boston Stadium, a place he'd only visited when it was empty. He could feel the excitement of the audience, people were trying to hold that last note with him, eyes beyond counting followed his every twitch and move.

He held it longer, mentally daring anyone in the audience to beat him, listening to the band's roar around him, supporting his voice. Then he was out of breath, and he leapt up. The final note of the song burst and ended as his feet landed on the stage.

Just as suddenly, he was in the hospital again, a machine breathing for him, a monitor tracking his heart, and bandages covering his face. Zachary was back in the dark, the Gentleman's comforting voice in his ear. "He said no to a dream that would have taken you with it, to glory, to fame, to riches and success beyond anything you've ever dreamt. That is what Maxwell cost you, even before this. Now you are about to die, and your spirit will wander without my guidance, so I'm here to offer you a deal."

Zachary could feel his mother at his bedside again, squeezing his hand, the cross between their palms. Her head was down on the back of his hand. "Tell me you didn't do it, Zack. Just wake up long enough so you can tell me you didn't do this to that girl."

"I can offer you three choices," the Gentleman said. "You die, a soul in the wind without direction. I save you so you can see what life brings before I take you into my arms when you die. The recovery will be painful, they'll put you in front of a judge, and they'll convict you of attempted murder. They won't find enough drugs in your system to say it wasn't your fault, and a psychiatrist will find you sane, so they'll put you in prison like this – without lips, without a nose, and missing even more than that. Then there's the last choice, you let yourself die, and I take your hand in mine. I live a life of true privilege, and every once in a while I find a soul with such a lust for life, with such charm and potential that I can't resist. I have to make my best offer to take you on, teach you the wheeling and dealing trade for souls, and get you working for me. You want details? Good. I teach you how these deals are made, how to charm people into giving them such a sweet time that they gladly trade their souls for it. Then you go on your own for a while, use my power to help spread the love, and take a crop of souls for me that will make Lucifer and Peter weep. You've got it in you, kid, I can feel it. I don't want to watch your soul get pulled off across that dark plain, so I'm going to dumb down the fine print for you too. You are mine until you trade for seventy souls under my supervision, using your cunning, your charm and my goods. Then, with all that you've learned, and the power you gather – and there will be power, traders like us always find the best things when we make the most of what people abandon for us – you will be free to make your own destiny. Who knows? Maybe we keep working together, and we find a way to shake down those pearly gates. You can always find someone who is willing to make a deal. It's paradise for a pittance, or you can suffer. Become a bitch to someone in the wastes of the afterlife, or in some prison cell. You give your mother's hand three squeezes if you're down for option three."

Zachary's mind was so muddied that all he could feel was his mother holding his hand, and the breath of the Gentleman against his ear. The pain was numb, but still there enough for him to know that he was damned to suffer through life if he chose it. He squeezed once, and rushed to the second.

His mother's head came off his hand. "He's awake!" she shrieked.

"The doctor said he was sedated," his father said. "It's not possible."

"He squeezed my hand two times," she countered. "He's awake."

"That's two, champ," the Gentleman said. "Give me one more, and it's a done deal. An 'A' grade training program, safety in the afterlife with me, and power waiting for you at the end."

"I know you can hear me," his mother said. "Stay with us."

The thought of dying on his mother, of not having a chance to tell her that he had no control over himself when he cut April and himself was almost too much. Telling her that something had him, that he had been possessed would be a gift to her. It was something she believed in, she was no rainy day Catholic, but a woman who went to church and believed. He could convince her that her son couldn't hurt anyone like that.

"But if you cut that girl, you can go," his father said. He would never convince him. His father was as much a churchgoer as his mother, but he was strict, a believer in the wrathful God, and a world determined to destroy itself. What was worse, his father never believed in him. He would rather believe a policeman or a judge once someone told him that there were no drugs in his system.

Zachary found the strength to squeeze one more time, and he did so with vigor, crushing the crucifix into his mother's palm hard enough to make her wince and pull away.

The Gentleman patted him on the shoulder, and then he was standing beside the bed, looking down on himself as his body went into a violent seizure. "Well," the Gentleman said. "If you can close like your father, you'll do just fine."

XV

Miranda led Maxwell to the bathroom in the main cabin, where she sat him down on the closed toilet and straddled his lap. He only suspected something strange was about to happen when he was through the bathroom door. By the time she was in his lap, straddling him and turning the sink's hot water on, he was full of questions. "Sure you have all this in the right order, luv? I'm thinking we're wearing a little too much clothing."

"I'm giving you a shave so we can get you ready for the initiation," she told him with a smirk. "Tie your hair back."

He had never met a woman who could lead him by the hand like she did, but there was a certain energy when she was determined, and it was best not to fight it. He took a hair tie from the sink's edge and pulled his hair back. "I'm pretty sure I can meet the spirits as I am," Maxwell said. "Then again, this is one of the only things my father didn't educate me on."

"They're secrets for a reason," Miranda said. She picked up a can of shaving foam from the bathtub's edge. Beside it was a straight razor. "I think the only good thing that's come of today is that we all remember why. Purifiers and circles that think there's some point in competing with others would never leave us alone if they knew how we're initiated."

"I was trained as a solo Weaver," Maxwell said. "I know how to work with people, but my father didn't expect me to for some reason."

"He didn't believe you would ever have to," Miranda answered as though it was something she had known as a certainty for a long time.

"How do you know?" Maxwell asked.

Miranda turned the hot water off and checked the temperature of the pool in the sink then piled some shaving foam in her hand. "Over the last year my aunt Gladys has been telling me all about you, and until I saw you a few days ago, I didn't believe that we were going to get together for a second. Among many other things, she told me as much as she knew about how you were trained by your father, and she knew a surprising amount." She used a brush to spread shaving foam across his face and smiled at him. "Tonight you're going to get all the attention, and when we finally get time together we won't feel like talking, but for the next few minutes, it's Miranda time. I'm going to have a razor against your face, and I have a few things to tell you."

Maxwell shared a look with her for a moment, they were both reminded of what was done to April and Zachary. "You all right?" he said quietly while trying not to move his lips.

"I'll be fine," Miranda said. "Someone did some horrible shit and we have to get over that so we can help April and Zachary through what's ahead. May as well start tonight, yeah?"

"You sure? I can shave myself," Maxwell said, eying the razor as she opened it with a flick of her finger.

"No talkie, Miranda time, remember?" she said with a little smile. "I've done this before, don't worry."

"Mmmm-hmmm," he managed.

"Like I was saying," she said as she slowly followed through her first smooth stroke down his upper cheek. "When I was in New York, and my aunts had me back in hand, you're all Gladys would talk about. I went back to them because I didn't want to lose my family, and I knew I would if I kept running from one stage, one band to the next. I was doing a sofa tour, and it got dangerous every once in a while, but I was okay. My family wanted me back, not just my aunts, but everyone in New York. They didn't understand why I was sofa surfing when I could stay with any of them, but I think you get it." She finished a stroke and looked him in the eye.

After a moment she smiled, nodded and continued. "You do. So, I promised my aunts I'd stay with them until we went back to Sudbury, I'd do them that favor. I thought I'd come here, meet you, have a nice time at the Gathering and then go back to New York. That's not happening anymore. Instead of putting my mom's house up on the market, I'm going to move in and see what happens because I'm in love with you. Keep smiling to a minimum, I'm no good with a moving surface."

Maxwell swallowed the smile he barely knew he had and tried to remain still.

"Better. It is a very bad time to have an accident with a razor right now. I have conditions if I'm going to stay. First, you have to stick around and give this a chance with me. Second, no working in the mine – my aunt Susan still prays for three people who were buried in there every night, one of them was my uncle. Third, if you're going to move for better work, or whatever, we stay together. We're both looking for a future, we may as well do it together. I know I want to be with you more than I want to go back to New York, but without New York, all my plans are shot." She finished a stroke and held the razor away. "You can nod now, that is if you agree."

Maxwell nodded, hearing everything she said and truly agreeing with all but one point. "Can I-"

"It's Miranda time," she said, cocking her head.

"You'll like it."

"Okay, shoot, but keep it short. We don't have a lot of time."

"Why don't we both go to New York?" Maxwell said. "A guitarist couldn't hurt."

She closed his mouth and started in for another sweep of the razor. "I honestly didn't think of that. You'd go with me?" Miranda wiped the razor on a towel and smiled. "You can nod or something, but just for a sec."

Maxwell nodded. "There's still real music there. I'd like to give it a shot, especially with someone I'm good with. You're magic on stage."

"Thank you, flattery will get you everywhere my love," she said. "Hold still, we're almost done. Okay, so we'll talk about New York later." She took a moment to concentrate as she shaved between his upper lip and nose. "I watched you at the hospital. What Panos did was horrible, and it's hard to stop thinking about it for a minute, I know you've barely stopped thinking about it at all. So, he's getting what he wants. Maybe Panos knows that you are so powerful that he doesn't want to face you until you're completely off balance. If that's his game, he's definitely winning."

Maxwell watched as she spoke. Her words seemed well chosen, and everything she said rung true. He was actually happy that she had him in a position to just listen.

"You know how to help April, and you can't do anything for Zachary until his family smartens up," Miranda said. "So, it might sound cold, but I'm going to tell you to do that, and then stop thinking about it until it's time to help them some more. You have your own shit to concentrate on, and if you bungle that because Panos got to you, then you're failing yourself and your friends. I know your instinct is to help everyone around you, I've seen it just in the last few days, but there have to be limits right now, capisce?" She swished the razor in the sink, and Maxwell took that as his cue to nod.

"Good, now I have to tell you a few things about the initiation, especially if your dad didn't prepare you. You're already open to the other side like I've never seen, but the initiation opens our eyes up in ways that would make other people crazy. We do not talk about what we see to anyone who isn't initiated. A lot of Circle members have been locked up in asylums over the last two hundred years. The next thing: Samuel wanted me to tell you that you're not joining with a Guardian and a Summoner, you're being initiated as a Solo Weaver like your father intended. That was Sam's decision based on what he knows, you will have to trust him. I wanted you as my Weaver, so you know, and both Scott and Bernie wanted to be your Guardians. I'm actually kind of sad I'm not going to see that scrap. So, what that means is that you can practice magic with whoever you want or alone. The other thing to be aware of is the Guardian circle. You've never seen one. In this kind of initiation circle there will be another circle outside of it with all of our strongest guardians, because we expect the veil to be extremely thin this year. We are going to bring the False Priest into the middle circle once the young initiates are finished and moved to the guardians. This will be your final rite. You will have to face the False Priest because he noticed you, if it weren't for you, he wouldn't be here. You know the rules of a powerful circle like this. Chin up," she instructed. "You'll have about half an hour to make final preparations, the ceremony will begin, the initiations will take place, and then they'll initiate you. When everyone is ready, you'll summon the False Priest into the center, proving you have mastered that art. Then you will bind him the way a Guardian does, and then you will dismiss or destroy him permanently. This is with everyone watching, and based on that, you will or won't be accepted by our Circle." She stopped talking so she could concentrate on shaving his throat, and when she was finished she briefly kissed his chin and smiled at him. "Yuck, soapy," she said, standing up and washing the razor.

"That's all," Maxwell said, wiping the traces of foam from his face with a towel. "Properly banish an angry, old spirit in front of the whole Northern Circle."

"There are people from all the circles in North America here, there have been rumblings about this one since the last one, seven years ago, but I'm not supposed to tell you that," Miranda said, drying the razor and closing it. "I'm also not supposed to tell you that no one knew who would be the focus of this Gathering until you cast a circle with us on the beach."

Maxwell stood and put his hands on her hips. "Nope," she said, pulling his shirt up. "Shower time, we both have to be clean and ready and there's going to be a line for this bathroom in fifteen minutes. No one meets the spirits after sweating all day if it's a special occasion."

"Thanks for the help," Maxwell said. "Is it still Miranda time?"

She ran her hand over his cheek and smiled. "For one more minute." Miranda kissed Maxwell, wrapping her arms around his neck and leaning against him. They remained that way for longer than intended, and he wished it could go on when they parted. "Okay, one more thing, and this is little Miranda talking, the one who wanted a Spanish prince to ride up with a black stallion in tow for her so she could ride off into the sunset with him. It's only been a few days, and it's passed like a minute, but sometimes it feels like we've been hand in hand for months, so I have to-"

"I love you," Maxwell said. "Never found it with anyone before, but you're the one, Love."

"Then I'm yours, but only if you'll be mine," she said with a playful grin.

"That's what I need," Maxwell said. "The rest is all details and window dressing." He finished taking off his shirt and started on his jeans.

Miranda's clothing was on the bathroom floor and she was starting the shower before his socks were off. He pinched the cheek where she had her protective tattoo and she shrieked. "I need to get one of those, maybe not where you have it though."

"We have a tattoo artist here, I was going to surprise you. Oh, and Allen will have his brands in the circle," Miranda said. "You know this shower is all business, right?" she said, slipping past the shower curtain.

"If you insist."

"I'm not meeting the ancestors with you dripping down my

leg," Miranda said.

"Well, that picture's sure to get me in the mood," Maxwell said, climbing into the shower.

"You're kidding," Miranda said from under the showerhead.

"I am," Maxwell said. "You've a foul mouth, but I love you anyway."

"You better."

"Did you have to banish something during your initiation?"

"I was thirteen," Miranda replied. "So, no, I was being introduced into the Circle as a legacy. That, and I didn't get the attention of something like you did, or have the knowledge you do. The Circle has to see how you use your knowledge."

"Ah, so mind my manners, then," Maxwell said. "No worries."

XVI

Maxwell barely had enough time to prepare for the fight he'd face during his initiation. The crossroads were so cold, he could see his breath in the air. Something had come into that space that was so hungry, that it sapped the heat from the place. He hurriedly took a cutting from the oldest oak he could find, feeling eyes looking at him from all around in the fading light. It was something he'd have to return to and remedy, removing the False Pastor would only be the first step.

He closed his hand around the bark and wood he cut from the oak and thought of the twisted hanging tree. Scant moments later, he was sure that what he held in his hand was a descendant of that old hanging tree, and retreated from the crossroads on his motorcycle.

Gathering what he needed from his father's hidden room was much faster, even though it took him at least five minutes to find where the scabbard for his family sword was hidden.

Bernie greeted him at the entrance to the cave leading to the private beach with a grin. "You know this would have been easier if you got initiated with Scottie and me." He was wearing a simple, two-paneled robe that was tied at the waist with a silk belt. Maxwell resisted the urge to comment on it.

"What fun would that be? Give me the choice between the easy way and the hard way and I'll pick an even harder way to do something every time," Maxwell said as he followed Bernie and his kerosene lamp.

He stopped a moment then looked at Maxwell. "You're not nervous, are you?"

"Not even a little," Maxwell said, shifting the sword scabbard on his back.

"You are," Bernie said with a chuckle. "You know, this is your only chance to turn back. Once we reach the other end of the cave, you're in until the end."

"A week ago I didn't believe in all this," Maxwell said. "Now I can't imagine how it was so hard for me to believe. If this will help me see more of the world for what it is and help me join a family that's wanted me along for most of my life, then I'll fight for it."

"You'll be a witness to most of what's about to happen, very little of it will involve fighting. What you do have to do is open your mind and your heart to everything you're about to see. Don't worry about guarding yourself until you feel you have to, and when that time comes, you'll have no doubt."

"You've fought in a circle like this?" Maxwell asked.

"No, but I've watched Samuel and my father do it on different occasions," Bernie replied.

"Any advice?"

"The circle removes two things that we have to face in the world: the ability for your opponent to create illusions, and their ability to get help. This is the only place where you can confront something like the False Pastor and trust what you see. Do you have a plan for defeating him?"

"I do, it's a good one," Maxwell said.

"Good, don't let anything else distract you," Bernie said. "Here we are, last chance." He held the lantern up so Maxwell could see the cavern exit clearly.

"Press on, ya blonde giant," Maxwell said. He took a step through and was confronted by Miranda, who was wearing a thin, cotton two-paneled dress that had no sides.

She smiled at him and held up a blindfold. "The next time you see the world, it will not look the same."

"I feel a little overdressed," Maxwell said as she tied the silk band around his head. It covered most of his nose, his forehead and everything in between. He couldn't help but smell the vanilla rose perfume she was wearing the first time they met as adults, only days before.

"We take you as you are," she whispered. "And celebrate what you become."

Bernie and Miranda gently led him down the path, across the beach, and to a short set of firm steps he didn't recognize. The hard surface under his boots was definitely stone, and he could hear the quiet rustlings of people around him.

"Maxwell Percival Foster," Samuel's voice addressed, sounding stronger than it had in all the time Max had known him. "Is your heart open to those who will stand with you in the circle?"

"Yes," Maxwell replied.

"Is your mind open to accept what you are about to experience?"

"Yes."

"Will you allow yourself to be bound against harming any of the trusted initiates and imitated inside this circle?"

"I will allow myself to be bound," Maxwell replied.

"Then you may approach," Samuel concluded. Bernie and Miranda finished guiding him across a stony floor. He was still outdoors, he could hear the birds, and feel the wind, but he could not imagine where he was.

"The young initiates who entered as uncontested legacy pledges now leave as full initiates who have made their promise to continue learning our ways. They have pledged loyalty to each other and everyone standing here, and go with our love, and our promise to continue to teach and nurture them as they become adults."

Maxwell heard the sounds of smaller feet walking past him, a little surprised and disappointed that he missed the initiations of the younger attendees. There were so many feet descending the stone stairs behind him that it reminded him of the rush between classes in High School.

When the shuffling of feet abated, a voice called out. "The Guardians have closed the circle once more."

"Relax," Miranda whispered. "I'll see you on the other side."

"Which Guardian presents Maxwell Perceval Foster to the Circle?" Samuel asked.

"Bernard Samson Webb. I present him as a Weaver," Bernie answered.

"Which Summoner presents Maxwell Perceval Foster to the Circle?"

"Miranda Alexa Larson. I present him as my Weaver," Miranda replied.

"Please take all he carries with him in the Circle and offer it to the altar," Susan said.

Maxwell allowed hands to slowly take his sword, his shirt, his knife and the rest of his clothes from him. As they did so, people offered comments to the altar. Bernie was the first, as his sword was carefully unstrapped from his back. "This man fights for his friends."

Miranda was next as his shirt was pulled over his head. "This man has shown deep love."

"This man has allowed his anger to provoke him to violence," Allen said as his knife was untied from his hip.

"This man can release his hate for all but two people in the world," said Scott as his amulet was removed.

"This man is playful at heart," Gladys said as she pulled his belt from its loops.

"This man speaks his mind," Bernie said as his pants were undone and they fell to his knees. Maxwell shook them down to his ankles and stepped out of them.

"This man would rather have a friend than an enemy," Miranda said as his boxers were taken down.

"Are those all the truths that you would have known?" asked Susan. "What of his flaws? I would hear three more."

"This man believes he is strong enough alone to bear any burden," Samuel said.

"This man is stubborn," Bernie said.

"This man is reckless," Samuel said.

"These things all sound true to me," Susan announced.

"And to me," Gladys agreed.

"And to me. The holders of the Inner Circle are satisfied," Samuel concluded.

"Do I get one of those lovely dresses now?" Maxwell whispered.

A few stifled snickers were his reward, then he heard a sword being drawn from its sheath, and Maxwell's demeanor became serious once more.

He winced as something sharp touched his chest, and he remembered a photo from an initiation rite still practiced in Europe. A strong hand kept him standing in position, and he straightened. A drop of blood ran down his bare chest, and he could picture himself in that old black and white image, standing straight in the middle of the circle, nude, with the Weaver in front of him. Sword in hand, the leader of the ceremony held the tip to his chest. "Maxwell Percival Foster, you are now known to the

Circle, and have earned the right to hear its true name. We are the Third Spiral. Now I ask the question you have come to finally answer," Samuel said, his voice strong and clear. "Do you swear to defend the secrets of our Order, protect the innocent from the hidden evils, and to return to the light with The Enlightened? Answer carefully, if there is betrayal in your heart, this blade will know."

"I do swear," Maxwell said.

The sword tip was taken back and lowered. "I reveal to you the laws and beliefs that have determined our course through one thousand three hundred and thirteen years," Samuel said. "There are five laws. All acts have a cost. Fear is the enemy. Secrecy is survival. We keep our own. Act for others first."

"Our beliefs are simple, but have shaken the pillars of society when proven to the innocent masses," Susanne continued. "The realms of life are endless, to die is to discover a different life in a new realm. Our common patron on the other side are travellers, spirits who have lived many lives. No person bound to this life can know all the secrets of the next. This world is nearing the end of the seventh and final Age of Innocence. The Third Spiral are stewards of the natural order, protectors of creatures that are innocent of the true darkness in this world and the next, and we prepare for the coming of the High Days. Our ancestors were present for the Arrival of the Goddess, and the Rise of the Sun Prince. We will bear witness to the Opening Door and The Calling Of Light."

Maxwell knew all the legends she mentioned. The Arrival of the Goddess was a story he was told as a child, about a brother and sister who was lost in the woods. When night came, and they could hear beasts closing in on them, thirteen silver haired wolves surrounded them, and a woman with grey eyes guided them out of the woods. When they arrived at their village, the woman introduced six of the wolves to the people, and they became their guardians. The woman left with the remaining seven wolves, but three nights later a giant silver and black matron wolf joined the village. War with another village came the next season, and the wolves would not fight unless their territory was breached.

When the decisive battle was fought, the men and women from the village the wolves protected were slain, leaving only a few at home for the wolves to protect. When the enemy came, they did so, and the neighboring tribe never intruded again. The few men and women left in the wolf village could not venture far to hunt because their neighbors were waiting for them, so they planted seeds instead. For decades, the wolves protected the territory, keeping fields of wheat and paddocks of other animals that sought the wolves protection safe so the small village eventually became a city, and when the neighboring hunter villagers sought trade, they were welcomed peacefully, but the wolves were ever watchful.

The Rise of the Sun Prince was something Maxwell learned through his own reading. The older books he learned about it from told it like a history. A young slave was born in Ancient Egypt under a bright star, and three great harvests followed. When he became a man, he travelled from one slave camp to the next, preaching peace. His popularity grew, and it was said that he was a great magician, able to extend days, heal the sick and ease spirits back into their graves. The Pharaoh was unhappy to hear about this slave, because it was said that the villages thought that the preacher was more powerful.

The preacher was in the desert, meditating and communing for three months during this time. When he returned, he saw that the slaves were mid-revolt with the Pharaoh, and thousands of lives were lost. Out of love for his people, he surrendered his power to the Pharaoh, and he broke the layman priest's walking staff, then put him upon a stone to be flayed. He survived a vicious flaying, and died after three days of being tied to a flat stone. They cut the bonds, but did not let the slaves take the body.

Another three days passed, and the layman priest returned to life, coming down from the stone he died on. He raised thirteen of his followers from the dead and visited numerous villages. Twenty-eight days passed, and the rumblings of rebellion were common amongst the slaves regardless of his message of peace. The layman priest confronted the Pharaoh again, who was deeply afraid. He handed the Pharaoh another walking staff, and invited him to break it, telling him that it would bring about a peace that would last the rest of his reign, and end the drought, but he would have to release any slave that wanted to follow him into the desert.

The Pharaoh did so, and the staff shattered into hundreds of pieces. The layman priest announced that he was the Sun Prince, and that he was gifting the Pharaoh's reign with abundance. He would take the followers he had risen to the desert along with all the slaves that were willing to come with him for the rest of his days. He would travel until he found his natural death, and his people would build a city upon his bones.

The drought ended, and, hearing that the Sun Prince would travel the desert for a decade or longer, a surprising number of slaves remained to serve the Pharaoh. To demonstrate his thanks to the Sun Prince, the Pharaoh built an empty tomb where his history was recorded, and then named his firstborn son after him. For twenty-one years the Pharaoh Ra was said to have miraculous power, which he used to create a son and a daughter and to maintain a period of plenty. It was often said that the Sun Prince returned to visit Ra on his deathbed to forgive him, then to take his power back so Ra would be allowed to die. They both disappeared at the same time, ascending to Godhood.

Maxwell had an idea that the Opening Door referred to the last breaking of the covenant, when another person would discover the secret of resurrection, then return to life themselves. The covenant between mankind and the divine, to keep the door between the mystical power and material laws closed, would be broken if the resurrected did not surrender the gift, allowing themselves to die, restoring the natural order. He hadn't seen anything talking about specific predictions or prophecies though, he didn't enjoy prophecy at all.

The Calling of Light was completely new to him as an event, but he knew the Prometheus Manuscript well. He spent years fascinated with it and the implied attachment to the Sun Prince, who was able to access magic that seemed more fantasy than occult.

"I ask you, Maxwell Percival Foster, do you swear to serve the Third Spiral, keeping its secrets and aiding our cause for the rest of your days and into the next existence?" asked Gladys.

"I do swear," Maxwell replied.

The blindfold was removed and Maxwell was struck by a rush of memories. This was not the sensation of remembering something he'd forgotten, but of experiences that were blocked from his mind coming to him in sequence.

The last year he spent with Miranda before she left for Italy was as clear as though it just happened. Handholding, spending hours playing music together. Finally, their first kiss, a perfect moment somewhere between the main house and the barn just after sundown. Recalling the cool air of twilight, his excitement and Maxwell's overwhelming love for her made his head spin. His father almost caught them in the act, coming around the bend as their encounter was ending and grins that would last hours split the bottom halves of their faces.

The seal between him and those memories were broken. His father put them there, and he understood at last. The weaver in him was a musician. That is how he understood the power between the incantations, the summoning of a being, and how those things affected the world. Seeing the power as though it was made of notes and understanding that there were harmonies to every ritual, spell, curse and especially between what one brings from the world beyond the physical was a revelation to Maxwell.

If he and Miranda were allowed to continue a romance they were too young for, he would not have built a foundation for magic in music, and she would have been stunted as well. Would they have been more powerful together? That was a question they could answer by being together. His father truly was working in his best interest, giving him the knowledge to exist as a Magus, while his music provided the art he'd need to wield the power he would eventually have.

Maxwell recalled discovering the opening to a cave blocked off by concrete and a steel door three times since then. Hidden in the forest, it was only a few hundred yards from the private beach. The last time he was taken there was at the beginning of his initiation ritual. After they blindfolded him, they guided him down the beach, then down a path in the forest, a path he was only just recalling. The way to the place he was seeing took him underground, then into the open night air. His memory of the journey to the present finally complete, Maxwell looked around himself to find the smiling faces of Samuel, Allen, Bernie, Scott, Gladys, Susan, and Miranda spaced around a circle etched on a stone floor. In the outer circle there were at least thirty people, most of whom he recognized as visitors who came to the farm from time to time as he was growing up.

Etched in the stone floor were circles of different sizes, all meant for different high rituals. In the dim light he could see that the black stone that was so common in the area was shaped into a henge that surrounded everyone inside the inner and outer circles. The space was closed in by flat stone faces in all directions past the henge, even in the starlight it looked like someone had cut a large recessed circle for all other circles to be placed in.

The space outside the circle had been decorated with wildflowers, cedar and oak leaves. There was movement on them, small things, some with their own inner light, using the decorations like rafts. Some were still, other small shadow and light bearing creatures moved from bloom to leaf, occasionally skipping through the air.

They all remained outside the two main circles, like an audience of faeries who didn't require protection or involvement. "Mother Maddock's Little Visitors," Maxwell said, naming the book he'd read and laughed at as a teenager. She claimed to have faeries in her garden, wrote about them and painted several who 'would sit still long enough' as she said.

"You're not the first to be surprised that she wasn't mad," Samuel said, amused. The Third Spiral is one of the few groups that are blessed with their protection, and our initiates are all able to open their minds enough to see a part of many different realms beyond our own. Some can only see the parts that are close to crossing into our reality, or overlap entirely, others, like you, Miranda and Bernie, will be able to see into other realms. Which ones, how far and when that gift will be under your control are questions that time will answer."

"We should get on with it?" Gladys reminded Samuel quietly.

"Yes," Samuel agreed. "Maxwell has stirred a spirit from the darkness. This being has embraced hate, and will only grow more powerful in its need to harm the living. You have the cunning, the knowledge and the power to face this spirit, and we want to know how you use those things without direction. Take what you need from your belongings and proceed." Samuel said.

Everyone inside the inner circle retreated to the ring of observers in the outer circle, leaving Maxwell alone with a short altar and the possessions he brought with him at his feet.

He knelt down, put his amulet on, took the wood he collected, a rough spun piece of twine, and moved on to the altar. In addition to what he knew he would find there, the athame, dishes of oil, water, salt, and other ceremonial instruments, he found a small brazier of coals with three branding irons inside. He looked to Allen, who was the only person he knew who had similar brands, and recognized that the older man was trying to passively observe.

Maxwell looked at the brands. One was a powerful protector against possession and curses, another was a symbol of channeling meant to increase the potency of the bearer's will. The third was the mark of the conjurer, made for practitioners who summoned beings to perform tasks for them. He picked up a damp cloth from beside the brazier and considered which ones may help him. Maxwell knew he could do without all of the brands, but intended to have at least two of them tattooed later anyway. Using the brands set out for him and whoever else was going to use them in a sacred space, in that time would be much more potent.

He chose the Silent Spirit circle, a match to Miranda's Tattoo that protected against curses and spiritual possession and pressed it to his chest. Even though the lines of the glowing red-hot brand were fine and delicate, it was still incredibly painful at first, dulling after the first few seconds. The smell and sound of searing made it much worse. He removed it when Allen nodded at him.

He put the iron back into the coals and couldn't help but smirk at Miranda, who was wide eyed and cringing as he picked up the more complex second brand: The Invoker's Seal, meant to assist him in projecting his will. With a wink in her direction he pressed the red-hot end beside the first brand. The pain wasn't as bad as the first time, but his body reacted to the abuse by sweating profusely. By the time he put the second brand back in the brazier drops ran down the middle of his back. He did not need the third brand at all, and no one seemed surprised when he turned his back on it.

Marking one of the man-sized circles carved onto the stone at his feet with a bit of bark, Maxwell took a step back so the altar was behind him. There was no need for him to summon his opponent using words or announcements. Instead he closed his eyes and imagined the defiled chapel in his mind as it appeared in his dream, with wooden walls that were the color of yellowing bone, and a pastor in its doorway that seemed to be at one with his shadow.

Imagining the False Pastor inside the circle was easy, the mental picture formed as though the being was eager to appear. Maxwell raised his hand, fingers splayed out across the star scape above and focused, shutting the world around him out. Faces of rotting children filled his mind, they clung to the black woolen robes of the False Pastor, and Maxwell recognized them for what they were: an extension of the Pastor's will, tools he used to frighten people who he had latched on to over the years. They only ever existed in the phantasm's imagination. With a thought, Maxwell was able to see past them in his mind's eye, and look directly into the eyes of the Pastor, grey and cold as they were. He lowered his hand and directed it at the circle he'd marked.

When Maxwell opened his eyes to look upon the False Pastor, he was already sure he would see him there. A few of the onlookers gasped at the appearance of a grey man surrounded by a black shadow-mist. "A wordless summoning," someone whispered.

"I bind you with tools you know," Maxwell said, presenting a thick sliver of oak he gathered from a crossroads tree near the fallen chapel. The Fallen Pastor sneered and loomed, trying to press past the barrier drawn on the stone. With great care, Maxwell looped the tiny noose he'd made of twine around the piece of wood and looked up at his opponent, smiling.

The face of the Pastor stretched long, it's pale visage staring on in shock and horror as Maxwell pulled the tiny noose tight. A rough rope closed around the neck of the False Pastor and hauled him up abruptly. The spirit clawed at the rope and Maxwell could feel all the frustration he had at being rendered powerless by the creature well up in him. It was not the time to follow that emotion. "You are bound," he growled before taking a deep breath in and letting his anger out with a long exhale.

Slowly he knelt and put the piece of wood, along with the noose tied around it on the stone at his feet and left it there as he stood again. The choking and struggling sounds filled the space, and the False Pastor kicked, clawed at the rope and made desperate gestures to the observers. "No one here pities who you are," Maxwell said. "They pity the child you once were, as we were all innocent once, beings of potential and light."

The False Pastor fixed his eyes on Maxwell and fought the rope furiously, no longer flailing, but straining, his hands reaching as far as they may, striking the edge of the circle boundary carved around him. "You are damned, Weaver!" he screamed hoarsely.

"I'm starting to reconsider that pity, spirit," Maxwell said, cocking his head. He took the blade his forefather made, unsheathed it and faced the False Pastor. "I am your deliverer. Look up, lost one, and find your path."

"Demons, the dark flame, the road of pain," the False Pastor said as he looked to the stars.

"They have come in response to what you are." Maxwell held the knife over his head and closed his eyes. "I call into the light, the Glade everlasting, I ask if there is any who would protect this spirit."

Maxwell could feel the fear from the bound spirit in the circle. Even if the False Pastor was completely evil, there was still something within him that feared his fate. There was no sign that relief was coming, and Maxwell waited as long as he felt he could, then longer. This was the true test, the act of it was easy, and he had done everything correctly and was in a place of great power. He hated the False Pastor enough to send him directly to the Pit, but doing so in a sacred space when there may be another option would make him seem vengeful and severe to everyone who was gathered there.

The words of his father came to him then, a recollection from his encounter at the crossroads; "Do what feels right, watch your back," and Maxwell knew exactly what to do. "No one's coming to save you, Pastor," he told the spirit. Without a moment's hesitation, he lightly kicked the piece of wood with the twine noose wrapped round it into the False Pastor's circle, then stepped inside with the spirit.

He felt his heart skip a beat as the False Pastor tried to possess him and failed, then the tug on his amulet as he attempted to dig his hands into his chest. Maxwell raised the knife. "I release you to the realms beyond our material plane," he reached out, expecting to feel nothing but air, but grabbed the cold, fleshy throat of the Pastor instead. He squeezed and looked into the cold eyes of the shocked being. "I banish you for all time, and release you to wander." With a flick of his blade, the noose that held the False Pastor aloft was cut.

The dark spirit screamed, the pitch was ear-piercing as he drifted up and out of sight. Maxwell could feel that it was utterly gone, even the memory of standing inside the circle with the thing was already something he found easy to doubt.

Susan, Samuel and Gladys returned to the inner circle, smiling. "You chose the method that does the most good. The spirit will never be able to return unless it is brought into this world by the living. If it is summoned you will know where it appears, and who is responsible." Susan said. "You have demonstrated the skills of a Weaver."

"You have demonstrated the skills of a Guardian," Gladys said.

"You have demonstrated the skills of a Summoner," Samuel said. "Welcome to the Third Spiral."

"That concludes the calling of this circle," Susan said. "Thank you and farewell to all the beings that bore witness, provided protection, and celebrated with us. You are welcome to stay for the evening if you do no harm, and depart peacefully by morning."

The glimmering creatures amongst the branches and their darker counterparts skittered back into the shadows, or took wing, flying for the stars. Miranda joined Maxwell, giving him a hug and a kiss before anyone else could congratulate him. "Now we can have a future," she said.

"It's about time," Bernie said, handing him a two-paneled robe like the one he was wearing then embracing him briefly. "Welcome to the real world."

"The crypt is a lot like the one just outside Liverpool, the original Third Spiral temple," Miranda said. "There's another one in Sicily, but it's smaller." They made their way to the outermost tunnel, it ran in a large circle underground, around the ritual site in the center.

"How long have you known about this place?" Maxwell asked.

"I knew this was here, but this is my first real look around."

The tunnel was wide enough for two people to walk through, and just tall enough so Bernie and Allen didn't have to duck as they walked. They led the way with gas burning lanterns that cast a white light in all directions. "Who made this place?"

"My grandfather, and my great grandfather," Bernie replied. "They made most of their living machining tools for the mining companies here, farming was a sideline."

"Ah, I'd forgotten that bit," Maxwell said. "I guess having the right tools for the job, they got to it."

"The outer expansion took the longest," Allen said. "The main areas took a month, it was easy to find experienced miners when my grandfather was alive. When my dad expanded the crypts, carving the outer ring, it took a summer and most of the fall. Most of his generation of the Third Spiral didn't work underground. Now, I think there may be three or four members who are miners. Expanding would take years."

They reached the crypt section and Maxwell couldn't help but notice that most of the spaces were empty, the plates covering the pre-dug shelves left blank. They made their way past dozens of unmarked spots. "Don't think you'll have to worry about expanding for awhile."

"True," Allen said. "There are enough spots for a couple generations of us, and our number is shrinking. Not as many people are finding their way to believing. Ah, here it is," he said, putting his lantern on a steel peg driven into the stone. "I've wanted to show you this for years, it's where your father is interred. Take as long as you like."

Maxwell looked at the polished silver coated plate covering a spot in the cave wall. "His ashes are in here?"

"Yes, you can look at the urn if you like," Allen said. "In your father's case, there's nothing to disturb. Some of the urns are locked to prevent any contact, like Fiona O'Dell's."

"Never heard of her," Maxwell said.

"Samuel's first wife, she became his spirit guide once she died. She talks to him through that pocket watch using a code," Bernie said.

"That explains a few things, and, considering how many wives he's had since, must be bloody awkward," Maxwell said.

"Sam says she got over it after wife number three," Allen said as he moved on down the hallway, letting Bernie's lantern guide him.

"Do you want me to stay?" Miranda asked.

"Yes," he replied. "Besides, there won't be any chattering here. As far as I can sense, this is a little dark hole with a pot of ashes inside. Good to know where the old man's ashes ended up though." Maxwell opened the door and found a key beside the simple bronze urn. "Hullo, Dad," he said as he took the key and tried it in the lock on the door protecting his father's remains. It worked, so he took a moment to look at the urn then locked the door. "Wish I believed sooner," he said.

Miranda took his hand, but didn't comment. Maxwell stared at the inscription on the door.

CHARLES FOSTER
LEADER, TEACHER, FRIEND
FATHER
1910-1969

"We were quite a pair when I was very young. I believed everything he told me then, and had to know everything he was doing, where he was when he was home. I remember departures and greetings the most, if I'm being honest," Maxwell said. "Wish I didn't forget magic when I got a little older. I think it was what he always said about my mother that killed that in me."

"What did he tell you?" Miranda asked.

"That she wouldn't answer if we called out to her spirit, she'd wandered too far and gotten into trouble, like she did when she was alive. He blamed her for a lot, I think. She was from a rough caste though, poor people who never recovered from being wrecked during the Second World War. I met my grandpa from that side, grizzled drunk who liked to tell people how worthless they are. Barely remember him, but I was afraid of him the one time I met him, that's hard to forget. Don't even remember why, but my father never let him near me again."

"What happened to your mother?" Miranda asked tentatively.

"Jumped off Humber Bridge when I was three. She had already left me and Dad, still can't picture my father changing diapers though." He traced the letters on the cold metal with his fingers and let a tear roll down his cheek. "Big lessons today. Finally feel like I'm almost all the way home, I even remember all that time with you when we were young, and you're here." He squeezed her hand a little. "But we're never all the way home again when the parents are gone, are we? Never thought I'd miss this old geezer again."

Miranda wrapped her arms around him as he allowed himself to think about the endless fights he had with his father, and all the discord his disbelief caused. The tears came.

"We'll build a new home," Miranda whispered to him. "Maybe we'll make one here, maybe in New York, but it'll be ours."

The celebration was well under way when Maxwell and Miranda emerged from the Third Spiral. By the light of their lamp they made their way down the path to the private beach, which was filled with almost all the attendees. The warm evening air was a relief after the cool damp of the underground temple and its catacombs.

The one thing he had to deal with nagged at him, and he wasn't the only one, from the look on Samuel and Susan's faces when they approached him and Miranda on the beach. "We have to talk," Susan said.

They were led to a circle of folding chairs around a small folding table, where Maxwell put his lantern and turned it down. "The Dawn Shard," he said.

"Are you sure you're not a little psychic?" Samuel said.

"Don't be silly, it's obvious," Gladys said as she sat down at the table. "Bernie is driving Scott home, he's going to the hospital early tomorrow morning. We'd be having a meeting of two good circles if he were here. It was good practicing with you again, Samuel."

"You think Bernie, Max and I are that good together?" Miranda asked.

"Anyone can see it when the three of you are in the same room, especially when you play music together," Susan said as though it was the most obvious thing in the world.

"You may even take your place in the Third Spiral as the Prime

Trio, but that's a few decades away, no need to get ahead of ourselves," Samuel said.

"That's not getting ahead, power is power, harmony is harmony, balance is balance," Gladys said. "All that's missing is wisdom, and I think they're catching up quickly."

"But are they ready to face what's growing at the crossroads?" Susan said. "I don't think so. Something old has come, Maxwell saw it earlier, when he was taking his cuttings."

"How do you know?" Gladys asked.

"I followed him with the sight," Susan replied, crossing her arms. "This close to the Gathering time, almost anyone with the right training can do it, we don't all have to be naturals."

"But that brings us back around to the question," Samuel said. "Are they ready to face something like that? Maxwell can discard fear like an old peel, but does he know enough to recognize the thing's true nature and find a way to send it on its way?"

"I don't think they realize we're still here," Miranda whispered to Maxwell.

"Let's see how long it goes on," he muttered in return.

"I'm sorry," Gladys said. "It's only that there's been no time for us to talk like this. Nothing was certain until you were initiated, dear," she told Maxwell. "And with you thinking about running off to New York together, we have to wonder how close your bond with Bernie really is."

"I hate it when you do that," Miranda told her. "Stop eavesdropping, just because you have the sight, doesn't mean my privacy goes the way of the dodo."

"There is a lot going on this week, dear," Gladys explained. "I gave you privacy when it was appropriate, and I was afraid we'd get left out on some important decisions, like you taking Max back to New York with you so soon. Give this place some time."

"I promised I would, so I will, just stop listening in."

"Can we get back to the point?" Samuel said. "We have to cleanse the crossroads, and then Maxwell has to calm the Dawn Shard again. He had it for weeks, and there were no problems, were there?"

"No, no bumps in the night or strange things happened while the book and the shard were together and we were on the road," Maxwell said. "Scott may have disturbed the seal when he went digging though."

"That seal is all that's keeping whatever's coming through at the crossroads in place," Susan said. "It won't last much longer, a night or two, maybe. Then there is Panos, we are sure he possessed Zachary to do his dirty work."

Maxwell couldn't believe that he'd almost forgotten Zachary's fate during the initiation and the tour afterwards. He hadn't forgotten the solution to Panos, however. "That is part of the same problem." He said. "The Dawn Shard knows him, I'm sure I can use it to call his soul out of whoever he's wearing now. It's a direct solution, but a good one."

"But there's a chance he'd be attached to the Dawn Shard then," Samuel said.

"Only until I find out how to release him, if it comes to that. Even if I fail in that for a few years, maybe decades, I think it would serve him right," Maxwell said. "Bugger deserves worse."

"So, we recover the stone tomorrow when the sun is high," Samuel said.

"Some people call that 'noon'," Susan said. "But I agree."

"So do I," Gladys said. "Until then, you two must enjoy, celebrate."

"No more watching," Miranda said. "Or I'll make sure you see something you wish you hadn't."

"Oh, I've seen it all," her aunt replied.

"I hope not," Maxwell said, suddenly feeling less than comfortable in a robe that had a tendency to slip.

"Don't worry," Gladys said. "I may do a fair bit of celebrating myself."

"Okay," Miranda said, throwing her hands up. "Now I'm glad I don't have the sight."

"Have fun," Samuel said, coughing. "This time of your lives will not come twice."

There was no end of food, drink, good people and even music as instruments were passed from one set of skilled hands to another throughout the night. The light of the stars and moon were only outdone by the bonfires, as Miranda and Maxwell made their way from circle to circle.

They were welcome everywhere, and when they became more interested in each other than the festivities, and made to retreat to the main cabin, there were boos and well-wishes in almost equal measure. Maxwell's hands kept on finding their way to her bare sides, her hips, and her lips sought his more often as midnight approached.

By the time the clock hands pointed up, they were in their room, the robes on the floor, and the covers pulled off. "I can only see my future with you," Miranda said as she wrapped her legs around him.

"I'll do anything for that," he told her, staring into her brown eyes. "Anything for you."

XVII

Maxwell and Miranda were up at ten the next morning, thanks to several knocks on the door. Maxwell answered the second, only to discover that no one was there. He returned to bed, pulling her into his arms. "Bloody ding-dong ditch."

"Something Gladys does, tells people to knock on my door if they're going in that direction. She's probably telling everyone whose going to the bathroom to do it as they go by."

"That's dirty."

"It works," Miranda sighed. "I'm awake."

They got up, showered and headed downstairs, where Maxwell immediately saw Bernie sitting alone at a table, coffee cup in hand, a newspaper in the other. It was immediately evident that his friend's mood was rotten. "I'll meet you in the kitchen," Maxwell told Miranda as they reached the bottom of the stairs.

"Uh-huh," she replied. "I'll get you coffee and make you a plate, you see what's up with Stormy Weathers over there."

"You're amazin'," he said as she split off.

"I know," she smiled back.

"Scott, his parents, and a whole bunch of people are at the hospital, blocking people from April," Bernie said. "Sands put a little piece in the paper this morning, there are so many lookey-loos at the hospital now that there are police guarding her room." He handed that day's Nickel City Gazette, a paper Steven Sands was part owner of, to Maxwell.

SUDBURY SLASHER MUTILATION-SUICIDE

There was a publicity shot of Zachary in mid-stage strut, screaming into his microphone, and another of the whole band. Set into the middle of the article that dominated the front page was a picture of April, most likely from her last year of high school.

Maxwell began to read, his empty stomach turning as the first line of the front-page article.

Police have halted the investigation into the mutilation of April Sands and the suicide of retired Ontario Provincial Police Officer Morley Parker after evidence has surfaced indicating that one Zachary Ross, lead singer to Canadian band Road Craft, committed the assault on April Sands. Authorities will not comment on the nature of the assault other than to say more than one bladed tool was used. Authorities also claim that, after witnessing the state of Ms. Sands and rescuing her, Retired Officer Morley Parker committed suicide in the basement of an abandoned house where she was found.

Some time that day, Zachary was found in his apartment on Elm Street in Sudbury, bleeding to death from self inflicted wounds that authorities state were similar to Ms. April Sands'. He died hours later after emergency surgery.

"Let me sum it up," Bernie said as Maxwell opened the paper more so he could read past the top of the fold. "They found someone to talk about Zack drawing symbols on the bus, probably one of those hippies he hung out with. They write about how what he did to April and might have been part of some ritual because, according to them, Road Craft wasn't just a band, but also a black magic coven. Yeah, their terminology is all wrong, and it isn't true, but it's in print now. Thousands of people who didn't know our names before will know them now, and it hurts everything here on the farm."

"Most of the people who matter won't believe this," Miranda said as she returned with a platter of left over pancakes, cheesy egg casserole, waffles, bacon and sausages. She carried two mugs of coffee in the other hand with care. He stood up and helped her put them on the table. "We'll share a plate," she said, picking up one of two forks. "Sorry, I could hear you from the leftover table."

"No problem, this is as much about you, because the Star had your picture with us on the front page," Bernie said. "We're all named as part of a black magic band, April is stuck in the middle of it, and people are going to come to the farm with questions like a few reporters did this morning."

"Bloody Steven Sands, using this to sell papers. You'd think people would ignore this rag," Maxwell said.

"Some of the owners are attached to the University," Bernie said. "The paper will always have credibility here. Anyway, the damage is done, people are packing up. In seven years, fourteen years even, the Gathering will happen somewhere else, there's too much attention here."

"I'm sorry, Bernie," Miranda said.

"I'm more sad for my father, and especially April. This is going to follow her around, we won't be able to tell people it was some accident."

"Zachary didn't deserve any of this either," Maxwell said quietly, feeling the weight of responsibility for his friend's fate. "He could be a complete waster, but Panos got into him."

"You're sure?" Bernie asked. "He followed you here and took Zachary."

"Absolutely. He tried to possess me, couldn't, so he went for someone he knew was close to me so he could find out where the book, or the shard was, or both. All this shit happened because I brought those things here."

"No, it happened because some crazed asshole started possessing and cutting people," Bernie said. "You don't get to shoulder this, man, I'm not going to let you. Just like I'm not letting you two go on the road alone. When you get the shard back, all three of us are heading out, a full trio, a circle, so we can all keep that thing on the move."

"Someone told you about New York," Miranda said. "We were going to invite you, but it just came up yesterday, there wasn't time."

"Don't worry about where," Bernie said. "My dad told me this morning about the Dawn Shard, how Sam's theory is right."

"What theory?" Maxwell asked.

"It has to keep moving," Allen said as he came through the screen door. "It can't be kept in the same place for this long, otherwise it gathers local spirits, and worse. There have been people at the crossroads since dawn cleansing the place. Samuel was there for a while, but they had to bring him back to his trailer. He wanted to be there when you got it out of the ground so he could give you his blessing before you left. I saw him for a minute, and he told me he hates being right, he believes you'll do the right thing and start travelling with it."

Maxwell thought for a moment, aware that Bernie and Miranda were waiting for him to say something, but the mouthful of egg casserole bought him time. The last thing on his mind was food, and his appetite was disappearing fast as he accepted the reality of the situation. He was cursed.

He swallowed and looked to Miranda. "It's the only thing that makes sense, that the bloody thing can't stay in one place for long. Looks like we're digging this up then I'm back on the road. I'm not going to let some poor sod volunteer to do this for me."

"We're on the road," Miranda said. "You don't have to go alone."

"It's worse than what you're thinking, Max," Allen said, sitting down. He looked right at his son as he went on, as though trying to get a point across. "Big populated spots, like hospitals, police stations, anywhere where there the Shard might come into contact with haunted places are the worst places for it, and once you pick this up, it leaves its mark. You attract things almost as badly. It's obviously marked you, otherwise that Pastor would have kept to his church yard like he'd been for so long." He looked towards Maxwell. "We didn't tell you because, well, I think you know."

"One last hurrah," Maxwell said. "So, you can't touch it," he nodded at Miranda. "And you can't touch it either," he pointed at Bernie.

"You won't have to worry about money," Allen said. "The leaders I was able to meet with this morning are happy with you being their courier, finding things for them and passing other things from one circle to another. The circles that are uncomfortable with you touching anything they want found or delivered are happy to take a collection for you every few months. They just don't want you anywhere near their communities."

"I understand," Maxwell said. "I don't blame either of you if you stay here," he told Miranda.

"No, you don't get to leave me behind," Miranda said. "Even if New York is too dangerous, I'd rather be with you on the road than waiting at home for someone to find a good place to stick the Shard for good."

"You're going to need help keeping that old Edsel on the road," Bernie said.

"You're staying here, Son," Allen said firmly. "Tibeault has a car for them, it's not new, but it's in good shape, straight from his dealership."

"I'm going with them," Bernie said.

"No, you're going to be here, answering the phone, setting

things up for them whenever you can by calling ahead. They don't need a third in the car, but they will need someone like you, with experience booking gigs, setting up hotels when they can afford it, arranging meet-ups on the road."

"He's right, Bernie," Maxwell said. "As much as I'd like you to come along, we'll need help from outside the car." His mind was already working as though he would be back on the road by nightfall. He remembered the deep cold at the crossroads, and had a feeling that the Dawn Shard was calling out to something no one wanted to face. It, and he had to go. "We'll need all the help we can get if we're going to be out there for a long time while you do research on putting the Dawn Shard to rest somewhere. There has to be an answer outside of the Book of Doors."

"What's the solution there?" Bernie asked.

"It's not a solution," Maxwell said, regretting mentioning it at all. "Nothing anyone would do. Nothing anyone *should* do."

"But there is something, maybe we can figure something else out based on that," Miranda pressed.

"It's a resurrection spell," Maxwell said. "Bring the bones of the deceased out, put a powerful vessel for souls on its chest, and sacrifice an innocent with the spirit belonging to that body present. The energy of the innocent, and the essence of the trapped souls restore the spirit to the body and make it whole again. Alive like you or me. Whatever vessel you use to gather souls for this is destroyed, but the resurrection requires the death of an innocent and violates the covenant. The walls keeping big magic and bad things out would come tumbling down."

"Still, there has to be other magic that can trade the power in the Dawn Shard for something better," Bernie said.

"I've never seen it," Allen said. "But we'll both look. People across the world will look as we let them in on the secret. It's going to take time to decide who we tell, there will be people who want the Dawn Shard because it has so much potential for drawing power."

"We'll find a way," Maxwell said. "Should go pack, won't take long, then go get it now, though." He turned to Miranda. "Are you sure you want to come with me?"

"Don't you want me to?"

"Oh yes, but it's my burden, and we will eventually run into people who will do anything for it, as bad as Panos or worse."

"There had better be two of us, then," she said. "Besides, I can handle myself."

"I have no doubt," Maxwell said.

"We'll make it our time," Miranda said. "A long vacation, we'll see the sights."

Maxwell smiled at her and allowed himself to feel relief. "Grand plan. Thanks, luv."

"Your aunts aren't going to be happy, but they won't be surprised, either," Allen said. "Before we pick up the Shard, Scott and Uncle Desmond want to see you, and the police have things under control at the hospital, so I thought I'd give you a lift. Miranda's Aunts are there right now, so you can talk to them about your plans there, then come back to get the stone after."

"Last chance, can't take the shard there," Maxwell said. "How is April?"

"She's in and out, but Scott says she knows he's there. The doctors are happy he's sticking around," Allen said.

Maxwell took a breakfast sausage, some bacon and wrapped it in a pancake. "No time like the present," he said as he stood up.

"That's an idea," Miranda said, doing the same.

XVIII

Miranda and Maxwell were dropped off at the emergency section of the General Hospital so they could avoid the press, and it worked for the most part. One reporter, his hair a mess, tape recorder under his arm almost got in their way. He met them with his little black and silver microphone, pointing it into Maxwell's face. "Do you have any comment on your lead singer's-"

Maxwell brushed past, without saying a word, and the security guard kept the reporter from getting into the Emergency waiting room.

The elevator leading to the fourth floor was empty, so Maxwell took the opportunity. "I'm sorry about New York," Maxwell told Miranda.

She smiled at him, not a reassuring creak of the mouth, but one of her warm, full-lipped loving smile. "Even if we're on the road for years, New York will still be there. Besides, we're going to see so much together. It's happening fast, but I'm getting excited too. We'll be doing a good thing."

"You keep surprisin' me, luv," Maxwell said.

"I know," she replied.

The doors opened, and they started down the hall towards the family room. "Hello, Max," Darren said as he emerged from a hallway to their right.

"Where have you been, man?" Maxwell asked.

"Did you get the Dawn Shard back?" Darren asked. He looked like he hadn't washed or changed his clothes in days, and there was something different about the way he spoke.

"You all right?" Maxwell asked.

"Just wondering, I heard there are a lot of people waiting for you to pick up the Shard," Darren said. "Sounds important."

"Don't worry about that, mate. Where have you been? Just hanging about with some of the Gatherers?" Maxwell said as he moved to keep walking down the hall and put his arm around Darren. If he wasn't possessed, then there was surely something serious wrong with his friend.

Darren pushed him away, pulling a gun from his pocket. "Just give me the shard and the book and everything will be fine," he said.

Scott emerged from the bathroom behind Darren, saw the gun begin to turn towards him and lunged for it. The weapon went off, Maxwell rushed Darren, and he was forced to the floor under the weight of him and Scott.

He got a grip on Darren's wrist and another shot went off, firing down the hall. "Help!" Miranda shouted, waving down a hallway at someone he couldn't see.

Maxwell elbowed Darren in the face, stunning him just long enough so he could get the gun out of his hand and toss it across the floor. In the next instant, something grabbed him by the scalp. The florescent lights above flickered, and Maxwell felt a dozen hands on him, grabbing at his shirt, his wrists, and his legs as they tried to drag him down the hall.

Scott was on the floor, bleeding from his leg, and Darren began to stand with his hands raised towards Max. "Where are they?" he demanded through grinding teeth.

"What's going on here?" demanded a security guard who arrived with two nurses in tow.

Darren glanced at them, and they were pressed against the walls.

"Panos," Maxwell said as he struggled to fend off the unseen hands, their nails were digging into his skin. "Where'd you get the power for this."

"I started opening doors," Panos said using Darren's skin. "Oh, the things I've seen, the wonders a couple sacrifices gets you. I need the shard and the book to continue. Where are they?"

The hands closed around Maxwell's mouth and nose, and then he heard two gunshots. The side of Darren's face exploded into a shower of blood and bone. Everything that held Maxwell and the guards in place released them. Miranda lowered the gun, her face frozen in a stunned expression, and Maxwell rushed to Darren's body. No one could survive the damage the gunshot did. He patted his fingers in the blood pooling around the body's head and drew a circle on Darren's shirt. "I bind you to this body, though it be dead, though it be cold, may it forever hold your soul." He chanted as he drew symbols from the Book of Doors inside the circle using blood. He moved to Scott's side then, hoping he managed to catch Panos before he could leave Darren's broken and dying body.

"I'm going to be okay, hurts like a son-of-a-gun, but I'll be fine," Scott said as he held his leg. "It went through, not bleeding very much."

The security guard took the gun from Miranda gently, put it on the nurse's station and then yanked her hands behind her. "Gotta cuff you two while we wait for the cops," he said as two more security guards arrived.

"Never mind that, you git! My friend's been shot!" Maxwell said. Two of the nurses rushed to Scott's side, the third looked at what was left of Darren, who was absolutely still on the floor, and turned to the nurse's station. "Best place to get shot, a hospital. We'll get you fixed up."

Miranda allowed herself to be handcuffed, but when a security guard approached Maxwell from behind, he got a finger pointed at him. "She just saved your mate's ass over there, and I didn't do anything wrong."

"Don't tell them anything, Max," Miranda said as the security guard turned her towards the elevator. "They won't believe."

"Are you going to come with me quietly, Sir?" asked the tall security guard standing in front of Maxwell. His demeanor was calm, he was just doing his job.

"Your friend's going to be okay," one of the nurses said. "The bullet went straight through, and the bleeding has already stopped."

"If you're taking me where she's going, then I'm going with you then," Maxwell said, putting his hands up.

"We're all going to the same place," the guard said as he cuffed Maxwell.

"What happened?" asked Gladys, shocked.

"They're taking your daughter to the station, let her tell you what happened," Maxwell said, twisting so he could see her and Susan. "Someone has to do a warding on this floor. Panos."

"I'm going to be okay!" Scott called up from where he was on the floor with one of the nurses. The other was running off.

As the next act in the chaos began, with doctors rushing in, nurses helping Scott and what was left of Darren onto gurneys and visiting families coming almost as quickly to find out what had happened.

XIX

Maxwell had enough time to go through all the events in that hallway in his head, and came to one conclusion: any honest thing he said could be turned against Miranda. He could leave out all the mystical motivations behind what happened, but that made it look like Miranda shot Darren in the head while he was unarmed. He could say that Darren was about to attack someone again, and Miranda was only preventing that, but there was a guard in the room who saw everything.

If that guard started talking about being pinned against the wall by an unseen force, Maxwell would back him up, but that would make them both seem crazy. More importantly, it wouldn't help Miranda. Spiritual possession and mystical forces were not known as good explanations for anything in a court of law.

The police detective he sat across from in the interview room barely even registered on Maxwell's senses. He let the questions roll over him as though he were a stone and the detective was a breeze. Nothing he said mattered, no threat or promise he made caused Maxwell to so much as bat an eye. After two hours of questions and attempts to get him to respond to anything, Maxwell calmly put his head down on the table and closed his eyes.

"Are you all right, sir?" the detective asked.

"I am medically fit," Maxwell replied. "You have better things to do."

The detective didn't move for a moment, then he collected his note pad and pen, then quietly left.

The only thought in Maxwell's head was that he should have been the one firing the gun. It was his band, they were his friends, and Panos was his enemy. He brought the trouble into being, but Miranda was going to pay for its end.

By the time he was checked out of the police station, Maxwell was emotionally numb. The only urge he had and followed was to look for Miranda as he was walked out, given everything he came in with, then shown to the door by a lawyer he didn't know. He couldn't see her, which wasn't a surprise, but it was a disappointment.

He could see Allen on the other side of the doors, and he stopped the lawyer, who was saying; "-but they're not charging you with anything. It's obvious the knife you had on you was not used in the assault."

"What about Miranda?" Maxwell asked.

"I don't think I can discuss her case with you," the lawyer said.

Maxwell slowly turned towards the tall, grey haired man, resisting the urge to drag his face down to his level and force him to speak.

"The news is not good," the lawyer said quietly. "They have already charged her with first degree murder, it's the fastest I've ever seen someone charged with a crime that severe in this province."

"Bail?"

"Listen, I understand what happened in the hospital, I was at your initiation, I'm here because I'm good and I'm one of you, but I have to present the defense on what I can prove, on what a jury might believe. She is in a very tight spot, Max."

"Will she be able to get out on bail?"

"No," the lawyer replied. "She is a Canadian citizen, so she won't be extradited, but she just arrived in the country after a long absence, and has ties internationally. I'm going to fight for her to get out on bail, but I don't know of a judge who would grant it."

"So, she's going to go to jail for twenty-five years," Maxwell said, having difficulty finding the air in his lungs to finish the statement.

"I'm going to do everything in my power to get this down to second degree," the lawyer said. "I'll make it happen, Max."

Maxwell pushed through the doors and nodded at Allen. Bernie was waiting in a black four door Chevy Nova. It looked new, he knew it was the car they were setting him up with to take the Dawn Shard on the road.

"Bernie's all packed, he's going to take the shard."

Maxwell began shaking his head before he reached the sidewalk and didn't stop until all three of them were in the car. "You're not taking the shard, you're not going anywhere, Bernie." He said firmly. "You're going to stay home, you're going to guard the book, and you're going to read that fucking thing over and over again."

"Are you crazy?" Allen said.

"Panos made a mess of things," Maxwell told Allen, who was in the back seat. "He opened doors he'll never get a chance to close, and I trapped his spirit in Darren's corpse, and I'm sure Darren didn't get a chance to get out. I can't be the only person we know who understands what's in that book, especially since I'm going to take that shard down the road and maybe never find more than three days peace at a time."

"You're going to be needed here, Max," Bernie said.

"For what? To watch her go to jail for ten, twenty, twenty-five years because I dragged her into my bullshit? Bloody hell, I love that girl like I've never, and the best thing I can do for her is get as far away as I can, take my fucking trouble and artifacts with me."

"She's going to want to see you, even if it is just visiting," Bernie said. "Miranda is going to need you."

"Would you listen?" Maxwell asked, and was about to launch into another list of reasons, when Bernie's father interrupted him.

"Max is right," Allen said. "We'll go to the crossroads. You'll go on to the house in another car, get his bags together. We'll take care of her Max. Just remember, you may have brought this trouble here, but Miranda and all your friends, everyone who loves you would have rather you did. This is the kind of trouble that would have killed you if you faced it alone, so, even though it looks like it couldn't have been worse, I'm glad you brought it home. This is a better outcome in the end, we get a chance to take control of it."

"Darren and Zachary are dead, April won't be the same, and Miranda is going to prison," Maxwell said quietly. "If I knew this was the homecoming, I would have driven my bike into the Saint Lawrence. Drive."

The ride to the crossroads was a silent one. Maxwell could see the grey patch of trees surrounding the intersecting dirt roads well in advance. The grass in the graveyard was yellow, the oaks, pines and birch trees were grey for fifty feet in all directions as though they had been parched, dead and sun-bleached for a hundred years. When the car stopped, he could see their limbs had been twisted, hollow faces stared towards the middle of the intersection. A few of the grey faces were furious, their long, dark hollow expressions severe and jagged. Most were morose, rounded and drooping.

A dozen elders from the Gathering circle the night before were along the roadside, watching the car pull in, waiting. "You're my brother," Maxwell said to Bernie as he turned the car off. "Doin' this as much for you as for anyone."

"I know, Max," he replied. "Wish I was going with you."

"Not this time," Maxwell said. "I'll tell you where to find the book when I call from the road."

Bernie hugged him and got out of the car.

"Sure going to miss you, Dad," Maxwell said to Allen just as he was opening the door. "Thank the stars you were there to catch me when I was young."

"I'm sorry you're taking this on the way you are," Allen said. "But I'm proud of you."

Maxwell got out of the car and walked to the middle of the crossroads. The chill in the air was still intense, and he knew he'd be facing something evil if it weren't for the group of elders shedding their light on the crossroads. The sun was going down, there was no time for hesitation, so he picked up the shovel dropped in the middle of the road and dug down to his seal.

Sweat broke on his brow as he felt malicious eyes staring at his back. Whatever was coming to visit the stone was powerful enough to stare through the protection a dozen elders had drawn around the crossroads. He smirked at he struck the iron seal, and knelt down to pick it up. One of the elders took it in oiled cloth marked with protective symbols. "Not going to want to use that until it's blessed again," Maxwell told him.

"We're going to melt it down and cleanse the metal," the elder said. "Thank you for doing this, man."

Maxwell looked up and recognized the man who joined them for a few songs, his blonde and silver hair was bound up in a long braid. "The road is a second home," he told him.

"Come see me in Arizona sometime," the elder replied as he closed the oiled cloth and returned to his place on the roadside.

Maxwell looked at the Dawn Shard in the hole and shook his head. "We're going on a trip, you and I," Maxwell said. He could feel the evil staring at him from a distance recede as soon as he made contact. The feeling that hundreds of other worldly beings were pressed back filled Maxwell. They were still there, he could faintly feel their desperation and hate. "I'm going to find out what you're really for some day." He shoved it into his pocket.

Bernie was behind him with the keys to the Nova. "I'm going to miss you, man." He said with a hug.

"Me too, but you'd better get back to the farm, I don't want to wait around her long," Maxwell said.

"The car is all loaded up, I even had time to get your amp in there, just in case," Bernie said.

"I lost a minute somewhere," Maxwell said. "Take care of Miranda and her aunts for me, make sure they know I'm sorry."

"They know," Bernie said. "They don't blame you, but they know."

With a final, firm hand shake, Maxwell left his friend behind. He got into the black Chevy Nova, moved the seat up, started the engine, and put the car into drive.

Epilogue

October 31, 1976
A gas station just outside Big Wreck, Arizona.

"I hear you," Maxwell said as he turned the ignition key of the Chevy Nova off. He could feel the lady in the passenger seat, if not see her. Harriet McCullen had a son who had run off as a teenager, and she was deeply worried. She had been deeply worried for a very long time. "I know where to find your boy Daryl, and you'll be seeing him tonight, just be a little patient. I've got a call to make, so I'll be minute, luv."

He stepped out of the car and into the merciless Arizona sun. "Missing Canada fall today," he said to the gas attendant, a dusty looking fellow in an EXXON hat. "Fill it up with regular."

He stepped into the telephone booth and connected to the operator. "Collect call to Canada, here's the number."

A moment later the line rang and Bernie picked up. "Max! How's the road?"

"Road's doing fine," Maxwell said, leaning against the glass and looking out towards the parched highway. "Driving almost pothole free out here, makes me wish I had my bike. Might not have room for this week's passenger though."

"You picked up another lost one?" Bernie asked, surprised.

"Lots of 'em out here. This one's as pleasant as you please, just wants to be reunited with her son, says he wandered off to a mining town called Big Wreck. I asked around, and sure enough, I wasn't too far. Place has been abandoned since the early nineteen hundreds."

"Big Wreck? You're kidding," Bernie laughed.

"Couldn't make it up, mate. Drew the sign on a quarter, threw it on the ground and the Shard moved it in the right direction. Her son's spirit's trapped there, who knows why, but I bet bringing his mother for a visit will jostle it free. Then their happy reunion will get them clear of the Dawn Shard, on to the other side at last. That's if it's like last time. Good way to spend my Halloween."

"I wish I could see that, man," Bernie said. "I guess you found out what the shard's good for."

"Maybe, I'm pretty sure that's not why it was made, but maybe I can make this more of a regular thing, give me another reason to crisscross the continent. How's the farm?" Maxwell asked, bracing himself for bad news.

"Mixed news, man. Things are quiet here, having a little Samhain thing. Got a call from the record company. Raw Dog has officially been bought by S&K records. They're reissuing our album, apparently people are looking for copies thanks to everything that happened last summer. They want us to go along with it, are asking if we can get another tour together."

"You told them our lead singer is six feet under?" Maxwell asked without thinking.

"Well, yeah, they want to set us up with some guy who looks and sounds like Zack."

"Bloody vultures," Maxwell said.

"I'm thinking about it," Bernie said. "Not with the new singer, fuck them, but they say we can make appearances in record stores, sign some records. Maybe something good can come out of the band's reputation, I could meet you in a few cities, they'll pay."

"If we don't have to dance behind some new wanker they put in front of us to sing our songs, then yeah. Guess it's a good way to stop asking for handouts so I can keep gas in the tank."

"That's what I was thinking."

"And I'll get some living company on the road for a while," Maxwell said. "I'm fine out here, mate, but it would be good to see someone breathe in the passenger seat." He did his best to suppress his excitement at seeing his long time friend again. "Just wondering, how many they pressing?"

"They say fifty thousand plus another twenty thousand if we do the record store thing," Bernie. "We're getting radio play in the States because of our new dark reputation, so they're sure they can move the records. It's a lot of money."

"I'll believe it when we're signing albums in a store," Maxwell said. "But, yeah, let's do it. Scottie?"

"He won't be going with us. Taking care of April."

"Good, that's where he wants to be," Maxwell said. "In the main house?"

"The two bedroom cabin," Bernie replied. "Think I heard April laugh for the first time since they moved in yesterday. She's come out a few times since she got a mask for her mouth. They were able to save most of her nose, so I think she's going to come through this."

"See Miranda this week?" Maxwell asked.

"Yesterday, and Wednesday," Bernie said. "I have good news and bad news. The hospital guard who saw it all go down is in Algoma Sanitarium. The Crown is still looking to prosecute, but they offered her a deal. Second degree murder instead of first degree, and fifteen years, but someone high up pulled some strings when they got new information, nothing was signed yet."

"What new information? No one's talking, everyone expects a trial," Maxwell said, bracing himself for the worst.

"Max, she's pregnant. They're dropping it down to the minimum, ten years," Bernie said.

"What? She's pregnant?" Maxwell asked.

"You're going to be a dad," Bernie said. "Man, she needs you to say something, especially now. I know this is a lot to take, but write her a letter. We can set up a telephone call too, just say the word."

"I will," Maxwell said. He squeezed his eyes shut, clamped his jaws together. "Fuck, she must hate me."

"Not in this lifetime, brother," Bernie said.

"She will. I can't put the Shard down. This thing, it's doing something to me, Bernie. What I can see, the things that turn their heads when I drive through a town, I can't pass it on. I need to ask you and her something, I'll write her about it myself, but I have to ask you to be a father. At least until I can come home, at least until we can find a grave that can hold this thing."

"Max, you know I'd do anything for you," Bernie said. "Is it really that bad?"

"It's a part of me, mate. Can't let anyone else near it, especially someone I give a shit about. I pass it on, and it'll stay connected to me anyway for years longer. I can't be around kids with what follows me, with or without the Shard."

"I'll take care of your kid while you're out there, no problem," Bernie said.

"No, I'm asking you to get on the birth certificate. That way I'll know no one can take that kid away, and it'll always be in a good place. I'll make it sound right to Miranda, I know she'll agree. I won't have my kid grow up with a rainy day dad."

"You're sure?" Bernie asked. "I love you man, and Miranda, I'll do this for you, because I know where you're coming from, but if you have any doubt."

"I want to be there," Maxwell said, pulling the shard from his pocket and looking at it. "It's not good for the kid, though. I need you for this, brother, though I've no right to ask."

"I can do this for you, Max," Bernie said. "Yeah, I'll do it."

"Don't let her get lost like I did," Maxwell said. He hung up the phone.

The gas attendant met him on the way to the car. "Six ninety-three," he said.

Maxwell pulled a ten from his jacket pocket and handed it to him. "No change, mate." He got into the driver's seat and looked to the sun visor, where the Polaroid of him and Miranda on his motorcycle was pinned. He stared at the photo for a moment before wiping a tear away and starting the engine.

"Only a few more miles now, Miss McCullen," he told his spectral passenger.

www.ingramcontent.com/pod-product-compliance
Lightning Source LLC
Chambersburg PA
CBHW052044240626
47153CB00006B/2202